ONE SUMMERHILL DAY

KEIRA MONTCLAIR

Enjoy!

Keira
Montclair

Cover Design and Interior format by The Killion Group
http://thekilliongroupinc.com

DEDICATION

A HUGE thank you to the best readers I could ever ask for in this JOURNEY OF MINE AS AN AUTHOR. I appreciate your support and am grateful for every chance I get to share thoughts with you. Please keep sending me messages, emails, and updates on my Facebook page. I thoroughly enjoy getting to know you and I look forward to hearing how you like my first contemporary romance. Only through this medium can I now say I have friends all over the world-South Africa, New Zealand, Australia, England, and across the fifty states of the USA, my country.

THANK YOU!

CHAPTER ONE

Caitlyn McCabe's hands gripped the steering wheel of her car as she headed east on the New York State Thruway. Her hands should be shaking due to the icy road conditions, the frequent black ice, and the occasional sliding of her wheels. In truth, it was the scene she'd left behind that had her on edge, not to mention the big question mark that lay ahead of her.

After twenty-five years, she was alone. Her biggest fear had come true. The last conversation between her and her husband played out in her mind again.

"Caitlyn, I'm sorry. I made a mistake. She means nothing to me. Please stay so we can talk about this. Besides, where will you go? You don't have any family." Bruce had done his best to convince her not to leave him, but she was done. Their relationship had deteriorated over the last year. This was the final straw.

"Wrong. I have my Aunt Margie, and as soon as I pack, I'm heading out this door to go stay with her." She stomped up the stairs to make her point, then proceeded to pack everything she couldn't give up. For all she knew, anything she left behind would probably be sold or tossed into the garbage by her cheating husband.

"Fine, do what you need to do," he shouted behind her. "I'll be waiting when you come to your senses. I need you, Caitlyn. You know that, and you need me."

Humph. He needed her. Hadn't looked like it with her best friend from work in his arms. At least he seemed to feel a little remorse for having been caught in the act. Well, he could have Lynn, along with the house and all the bad memories it held. She had only moved to Philadelphia for him, so there was no reason for her to stay. After packing most of her belongings into her small car, she'd left the house without looking back. She'd spent the night in a hotel room, so she could make initial divorce arrangements with her lawyer, and phone in her resignation. Though she'd normally only leave a job after giving her two week's notice, desperate times called for desperate measures.

There had been one slight hitch in her escape plan. When she finally reached her aunt's house in the south of Buffalo, she'd been shocked to find out her aunt wasn't there. A stranger had answered the door of the house Aunt Margie had owned for over forty years. They had bought the house from an estate sale.

Her only living relative was dead, and no one had thought to tell her.

Tears slid down her cheeks, blurring her vision, something she couldn't afford right now, not in these driving conditions. Why hadn't she spoken to Aunt Margie for so long? She had been so busy taking extra shifts to help out at the hospital that the months had flown by. Had it really been since Thanksgiving? She'd called and left a message at Christmas, but Aunt Margie had never called back. What a terrible niece she was.

She brought her focus back to the present. What the hell was she doing driving in this weather in western New York? Simple, she had been so upset by the disappearance of her dear aunt she hadn't been thinking clearly. Now she realized what a foolish move it had been to leave Buffalo in this state. It didn't help that she had no idea where she was going. She had to pay attention to the weather and stop thinking about the mess she'd made of her life.

The snow flurries had turned into a squall, and the road was now coated in a thin white blanket that hid the black ice she feared so much and covered the white lines on the edge of the highway. She had to make a decision soon, because she couldn't stay out here in this mess. The wind whipped the snow in her headlights in blinding whorls.

She passed one car in the ditch, then another. Though her fleece gloves hid her knuckles, she was sure they were pale white from their grip on the wheel. As she passed over the next bridge, the wheels of her car lost their grip on the pavement, and the car went skating across the crystalline black surface. Just like that, the control of the vehicle was yanked out of her hands and left up to the mechanics of her vehicle and fate.

She held her breath, waiting and praying for the comfort of traction again. A sigh of relief escaped her lips when the tires grabbed the asphalt again on the other side of the bridge. Okay, she had made it through that one, but how many more close brushes could she handle? A car directly in front of her skidded, but managed to regain control.

She had to get off and find a place to spend the night. *Yes, she thought, all you need to do is find a hotel, get your most important belongings inside, and make a plan for the rest of your life.*

The black of the night made the snowflakes hypnotizing in her headlights. A few minutes later, she sighed in relief when she caught sight of a distant green sign indicating an exit off the thruway. In the reduced visibility, the text was illegible. She squinted to bring it into focus, hoping it was a place with hotels, not just an exit to another highway. Without realizing it, she pumped the gas slightly and her back tires spun to the right. She squealed, praying the car would keep on the road and she wouldn't miss the exit. There was no alternative in this weather; she had to get off the thruway as soon as possible. She took her foot off the gas pedal and managed to hold onto the spin before straightening her vehicle.

The sign finally came into view: Summerhill—two miles. She relaxed and said a quick prayer of thanks. She *remembered* Summerhill. It had been her father's favorite place to vacation back when they lived in Buffalo. The city of Summerhill sat on the northern end of one of the Finger Lakes—Orenda Lake.

She hit her right turn signal and allowed her car to slow, only lightly touching the brake pedal, since she knew, as did any halfway decent driver in the northern states, that braking too hard or too fast could send her into a tailspin.

The sign at the end of the exit ramp was covered in snow, but it showed an arrow to the right. Though she had no idea what it was advertising, she was convinced it was the correct way to go since all of the Finger Lakes were south of the thruway. She vowed to pull into the first hotel she reached. A few more minutes and she would be safely ensconced in a warm hotel room with a TV and hopefully Wi-Fi so she could use her laptop.

The snow was heavier on the roadway here. The plows hadn't been out yet, but she could follow the tracks of the car in front of her. Besides that car, there were two others coming toward her and one behind her. The crest indicating the City of Summerhill loomed not far in the distance, a beacon in the chilly, dark night.

One of the dark SUVs headed toward her was going way too fast for the road conditions. Foolish SUV drivers thought they were impervious to snow. Right before it came abreast of her, it skidded out of control.

Caitlyn braked her car harder than she should have in the hopes of avoiding the oncoming vehicle, which was now headed straight toward her. She stepped on her anti-lock brakes until they grabbed, but she still skidded. The sound of crunching metal and a small jolt from behind her indicated the car to her rear had collided with her bumper. Her instinctual reaction was to keep her brakes pushed into the floor as far as possible, which sent her careening sideways down the highway, directly into the path of the skidding SUV. The car from behind hit her again, guaranteeing her fate. The SUV crashed into the left side of her car, inflating her airbag on impact and destroying the front end of the vehicle. The ruined remains of her car skidded sideways off the road, and she screamed as cold metal met the skin of her left leg, followed by a rush of warmth.

The clamor of skidding tires and crunching metal drowned out the sound of her screams. As her car spun, she glanced across a field and noticed a young boy dressed in scruffy old clothes. A big Scottish Deerhound stood next to him, and both of them were staring directly at her.

Somehow she heard the urchin when he whispered, "Do no' worry, missy angel."

Blissful darkness took over as she passed out, still clutching the steering wheel.

Police Officer Ryan J. Ramsay III and his partner had been cruising town when they crested the hill at the entrance to Summerhill. Dave pointed just as the gruesome scene unfolded. Two monster SUVs skidded on the snow and crashed into a small sedan, shoving it sideways off the road. He hit his siren and called the accident into the station, requesting at least two ambulances from Summerville Memorial Hospital, though he expected to find a fatality in the little red car.

Another cruiser met him at the scene, this one driven by his brother Jake, who offered to manage traffic while Ryan and his partner, Dave Oglesbee, checked on the occupants of the vehicles. The black SUV that had caused the accident had stopped on the side of the road, and the driver was already stepping out of the vehicle.

"Anyone hurt in your vehicle, Sir?" Oglesbee yelled as he moved toward the SUV.

The driver shook his head, stunned, but apparently uninjured.

Ryan ran over to the small red sedan. The driver's door was partially crushed, and the glass in the window had blown out, sending shards of glass everywhere. He tried to open the door, but it wouldn't budge. Flinging open the back door, he found loads of boxes in disarray but no passengers, and only noticed one casualty in the driver's seat. A young woman didn't move, blonde curls covering her face, her head leaning to one side.

"Miss?"

Nothing.

"Miss, can you hear me?" He reached his hand around the back of the seat to feel for a pulse in her neck. As soon as he felt it, he yelled to Oglesbee. "She's alive." He peered at her closely and noticed her shallow breaths were punctuated by slight visible puffs as her warm breath hit the cold air around her.

Then he glanced over the rest of her body, and what he saw was like a fist to the gut. Blood, too much blood, pooled in her lap, probably coming from the wound around the thin piece of metal protruding from her leg.

He yelled at his partner. "I need some help."

She moaned and released the steering wheel, only to search for something else to grab onto.

Afraid to touch her because of the possibility of a neck or back injury, he hopped out of the other side of the back seat and opened the front passenger door so he could slide in beside the wounded woman. He grabbed a piece of clothing he saw on the back seat and shoved the now deflated airbag out of the way.

"Miss, I'm Officer Ramsay, and you've been in an accident. Can you tell me your name?"

No response.

Oglesbee appeared outside the broken window. "She's still alive? Wow. Lucky."

"Yeah, but I have a bleeder. I need to tie a tourniquet above the spot on her leg."

"What spot?" Dave Oglesbee peeked over the jagged edges of glass.

"That spot." Ryan pointed to the protruding piece of metal dripping blood.

"Don't pull it out," he said with a whistle. "You could kill her."

"No shit. Really?" Ryan glared at his partner. "Find out how long before the ambulance arrives."

"She the only one?"

"I don't see any evidence of passengers. Call the EMTs. Find out what's going on. And send them straight over here when they arrive."

Oglesbee pulled back and surveyed the area again before turning back to Ryan. "I already checked the car behind her. The guy's fine. She's the only injury. The other two were blessed." Suddenly, the car behind him took off, spinning in the snow. "Asshole."

"Get the plate?" Ryan yelled. Not that he needed to ask, any law officer would know enough to have taken the number.

"Yeah, I got it. Getting in my car to report. I'm not going to chase him. I have all the information we need to find the guy. Holler if you need anything." Oglesbee headed over to their patrol car.

Ryan attempted to get the cloth under her leg without

moving her, but it wasn't possible. He placed pressure in the spot above the injury, hoping to slow the bleeding. He had seen enough injuries in the army to know what to do.

Her leg, she could lose her life or her leg. He knew what that was like. "Miss, I need you to wake up." Nothing again. He would love to shake her, but a person with a possible neck injury should not be touched. He leaned into her ear and yelled. "Miss."

Her eyes shot open, and he was startled to find himself staring into a pair of beautiful blue eyes. "Miss, my name is Officer Ramsay. You've been in an accident. I need your help, but please don't move."

Her dusky lips parted enough for a whisper. "Okay."

"Can you wiggle your toes for me—just a bit?"

A pause, then, "Yes."

"Okay, I need you to try to lift your left leg without moving your neck or your back. Half an inch is all I need."

After a few moments, she whispered, "Is that enough?"

"Yes." He slid the cloth underneath and quickly tied a tourniquet above her injury. "I know this isn't the best solution, but I can't put compression directly on the wound."

"Why not?" Her gaze caught his and her right hand touched his arm.

"Because you have a piece of metal in your leg and I don't want to remove it."

His brother's face appeared in the window. "Oglesbee is watching traffic. How is she?" Jake asked.

"Stable for now, but where's the ambulance?"

"Oglesbee said ten minutes out. Lots of accidents tonight."

"Good. We can last that long. Bring me a blanket." He needed to try to stop the tremors that were spreading across her body. True, she was probably in shock, or headed that way, but the blanket would help protect her from the cold temperature.

His brother disappeared.

"Tell me the truth, Officer," the women said to him in a quiet, musical voice. "I'm a nurse. I can handle it. There's definitely major blood loss. Will I make it? It's okay if I don't."

Ryan's eyebrows rose as he caught her gaze. Had she really

just said that?

Damn, it was exactly what he would say in this situation.

CHAPTER TWO

"What's your name, Miss?"

"Caitlyn McCabe." He hadn't answered her question. Was she going to die? Didn't matter if she did, did it? No one would miss her. Her husband wouldn't have to deal with the divorce. Everything would be his. She scowled as the implications of her death crossed her mind. Like hell would she give him everything after what he did to her. She would fight.

"Caitlyn, are you allergic to any medicines?"

"No."

"Are you taking any medications?"

"No."

"Where are you from? You're going to have to go to the hospital for treatment. Is there a family member I can call?"

She flinched as the officer retied the tourniquet on her leg a bit tighter. That one small movement brought the pain in her leg to the forefront of her mind in a very big way.

"Hurts pretty bad, huh?"

She nodded, afraid to open her mouth lest she scream in the poor policeman's ear.

"So, your family? Husband? Mother? Father?"

She shook her head.

He scowled at her. "Try not to move your neck."

She could tell he didn't believe her. Well, it was true. Her parents were both dead.

"Where do you live?"

She didn't respond, unsure of what to say. How could she even answer that? She had left her husband in Pennsylvania; her aunt in Buffalo was dead. Where *did* she live? She gripped his arm tighter as if he were the only thing holding her together, keeping her alive. Her mind felt cloudy, which couldn't be good. She was experiencing oxygen deprivation. Was it from losing so much blood? She glanced at the officer's hands wrapped tight around her leg, gripping her so hard it hurt.

"Don't look at the blood. You'll be all right. The ambulance will be here soon."

"There's too much," she whispered, clutching his arm in her hand. She closed her eyes, hoping to blot out the pain. If she could just take a little nap, everything would be better when she woke up.

A voice echoed in her ear, strong and commanding. "Don't close your eyes. Stay with me, Caitlyn. I need you to stay with me. You're not going to die."

She opened her eyes again just to let him know she was still conscious. "My leg. It hurts really bad. There's something sticking out of it. My leg."

"The bleeding is slowing. There's a tourniquet and I'm applying pressure. Don't worry about your leg. Where do you live, Cait?"

"I'm going to lose my leg, aren't I? My toes are tingling. There's too much blood."

"No, you're *not* going to lose your leg. Not if I have anything to do with it."

He was shouting at her and she didn't understand the expression in his face, like he was angry about something. Another police officer appeared next to her window with a blanket. Officer Ramsay covered her with it and the warmth made her sigh. She closed her eyes again.

"Stop worrying about her leg, Ryan," the second officer said in an undertone.

"I can't let her lose it. The ambulance will be here soon and she'll be fine."

"And she'll be fine if she loses it."

"No, she won't. That's why we can't let it happen."

She couldn't understand why they were arguing about it. Why should they care about her leg?

"Caitlyn!" A sharp voice forced her to open her eyes again.

"You need to stay awake." Officer Ramsay turned to address the man by the window. "I got her name, but she can't tell me where she's from."

Both of the men turned to look at her, and she noticed a similarity. "Are you brothers?"

"Yeah. Jake's my younger brother," Ryan said. "What kind of nurse are you?"

"Emergency room, RN."

"Around here?" Jake asked.

"No." She closed her eyes again. Tired, she was just so tired.

"Caitlyn!" Ryan bellowed.

She whispered something, but he mustn't have heard because he said, "What? I can't hear you. Say it again."

He leaned his ear down next to her lips. "Bossy," she whispered, her lips feeling dry from dehydration. "You're very bossy."

Jake laughed. "I like her. Hey, Caitlin, when you're better, you want to go out?"

"Like hell." Ryan gave his brother a long stare that was hard to interpret. "She's not for you."

Sirens could be heard in the distance. She hoped they would get here soon, because she was very cold. The two officers kept talking, but she couldn't understand either one of them anymore. She closed her eyes again.

"Caitlyn!"

Her eyes flew open. "But I'm cold. Please let me sleep." The sirens rang and rang until she wanted to shut them off. Finally they stopped, and she closed her eyes again.

The last thing she heard was Officer Ramsay's voice. "Tell them to hurry up. We don't have all night." He didn't sound the least bit happy.

Ryan Ramsay stood outside the Summerhill Memorial Hospital's triage room, waiting to talk to his sister, Mallory. Ryan had a large family, which was very convenient whenever he needed information about anything going on in the city of Summerhill.

After she processed the last patient, Mallory motioned him

forward. "What's up, Ryan? Tough night?"

"No tougher than yours, I'm sure."

"I don't know about that. I'm working the night shift, so it makes sense that I'm still on the clock, but you were supposed to be done at eleven and it's two a.m."

True, it had been a busy night. He shrugged. "The calls kept coming and we didn't have the manpower. You'd clock the extra hours in my situation."

Mallory nodded. "True. What can I do for you?"

"I want to see the woman who came in with the puncture in her thigh, MVA around eleven. How's she doing?"

"You know I can't tell you that…or did you forget HIPAA laws prevent me from giving out any of her personal information?" Mallory scowled at him. By the book Mallory, he'd always called her.

"Damn, you like to throw your title around, don't you, Mal? I'm not part of the healthcare team. Being an RN doesn't mean you have to act like a guard all the time. I found her first, and I'm the one who put pressure on her wound. I need to know if she's going to lose the leg."

"You were the first on the scene?"

"Yes."

"Then do you know anything about her family?" Mallory punched the keyboard of her computer, checking for information.

"No. I think she was too weak from the blood loss. She just kept shaking her head no when I asked her about them."

"Hmmm." Mallory rested her chin in the palm of her hand as she stared at the screen. "She's awfully young to have no family."

"Please just tell me how she is."

"I can't. You know I can only give information to certain family members, plus she has a restriction."

"Well, I have her belongings and I want to bring them to her."

"Give them to me." She held her hands out.

"No, I don't think so. I am the officer involved. I can only release her belongings directly to her. How do I know you'll give them to her?"

"I'm your sister, for God's sake. What do you think I'll do with them?"

"Give me clearance, Mal. I want to hand them to her. I was the officer who kept her from bleeding to death. This one's important to me."

Mallory stared at him. "Fine, she has a restriction on her chart, but it isn't you, so I'll show you where she is."

Ryan smiled at her. "Thanks. Can we go now so I can get home for some shut-eye?"

"Follow me." Mallory traipsed over to the swinging doors at the end of the waiting room, glaring at him as she pushed it open.

Most patients in the emergency room were cared for in curtained areas, but there were a couple of private rooms. He was pleased to see Caitlyn had been given one. There was a window in the wall of the room she'd been given, but at least he could close the door so his sister wouldn't have to listen in on their conversation.

For some reason, he hadn't been able to get Caitlyn McCabe out of his mind. He wasn't sure why she was affecting him this way—if it was her piercing blue eyes, her injuries, or what she'd said, but he wouldn't be able to sleep if he didn't at least come check on her.

Mallory waved at him on her way out. Caitlyn was resting, her eyes closed, her head turned away from the doorway. He moved around the bed so he could get a good look at her. She was serenely beautiful in the glow of the hallway lights, even with the multiple scratches from the shattered glass of her car windshield on her strong cheekbones. The light coming in through the window reflected off her golden strands. Her hair wasn't short or long, but in between, just below chin length. The silky strands lay on the pillow behind her, begging for him to run his fingers through them. It had been a long time—too damn long—but why was this woman the one who moved him? He refused to stare at her lips. Somehow, he knew that temptation would be too much.

He took a step closer and her eyes flew open. Jumping back, he cringed at how this probably looked to her. The last thing she needed to feel right now was threatened. Clearing his throat, he plunged ahead. "Caitlyn?"

"Yes?" She followed him with her gaze, and suddenly recognition set in; he could see it on her face.

"Officer Ramsay? Is that it?"

"Yes." He gave her his best smile, one he didn't flash often. "You have a good memory."

"Thank you for helping me in my car. You're just about the only thing I remember after the crash." She smiled, then waited for him to speak.

"I brought some of your things, Ms. McCabe. I found your purse, a laptop case and a small bag in the back seat of the car. I left the boxes alone. I figured there might be some personal things you could use. Your other suitcases were left in the trunk of the car and you can retrieve them along with the boxes when you're released from the hospital."

He placed her purse in a drawer in the nightstand and her laptop case on the bedside table. The small suitcase he set in the patient closet.

"Thank you so much, Officer."

"Ryan, please call me Ryan." As soon as he closed the closet door, he returned to her bedside. "Feeling better?"

"Yes. They removed the chunk of metal from my leg and stitched me up. As you can see, they're loading me with fluids as well." She nodded toward the IV pole. "I'll be here a night or two, I lost quite a bit of blood, and I may need a transfusion. Thank you for trying to keep my blood loss to a minimum."

"Ask for medicine. You shouldn't have to deal with the pain."

She laughed. "Oh, I did, and that's why I have a smile on my face. Vicodin, thank goodness. Thank you for returning my purse and my laptop. I was worried about them."

"You're welcome." He paused, gathering his thoughts before he spoke. "Can I be of assistance in any other way? You said you don't have a family. Is that true or was it just the shock talking?"

Caitlyn sighed. "No, it's true. My father died when I was younger and my mother passed a few years ago. No siblings, unfortunately."

"Well, I have more than enough to go around, if you ever

want any. Twelve of us at last count."

"Twelve?" Her eyes widened.

"Yep. Five siblings and six step-siblings."

"Wow, you're so lucky. I've always wanted a sister."

"I have a few I would be happy to give you, no lie."

They both laughed, but he could tell she was tiring. He reached over and covered her hand on top of the blankets with his, wrapping his warmth around her. "Good luck to you. If you ever need anything, call me or stop by the station house and ask for me. When you're ready to pick up your car, I'd be glad to help you."

"Thank you, Officer Ramsay. I think I'd like to rest again for now."

He was about to release her hand, but at the last minute he held on instead. For some reason, he didn't want to let go of her. Who was she, really? He forced himself to place her hand on the blanket, nod and walk out of the room.

Walking away from her felt wrong, just wrong.

When he grabbed the door handle, he heard his name, so he turned back to her.

"Officer Ramsay, you limp."

Caitlyn gave him a puzzled look as she stared at his leg, the same way everyone stared at his leg. She would get that familiar pitying look in her eyes next, the look he hated.

"Yes, I do." He wasn't about to explain his injury to her.

"Oh." She smiled at him. "You have a previous injury?"

He nodded, waiting for that look to come into her gaze.

"Then we have something in common—" her face lit up, "—don't we?"

He was stunned, because there was still no pity in her eyes. That was a first. Caitlyn McCabe was different.

CHAPTER THREE

Two days later, Mallory Ramsay, RN, strode into Caitlyn's room carrying a bundle of papers. "Are you all set? I see you've dressed. Did you get everything you wish to take home with you?"

"Yes, I have everything. I'll have a seat while you go over my discharge instructions."

Mallory raised her eyebrows. "You talk as though you understand this process."

"Yes. I'm a nurse, also."

"Oh. An RN?"

"Yes, in fact, I spent the last year in emergency room nursing. I loved it."

Mallory perked up. "You did? Where did you practice?"

"I was in a hospital in Philadelphia. I just moved from there. I was going to relocate to Buffalo, but things were not as I expected there, so I'm actually not quite sure where I'll be settling."

"Well, if you're looking for a job, we have two full-time openings in our emergency room. We sure could use the help. The pay is good, not great, since we're in a small, somewhat rural community here, but I like it. It doesn't hurt that we don't get many gunshot wounds or stabbings. Anyway, we are always looking for good nurses. I'm only on this floor today because they were short and I need the extra money. I pick up extra shifts a lot."

"Do you have pediatrics here?"

"A little in emergency. We usually stabilize and transfer the kids to the Children's Hospital in Rochester, so our pediatric floor isn't usually full. Why, do you like peds?"

"Actually, no. I was afraid your emergency room did both, and I don't like pediatrics because I don't know how to handle children. But I'll give it some thought. Maybe I'll decide to stay here for a while. My father always loved Summerhill. We used to vacation at the lake when I was little."

"I've lived in Summerhill my whole life, even went to Summerhill College for Nursing. I love it here, but I have a huge family, so my roots run deep."

Caitlyn's brow furrowed. "The policeman, Ryan? He told me the same thing. Do you know him?"

"Yep, that's my brother," Mallory said with a laugh. "He can be a little overbearing and serious at times, but he's a good guy. Okay, let's go over your instructions."

When she finished all the paperwork and signed her name, Caitlyn said, "Is there a nice bed and breakfast you would recommend here? I think I'll probably need to stay a few days. I need to locate my car and see what's going on with it. Your brother said to contact the police department when I was ready."

"I'll check with Ryan and find out where it is. Why don't you find a place to stay, settle your things, then worry about your car? There's a lovely bed and breakfast just over the hill on the other side of town as you head to the lake. Do you remember the town at all?"

"A little."

"The next intersection after your accident was Main Street. If you go through that and up over the hill, you'll see a couple of hotels. The Lakeview Bed and Breakfast is on the right as you head toward the lake, and it has a beautiful view."

"Would you mind calling a cab for me?"

"No problem, but the cabs are expensive. I'm sure my brother would take you over there if he's on duty."

Caitlyn shook her head, not wanting to burden anyone. "Please, just call me a cab."

A volunteer came along and brought her down to the front entrance, where she was required to sit in a wheelchair until the cab arrived.

Mallory ran over at the last minute. "Here's the place your

car is being kept, according to my brother, and here's the address and phone number." She handed her a yellow sticky note with the information.

"Thank you, Mallory, for everything." She took out her phone and dialed the number right before Mallory came running out again with another sticky note outstretched. "Here's my cell phone number. If you ever need anything or decide you want to apply for the job, give me a call."

"That's very sweet of you. Thanks, Mallory." Mallory left so Caitlyn talked to the person at the car repair shop while she waited for the cab. Unfortunately, the car wouldn't be ready for at least a couple of weeks. Maybe that would give her time to think about her situation.

The cab pulled up and the transporter helped her move from the wheelchair into the cab, handing her all her belongings before closing the door.

"Where to, Miss?"

"The Lakeview Bed and Breakfast."

A few miles through snow-covered streets and an hour later, she stood inside a lovely room with a queen-sized bed, staring at her laptop and trying to decide what to do. It looked like she wouldn't be leaving Summerhill anytime soon. Fortunately, she had found a nice place to stay, and since money wasn't an issue for her, she could stay right here and enjoy the beautiful view of the pristine lake.

She refused to go back to Philadelphia. She never wanted to see her husband, Bruce Dalton, again, and she had already quit her old job. Besides, she wanted to find out what had happened to her dear Aunt Margie. Maybe it would help her get answers if she was in New York State, close to where her aunt had lived. It was another reason to stay.

Her decision was made. She would stay in Summerhill for a while. When she felt a bit better and had her car again, perhaps she could find a place to rent on the lake. Yes, that was it. A piece of her father's heart was here, so why shouldn't she learn to love it, too? She would make her father smile down on her from his place in heaven.

She would spend a couple of months in Summerhill. All she needed were her belongings from the trunk in her car.

Ryan left his apartment on Saturday and headed to the family inn. His stepmother hated for people to call it the inn, but with all the siblings and step-siblings and the size of the place, the name fit. The house sat on a small hill overlooking the lake with enough bedrooms to house his new family of fourteen, if need be. Some of his siblings had their own places, some were at college, and the twins were in the military, but the Ramsay-Grant rule was everyone who could be at the lake house for the Saturday picnic at noon—summer *or* winter—needed to be there. It was a new tradition his stepmother, Lorraine Grant, had started.

At first, it had bothered him since it hearkened back to an older time, when family was seen as a more uniting concept. But now he loved his huge family. This was especially true since Lauren had started researching their ancestry and discovered both families were descendants of great Scottish clans. The Grants were related to the famous Alexander Grant from the Scottish Highlands, while many Ramsays were found in the Lowlands of Scotland. Somehow, the two families had combined in the past just as they had here in the Finger Lakes.

Ryan didn't mind the Saturday tradition, especially since his stepmother was such a great cook. When he was in the army, he had always envisioned his homecoming would be on a Saturday. He had dreamed of being welcomed home as a hero, just as his grandfather had been before him. Unfortunately, things hadn't happened that way. Instead of a hero's welcome, he had come home injured, depressed, and a failure.

Jake had been in the same unit, but he'd been honorably discharged. He had missed the bomb that had caught Ryan in Iraq and been able to finish his tour, so his homecoming had been exactly the way Ryan had wanted his to be. The third Ryan Ramsay hadn't had a great Saturday homecoming, but at least he had somewhere to go on Saturday so he could forget about his past.

He sighed, angry with himself for being jealous of his brother. He loved Jake, and they had become very close while in the army together. Things didn't always happen the way you planned, and it was hardly his brother's fault Ryan had come home in disgrace.

Ryan pulled into the sloping driveway, pleased to see the number of cars that were already there. He parked and got out, walking into the large family room that had been added to the back of the house for the winter picnics. He strolled inside the back door to a chorus of greetings that were delivered as he stomped the snow off his shoes and yelled back greetings of his own. The room had a huge fireplace on one end, but it consisted mostly of windows.

In the summer, the windows were all kept open, or at least the ones facing the lake were. In the winter, the fireplace was usually going. Three different seating arrangements allowed for smaller gatherings and a pool table sat in the corner, the usual place his brothers congregated. A large flat screen television hung on the wall for all the sporting events they loved to watch.

Lorraine greeted him. "Hello, hero." Tall with dark hair and blue eyes, Lorraine Grant-Ramsay had a warm smile. She had always wanted to be a doctor, but had never made it to medical school. She fell in love and married instead, then married Dr. Ramsay after she was widowed.

He kissed her cheek. "Lorraine, you know I would rather you not call me that."

"I can't help it, but I'll try, Ryan. Like father, like son, as they say." She smiled and patted his shoulder.

Hero. Hardly a hero in his mind. His father was the hero, not him.

He had to admit, he had never seen his father this happy before. He'd worried his father would never adjust after losing their mother to breast cancer. But Lorraine Grant and her six children had pulled his father—along with the entire family— out of their slump.

"RJ!" his father barked from across the room. He made his way over, carrying a basket of rolls to set on the buffet table. "You survived the snowstorm? I heard it was a busy week for the police department. You must have clocked some extra hours."

"Yeah, I had over fifty hours this week, Dad. Fortunately, no fatalities." He brushed his hair off his face.

"Jake said you saved a woman's leg in a pretty bad car accident near Main Street."

"I think Jake has an overactive imagination. She just had a gash on her leg."

"That's not what Jake and Mallory said, but I'm glad to hear it ended well."

Ryan waved to his brothers at the pool table, but he passed them to follow his stepmother into the kitchen. He was starving and Lorraine was a great cook, capable of far better meals than anything he could hope to make in his apartment. "Lorraine, anything I can do to help?" He'd do anything to help get that food out so they could get started.

The kitchen was dark wood cabinets with caramel-colored granite countertops. A center island had stools for six to eat when they were in a hurry. The countertop was covered with Lorraine's many dishes, including chocolate chip cookies for dessert. Ryan grabbed a cookie and popped it in his mouth while his stepmother pretended not to notice. Macaroni salad, tossed salad, cut up watermelon and berries all called to him. But none as much as the Sloppy Joe creation she had simmering in the crockpot.

"Here, dear." She picked up two bowls and handed them to him. "Why don't you take the salad out for me? We'll be eating in a few minutes. Everything alright?"

"Yeah." He grabbed the bowls and headed out to the family room. This week had been better than most weeks, except for the new conundrum in his life... He had met a fascinating girl who haunted his dreams, but she had left town and he would probably never see her again. He hadn't been able to stop thinking about Caitlyn McCabe, though he was sure she was long gone by now.

Mallory came over as he stepped out onto the porch with the bowls. "Ryan, have you seen your friend?"

"Who?"

"Caitlyn, the one in the accident with the leg injury."

He stopped, but then walked over to the table and set the bowls down before turning toward Mallory. "Why aren't you worried about your HIPAA laws now?" He glowered at her, recalling the way she had harassed him in the ER.

Mallory's classic defensive posture of her hands on her hips settled into place. "You already know about her and I didn't use her last name. Besides, no one else is listening and you are police, not health care, as you reminded me."

"Why would I see her?" He ushered his sister into a corner away from the table and prying ears, pushing her shoulders a little too enthusiastically. He was not about to let her disappear until she explained herself. "I'm sure she was discharged and has headed back to Pennsylvania."

A wry grin crossed her face. "Ah, but she didn't."

"Didn't what?"

"Didn't go back. She's still in Summerhill."

And this was the best damn news he had heard in days. "What happened?"

"The transporter came back and told me how sorry he felt for her because her car wouldn't be ready for two weeks. She asked for the address of a bed and breakfast because she doesn't have anywhere to stay."

"Which one?" The weekend held definite possibilities now.

She raised her eyebrows at him. "Interested, huh? She's at Lakeview."

"I'm only asking how she is, that's all. Plus, as soon as her car is ready, she'll be gone."

"I don't know. There's something going on with her, but I can't put my finger on it, and I can't say anymore. HIPAA, remember?" She tossed her hair back and spun around to head into the kitchen.

Ryan couldn't argue with that statement. There was something about Caitlyn that didn't make sense…or, really, a few things. For one, he'd checked her license in her purse to verify her identity and her name didn't match the one she'd given him. Now, he'd find out why.

CHAPTER FOUR

The next day, Caitlyn wrapped a scarf around her neck and headed out the door of Lakeview Bed and Breakfast. It was chilly, but the sun sparkled on the freshly fallen snow and she needed to get outside and think. Her leg still ached and she didn't have full use of it yet, but she could trudge around enough to make it down to the lake, especially since there was a path through the snow.

She was almost down to the bench in the park when she heard her name. Turning around, she was surprised to see Officer Ryan Ramsay in street clothes striding toward her. She smiled and waved. "Hello, Officer Ramsay."

"Caitlyn. Nice to see you moving around."

Ryan trekked down the slope of the hill toward her, his limp more noticeable on the uneven terrain. She was curious about what had caused his problem, but didn't feel she knew him well enough to ask. If he wanted her to know, he would tell her.

"Mind if I join you?"

When he reached her side, she summoned all the self-control she had not to stare at him with wide eyes. How had she failed to notice how good-looking this guy was? Brown hair, just the right amount of beard, and green eyes she could fall into all invaded her senses at once. She'd never felt such an immediate and powerful reaction to a man. Turning toward the water to hide her reaction, she said, "No, not at all. Though I warn you, I'm only going as far as the bench." She pointed to her destination.

"How's your leg?" he asked as he came up beside her and

placed his hand on the small of her back.

Such a small gesture, yet she liked his hand right where it was. "Improving every day. I just wanted to get outside and enjoy the sun. It's so beautiful with the pines around the lake."

"It is. Waiting for your car to be repaired?"

"Yes, I'm afraid it will be at least another week." Her foot landed in a small hole and she lost her balance. She reached for him, and he caught her in a matter of seconds, even with his injury. He grabbed her around the waist and she found herself staring into his green eyes, mere inches from hers. Her gaze veered down to his lips, and she found herself wondering what it would be like to kiss him.

She jerked her gaze back to his eyes and blushed, shocked at the path her thoughts had taken. After all, she had just left her husband. But when had been the last time they had kissed? Their love life had become almost non-existent. Maybe if she had been more observant, she would have noticed the decline of their marriage. Maybe it wasn't all Bruce's fault if she could be turned on by another man this easily.

Once Caitlyn straightened herself, they continued their stroll toward the lake, but Ryan didn't move far from her, almost as if to say he had enjoyed the close encounter as much as she had. "Since you have no vehicle, then I insist on taking you to dinner tonight."

"Oh, heavens no. I couldn't impose."

"You wouldn't be, and I am only offering to take you to the little place on Main Street, Deb's Diner. Have you tried it yet?"

They reached the bench and she sat, positioning her leg so it was straight. "No, I haven't. Is it good?"

"It isn't as good as our five-star restaurants, but I eat there often," he said as he settled in beside her. "Suits me better than my bachelor apartment. Plus, we policemen like our diners."

She laughed. "But..."

"Please, I insist. Otherwise, I'll be eating there alone."

He slung a hand over the back of the bench, and for some reason, his closeness warmed her insides. "Sure, in that case I'd love to come." She gazed into his eyes, and he nodded and smiled as if to affirm their agreement. His eyes were mesmerizing. "Have you lived here long?"

Ryan said, "I've lived here all my life except for when I was in the army. I grew up with my parents, two brothers, and three sisters, but my mom died a while back from breast cancer."

"Oh, I'm so sorry. That must have been terrible for you."

"Losing her was hard on all of us, but especially my dad. Fortunately, he met someone and married again, which is how I ended up with six step-siblings—four brothers and two sisters. Now we have enough for any team sports we want. When the seven guys get together on the basketball court, it can be dangerous, but we have a great time."

"So, you get along with all of them? Wow. No sibling rivalry?"

"A little when we were younger, yes. But I love having such a large family. We get together every Saturday for lunch, and I rarely miss it." His expression turned from cheerful to serious. "Their continued support means everything to me."

She found herself wishing she could see him without his coat on so she could have a better look at him. In his police jacket, he had looked massive, with broad shoulders, thick biceps, and a narrow waist…Did he have a six-pack for abs?

He stared at her expectantly.

"I'm sorry, what did you say?" The man was distracting. He laughed and his white teeth sparkled at her almost as much as the snow at her feet.

"Can I pick you up in a couple of hours?"

"Yes, that sounds wonderful, Officer Ramsay. In fact, I think I will head back. It's a bit chilly out here, even with the sun."

"Ryan. Please call me Ryan. I'm not on duty today." He grabbed her arm to steady her as she stood, trying not to bend her leg too much. As they headed up the hill, he said, "Do you mind if I hang on to you? I know from experience that it's much more difficult to walk up a snowy hill with a bum leg and I don't want you to fall."

She nodded. "Thank you." The simple kindness spread warmth from her head to her toes. She grabbed his elbow, hoping he would use this opportunity to tell her how he'd been injured, but he did not.

When they hit the steepest part of the hill, they both slowed,

Caitlyn struggling to push off without too much pain.

"You all right?" he asked, the concern in his gaze shooting straight to her heart.

"Yes, thank you." She paused for a moment to absorb the pain, but then kept moving. When she turned her head to glance at him, she couldn't help but laugh. "We certainly are a pair walking up this hill together, aren't we?"

He nodded and gave her a strange look. "Yep, we are."

Ryan couldn't believe he'd had the nerve to ask her out. Was this a real date or not? It was Saturday night, but she could consider his offer a friendly gesture. He checked his reflection in his rearview mirror before he got out of the car. He'd put on cologne, even though he had left most of his beard scruffy. Mallory always bugged him about smelling nice for the ladies. He wasn't sure if it genuinely made a difference, but he'd decided to take his sister's advice for a change.

As soon as he walked into the foyer of the bed and breakfast, he caught sight of Caitlyn as she limped down the hallway toward him, a smile lighting up her face. He took a minute to appreciate the effect she had on him. There was a sort of glow that emanated from her, one capable of cheering anyone up. Her smile reached all the way to her eyes, making them shimmer in the light. All he could think of was rubbing his thumb across the plump surface of her bottom lip, and then kissing her until she melted in his arms or until she couldn't speak, one or the other.

What a fool he was. That type of thing only happened in the movies.

"Hi, Caitlyn. You look nice." She actually looked gorgeous, not just nice, but he decided that would be a little over the top for a first date. She was dressed in jeans and nice boots, with a black sweater and a red trimmed scarf wrapped around her neck, and the black set off her blonde hair.

"Thank you, Ryan. You look nice, too."

He helped her on with her coat, then held the door for her as they walked into the parking lot of the B & B. He had parked close to keep her from having to walk too far, and he helped her slide into his car before he climbed in the driver's side.

Maneuvering yourself into a car after a leg injury took practice, he knew better than anyone. He noticed the way she gripped the door before she sat—she was still in pain. As soon as he closed the door, he put the keys in the ignition and turned to look at her. A warm feeling washed over him.

"You smell good, Ryan. What kind of cologne?"

"Honestly? I have no idea. Whatever my sister gave me for Christmas." Damn, score one for Mallory.

It didn't take more than ten minutes to get there, and several patrons greeted him when they walked into Deb's Diner. He waved to the hostess and indicated a booth in the back corner, hoping for a little privacy there. When he and Caitlyn reached their table, he helped her off with her coat. His hand accidentally brushed hers, just enough to shoot a spark up his arm. What the hell was that? Shit, all of a sudden he felt like a middle schooler with his first crush on a girl. He swallowed as he sat opposite her in the booth, suddenly very conscious of how beautiful she was. Even with the little wounds on her face from the accident, she was stunning. When had he ever dated one like this before? Shit, this *was* a date. He needed to text Mallory and ask her for guidance. He knew nothing about dating anymore. Before the army, he would have texted Jake, but since the army, he had grown closer to Mallory, though he wasn't quite sure why.

The waitress handed them each a menu, so he opened his. His stomach flipped at least ten times. Somersaults, if he had to guess. He tried to stare at the menu, but it was hard to concentrate with Caitlyn so close to him.

"What do you recommend? You must have a favorite." She set the menu down to await his answer.

"Deb is a great cook. I like the turkey, gravy, and mashed potatoes. One of my sisters likes the grilled chicken wrap, the spinach salad, and the quiche. The nachos are great. My other sister and my stepmother like the meatloaf." He peered over his menu, hoping he could gauge her reaction by her facial expression.

"I'll try the grilled chicken wrap."

The waitress returned and took their order. Caitlyn glanced around the room. "They're busy. That's always a good sign for a restaurant." She took a sip of her ice water, then settled her hands on her lap. "So would I have any chance of renting a place here for a couple of months? What do you think?"

"You want to stay in Summerhill?" He tried to keep his expression neutral, though he'd love for her to stay so they could spend more time together. "I'd be happy to help you find a place. I know a couple of the real estate offices that handle rentals. On the lake or off?"

"On, if possible." She stared at something across the room. "I want to stay until I can figure out something…"

"Anything I can help you with?"

She returned her gaze to his. "I don't know. Maybe." She paused for a moment before continuing. "I was on my way to visit my aunt in Buffalo. That's why I came to New York. I was leaving her house when the storm hit, which is why I took the turn-off to Summerhill."

"What is it you're looking for?" He played with a napkin, folding and unfolding.

"My aunt."

He frowned. "But didn't you just visit her?"

"Yes, I went to her house, but she wasn't there."

He stared again, not knowing how to respond. "Where was she?"

She leaned toward him. "That's just it. I don't know." Her breath caught, but she cleared her throat and continued. "My Aunt Margie lived in Buffalo in the same house for over forty years. When I knocked on her door, a stranger answered. He said he'd bought the house from an estate."

"Wait, your aunt's dead?" He hadn't expected that. How did you not know your aunt had died?

"Yes." Her voice sunk to a whisper. "She died and I had no idea. I don't know how she died or when, and she was my only surviving family." She stared at the ceiling.

Ryan could tell she was fighting to hold back tears, so he reached across the table and grabbed her hand, brushing his thumb across the back. He was surprised when she didn't pull back. "I'm sorry. How can I help?"

She dropped her gaze from the ceiling and stared into his eyes. "I need to know what happened. Can you help me?"

"Of course. I'll see what I can do. I go back to work on Monday and I'll call the Buffalo Police Department. How about if we find you a place to live first?" His thumb was still lightly caressing the back of her hand, and he had absolutely no desire to stop.

She nodded, now staring at their intertwined hands. She brushed the tears away with her other hand. "I can look for a place by myself. I really am independent."

"But isn't your car still in the shop?"

She laughed. "Why yes it is, isn't it? Then your assistance with a realtor would be much appreciated."

"I'm not working tomorrow, so we can do it in the afternoon if you'd like."

Dinner arrived, so she pulled her hand back. "That would be great."

Ryan's phone text notification went off, so he pulled his phone out of his pocket to check the message. He hated to do it, but being a police officer, he was required to keep his phone on him at all times in case of an emergency. "Excuse me. I have to make sure it isn't the department."

"Sure." She settled her napkin on her lap and politely looked at her food.

Ryan put his code in and checked his texts.

Mallory: *Come on over. Family meeting.*

Ryan typed in, *No*

Mallory: *Why not?*

Ryan: *Busy*

Mallory: *Could you not be such a guy and type in more than a one-word answer?*

Ryan: *No*

Ryan set his phone down and smiled at Caitlyn. "Sorry. Annoying family."

She chuckled. "With a family that big, you must get text messages from them all the time."

"Very true, that's why I ignore a lot of them."

His phone buzzed again, and he sighed before checking it.

Mallory: *Where are you?*

Ryan: *Diner*

Mallory: *Eating dinner?*

Ryan: *No, dancing. Don't come over. 5*
Mallory: *5??? Dancing with 5?*
Ryan: *5 words. I'm eating. Go away. 6*

Ryan shut the sound off on his phone and set it on the table. "Very sorry. Done." He got his knife and fork out of the wrapped napkin. The vibrate went off on his phone—and again and again.

"Damn it." Ryan picked up the phone just as it went off four more times. He looked at the screen and saw the texts were from Mallory, Lauren, Mallory, Jake, Mallory, Lauren, Mallory. He sighed and shoved the phone into his pocket. He was tempted to just turn it off, but he couldn't. "Sorry. Now they're being obnoxious."

"Is it your sister Mallory? She's very nice, you know."

"Yeah, but she can be a pain in the ass sometimes. And now she's apparently roped in my stepsister and my brother. They do this group texting that gets really annoying. Mallory thinks she can annoy me so much that I'll have to answer."

"Still, you have family that loves you."

He paused for a moment, thinking about how it would feel to be in her shoes, with no family at all. "Yeah, I do. A lot." He speared a piece of turkey.

She laughed. "A lot of family or they love you a lot?"

He grinned. "Both, I guess. I didn't think I would like having all the stepbrothers and sisters, but I do. Makes for great holidays and my dad is so much happier." He changed the subject. "So I can pick you up tomorrow at noon to look for a place. Maybe a cottage?" He stuck a forkful of mashed potatoes in his mouth.

"That would be great. A cottage on the lake. Hmmm." She gazed off into space for a moment. "Has a nice ring to it."

They ate in silence for a bit until the front door banged open to admit a boisterous group, laughing and stomping their feet as they came inside.

Ryan heard the waitress say, "He's over there." He dropped his fork with a clatter and said, "Really?"

And yes, it was really them. In a matter of seconds, Mallory, Lauren, and Jake stood in front of the booth with grins on their faces.

"Uh-oh," Jake whispered. "Maybe we should leave."

"Hi, Caitlyn," Mallory said with a sharkish grin. "How nice to see you again. How are you doing?"

Ryan introduced Caitlyn to his family, but he glared at them all the while, letting his ire be known. "What happened to the family meeting?"

Jake said, "We ended it. More important things to do."

Caitlyn said, "How nice to see you here! Join us."

"Not nice," Ryan grumbled. "Go home."

"We're actually headed to the Brew House, so we thought we'd drag you with us," Lauren said, brushing her long brown tresses behind her ear.

Caitlyn said, "Lauren, are you in health care or with the police?"

"No," her eyes grew wide and she scowled. "I'm doing graduate work at Cornell University majoring in History. I'm the odd one more interested in the arts."

"Oh, how interesting. The Brew House?" Caitlyn asked. "Where's that? I know very little about Summerhill."

"Well, if you haven't spent too much time in Summerhill before, you definitely need to go to the Cobalt Brew House," Jake said. "They make their own craft beers, most of them quite good. The food's great, too. In fact—" he gave Ryan a teasing grin, "—I'm surprised my brother didn't take you there."

"Well, I don't think he could have picked a better spot," Caitlyn said.

Mallory stood and grabbed Jake's arm. "Come on. We'll go to the Brew House. Why don't you join us when you're done?"

After they left, Ryan said, "Sorry. I told you they could be obnoxious."

"Don't be sorry. I think you're fortunate to have so many siblings. Are all three of them siblings?"

"Lauren's a Grant. But I love all my step-siblings. Would you like to join them at the Brew House when we finish here?" Ryan gazed into her blue eyes, hopeful that she wasn't about to shut him down. He liked Caitlyn, that simple. He wanted to know more about her, and he hoped she felt the same way.

"Sure."

Ryan was surprised she had agreed to go, but he couldn't be happier. She didn't seem to mind his family interrupting their time together, and they did help with the awkward side of the first date. Yep, this was a first date, and he hoped it would be one of many.

Before Ryan knew it, he was leading her into the Brew House, which was crowded and noisy, the usual ambience for a Saturday night. He kept Caitlyn tucked in front of him, his hand on her waist, afraid she would get knocked over by someone and lose her balance in the crowd. They found his family at a high-top table in the corner, and as soon as they maneuvered their way over, Jake hopped out of his chair and offered it to Caitlyn.

"Caitlyn, what would you like?" Jake asked.

"I'll have a diet coke, please."

Jake said, "You sure? Their craft beer is quite good, and they carry wine from the local wineries."

"No thank you. Still on pain meds for my leg."

"Oh, of course, sorry," Jake said. "Any better?"

"Yes. Thank you."

"So Caitlyn," Jake started. "Did Ryan tell you I'm the smartest and the strongest of all the siblings and step-siblings?"

Caitlyn laughed. "No, he didn't mention that."

Lauren added, "And of course he's the most humble."

"She already knows I'm the best looking. Right?" Jake winked at her.

Mallory said, "As you can tell, Jake and Ryan are a little competitive. They always have been."

"Who was always the first one to the bottom of the hill when we went sledding?" Jake bragged. "You guys know it was always me. It was an early sign of character."

Ryan didn't have much to say, since his siblings talked non-stop, though it was all in good-natured fun. After about forty-five minutes, he noticed Caitlyn was tiring, so he leaned over to whisper to her. "If this is too much for you, I can take you home. Don't be embarrassed. I'm sure your leg hurts and I know how exhausting that type of pain can be." He stepped back and gazed into her eyes. He could see the pain there, though she was making a valiant effort to hide it.

"Let me take another pill and see how it goes. I'm trying to take as few as possible, but sometimes the pain gets to be too much." She smiled as she dug in her purse for one of the pills.

A few minutes later, she tugged on his arm and he leaned down to her.

"I think I need to go."

They said their good-byes and Ryan led the way through the crowd, holding her hand to keep her directly behind him so she wasn't jostled too much. As they neared the door, a guy leaned over, clearly inebriated, and said, "Hey, cutie."

Ryan reached over and tucked Caitlyn behind him. "Do *not* touch her."

The guy grinned and backed off, raising his hands in the universal gesture.

And all Ryan could think of was putting his fist in the fool's face.

CHAPTER FIVE

Caitlyn had enjoyed watching the family dynamics of the Ramsay-Grant clan. At first, she could tell Ryan was really annoyed that his siblings had followed him to the diner, but after all the joking, he had finally settled back and started to laugh with them. The siblings' camaraderie had been so fun to watch at the Brew House. She hadn't wanted to leave, but the pain just became too much for her.

When a drunk made a move on her on the way out of the Brew House, she had been happy to stand behind the massive shoulders of Ryan Ramsay, almost leaning into him. His concern for her was quite surprising. He had gone out of his way to take good care of her, a quality that was definitely lacking in her husband...or soon-to-be ex-husband.

They were driving toward the bed and breakfast when he veered off the road toward the lake. "How about a closer view of the lake? I know a perfect spot that won't require much walking. But if it's too much, I'll understand, especially since it's cold out."

"I'd like that. I'm just not into crowds much, though I enjoyed spending time with your family." The idea of spending more time with him excited her. At first, she had been uncomfortable about the dinner. She'd hoped he wouldn't consider it a real date. After all, she wasn't divorced yet, though she'd spoken with her lawyer since the accident, and was well on her way to having that settled. Still, somewhere along the way, her feelings had changed.

She *liked* Ryan Ramsay. He was a good looking man, hardworking, warm, funny, and she was comfortable around him. That feeling was new, since she and her husband had grown apart a long while ago. Watching Ryan's interactions with his family had made her like him even more. But it was time to be honest with him about her situation—and not somewhere they'd be surrounded by potential eavesdroppers. Sitting with him by the lake would give her the perfect opportunity to do just that.

He parked the car by the boardwalk at the end of the lake and helped her out. The moonlight cast a golden haze on the surface of the lake, which was frozen in some spots, still running in others. There was enough water to make the slight lapping noise that she so loved to hear. When she used to vacation here as a child, her parents would leave the windows open at night, and the sound of the water against the sandy beach would lull her to sleep every night.

They sat on a bench right near the car, basking in the serenity of the night. A cold breeze set branches rustling, and she wrapped her scarf up over her face as best she could.

Ryan took her hand and said, "Don't be upset, but there's something I want to ask you."

"I promise not to be upset if you promise the same, because there's something I need to tell you." She gazed into his green eyes and saw nothing but encouragement. There was no judgment, no censure, no insult waiting to be released—none of the things she was used to from men. "Please let me start, and then you can ask me anything you'd like."

"Sure." He tucked her arm inside his and waited.

She took a deep breath and decided there was no way to soften what she had to say. "I'm married."

"Okay."

She had expected him to pull his hand away, but he didn't, so she continued. If he had been quick to judge her, she would have gone home. She didn't need another man like that in her life. "We are in the process of divorcing. My lawyer's confident it will be finalized in a few months."

"Do you want to talk about it?"

"No. Not yet… Well, I'm not sure." She glanced at him and he grinned at her, the warmth of his breath leaving a trail in the air. "Well, we were only married for two years, but it didn't work out. My lawyer has all the paperwork drawn up; my ex just has to sign the papers. I don't know if he will agree or not. We'll see, I guess. I have never done anything like this before, so this is a new process for me."

"You lived in Philadelphia with him?"

"Yes. It just didn't work out, and that's all I'd like to say at this point."

"Accepted. And that answers my question." He smiled. "When I pulled your things out of your car, I checked your license to make sure you had given me the correct information. The name on it was different from the one you had given me."

"Oh." She gave him a sheepish look. "Caught, huh?"

He laughed. "Not usually good to lie to a police officer."

Without trying to interpret her desire to be close to him, she snuggled her head against his shoulder. His arm came around behind her and tucked her close. Oh, but he was warm, nice and warm. "Sorry, but I'm planning to take back my maiden name, McCabe. My married name was Dalton."

"Legally?"

"I suppose not yet. I guess I still have to be Caitlyn Dalton for a while yet."

He stopped and removed his gloves, cupping her cheeks in his hands, warming them with his thumbs. "To me, you'll be Caitlyn McCabe."

He kissed her then, a tender kiss that heated her all the way to her toes. A kiss so unlike her husband's that she reveled in it for that fact alone. His lips were soft and he tasted like peppermint, warm and inviting.

When he ended the kiss, he dropped his hands and tucked her arm into his again. "Do you mind if I call you Cait?"

"I would love that. My husband always called me Caitlyn."

"Cait it is."

"And I promise that's the last time I'll talk about my husband."

The next morning, Ryan showed up at the Ramsay-Grant inn for the late breakfast his stepmother often cooked. When he walked into the kitchen, a chorus of greetings echoed off the walls. Everyone present had a goofy grin on his or her face.

He took his jacket off and threw it on the hall tree, then turned to face his family. "Pardon me for being a bit suspicious, but you aren't normally all here for breakfast on Sunday. Jake? Mallory? Special occasion?" All he got for answers were more silly grins. "Look, I'm not telling you anything. All you get to know is that I'm helping her find a place to rent today. Got it?"

Mallory spoke first, as usual. "Did you tell her...?" She let it trail off, but all of them knew what she was talking about.

"No, I didn't. And you're not going to tell her anything about me, either. When I want her to know, I'll tell her. And that goes for anyone I date. Clear?"

"Oooh, he did call it a date," said Madison.

"That's what I heard, too. About time, Ryan." Jake barked.

Blake yelled out, "Leave the poor guy alone, would you."

Shit, at least someone had some common sense. Blake just won sibling of the year.

"Did you kiss her?"

"Did you like it?"

"Do you like her?"

"Enough!" Ryan bellowed. "I'm not saying any more, so stop asking stupid questions and stop acting like horny teenagers."

He pulled his chair out to sit as the table full of Ramsays and Grants fell silent, their faces now drawn down into scowls. "Lorraine, is there any breakfast left? Sorry that I'm late."

His father walked into the room and strode over to clasp Ryan's shoulders from behind his chair. "You're late, Three."

"Dad, you know how I feel about that." His father's favorite nickname for him was Three. His grandfather was Ryan James Ramsay, Sr., his dad, Ryan James Ramsay, Jr. Thus, the Three was for Ryan James Ramsay III. But he hated it. His father, unfortunately, wouldn't give up trying.

"Fine, RJ, you're late. What's going on?"

"Nothing. Now may I eat or do I need to go to the diner?"

The rest of the morning went as usual. He listened to all that had happened to his family over the past week. When he finished, he took his dish to the kitchen and put it in the dishwasher before grabbing his coat.

"Aren't you staying for basketball?" his father said. "Syracuse is on."

"I'll be back. I have something to do first." He grabbed a peppermint hard candy from a dish and scowled at his laughing siblings on the way out.

"What exactly is it you're going to do, Ryan?" Jake yelled.

Ryan ignored his brother. He was looking forward to helping Cait. Though his first thought had been to stay away from a married woman, separated or not, he hadn't felt this way in some time...and he wasn't willing to let it go without exploring the connection between them. Besides, she needed help with the cottage and finding out about her aunt, so he would be there for her now, and they could work out what, if anything, they wanted later.

Caitlyn's father had died when she was thirteen. A sergeant in the army, he'd died in a bomb blast in Iraq. The last letter she had ever received from him he had promised her a vacation on Orenda Lake in Summerhill. Perhaps it was time to take that vacation.

True to his word, Ryan showed up on time and drove her to meet his friend Tracy, who was also a realtor. They had graduated high school together. The first two houses didn't really work, but the listing for the third one had looked more promising than the others, and she'd dared to get her hopes up.

As soon as they pulled onto the property behind Tracy, a tingling feeling swept through Caitlyn. Was it because of the handsome man next to her or was it a sign that this was her house? As soon as she stepped out of the car, she stopped to savor the view of the cottage set against the white snow on the lake. Granted it wasn't the lovely blue she would see in the summer, but the scene of the rolling hills behind the cottages across the lake warmed her insides. How she would love to hear the roar of motor boats, the splash of friends swimming, and the friendly chatter that would carry up to the deck in the summer. It reminded her of a place she had once stayed with her family. Ryan came up behind her and gripped her elbow as they trailed behind the realtor.

Tracy said, "This beautiful three-bedroom home is available

to rent, but it's also for sale if you decide you really like it. There are also three bathrooms. I like this place because it has a gentle slope to it. There are only a few steps separating the levels. This makes it much easier for the elderly and people with disabilities." She gave a pointed look to Ryan, then glanced between his leg and Caitlyn's.

Ryan's grip on her arm tightened, and Caitlyn didn't blame him. Tracy's words and actions were entirely too rude, whether she'd intended them to come out that way or not. "Excuse me, Tracy. People with disabilities find a way to work with what they have. There's no reason to treat us differently."

Tracy blushed first, but she recovered quickly. "It didn't mean to embarrass you, but the two of you obviously have a similar problem, so I thought it made sense to point out that it would be particularly easy for you to get around this place. Ryan knows I didn't intend any harm."

Caitlyn chose her words carefully. "Thank you, but I think Ryan and I are capable of making that determination for ourselves."

Ryan's arm moved from her elbow to her waist, tugging her next to him.

"It's okay, Cait. Tracy didn't mean anything by it."

Damn it, like hell she hadn't. Caitlyn wasn't about to act like she wasn't upset to have been placed in a category with the elderly because of a limp. Then she felt a pang of remorse. Ryan's limp was probably permanent, so he had to face casual insults like this every day.

Ryan leaned in to whisper in her ear. "Let it go. This is a beautiful place. Don't let her ruin it for you. There are other realtors if you don't want to work with her. She's an acquaintance, not a friend really."

She gazed into his eyes for a quick moment and was lost. How wonderful it felt to be with a man who cared about her feelings. He was right, so she shook off her irritation and walked down the steps to the next level. The realtor stopped at a side door to unlock it. Caitlyn was about to head inside, but she took that moment to turn and glance at the lake. The view made her freeze in place. She turned to Ryan and said, "I'll be right back."

Treading carefully down the embankment and the remaining steps, she paused at the edge of the lake before walking to the end of the small dock. A peacefulness settled into her bones as she scanned the lake and the opposite shoreline. The glassy surface called to her, and a small smile crept across her face as she lifted her face to the cool breeze drifting across the waterway.

Just like that she knew: She was home. For some reason, it felt as if welcoming arms encompassed her as she stood on the warped boards of the dock.

Maybe Orenda Lake could give her what she had been searching for since her father's death—a place to belong. Both she and her mother had felt lost since that fateful day so long ago. Her mother had descended into a deep depression and alcoholism, and thirteen-year-old Caitlyn had needed to take care of her instead of the other way around. After a few years, her father's sister, her Aunt Margie, had finally insisted she come to live with her on the other side of Buffalo. At the age of sixteen, she had moved in with her aunt and started at a new high school where she had been lonely and tormented. The sense of being lost, of having no real place in the world, had followed her.

She had met Bruce in her last year of college and married him within six months—trying to belong somewhere, to someone. The idea of moving to Philadelphia—of having a fresh start—had excited her. But the marriage had not gone as well as could be expected a few months after moving to Pennsylvania. Rather than finding herself, she'd felt more lost than ever.

Until now. *This* was where she belonged. Uneven footsteps approached on the shoveled snow behind her, and she turned to see Ryan moving toward her, a concerned look on his face.

"Cait, are you alright?"

She wiped the tears from her cheeks and nodded. "Yes, Ryan. Oh, yes. This is the place. This is my home."

"But you haven't even looked inside yet. Wouldn't you like to explore the house?"

"Yes, I would." She pivoted around so she could look at the house from the front. The vinyl siding was grey and it had white shutters. There was a large wrap-around deck that overlooked the hundred feet of lake frontage and there were neighbors on both sides, but not too close.

"Do you like it, Ryan?" She grabbed his hands in hers, hoping he loved it as much as she did. For some reason, his opinion mattered.

"Yes. It's beautiful, but it's also the most expensive of the properties we've looked at. I think you need to examine it carefully and ask about the rental fee and the utilities. It does have the two car attached garage, which you don't often see in cottages. It'll definitely come in handy this winter."

"Let's go inside. Do you trust Tracy, though? I don't like what she said before."

"I do. It was a stupid thing to say, but I think she had good intentions." He stared at his feet. "I'm used to it by now, Cait. It's not a big deal and it happens all the time. But we can find another realtor if you'd prefer."

"No, let's take a look."

Tracy gave them the tour of the interior. The kitchen had been redone with white cabinets, black granite countertops, and tile flooring that looked like weathered wood. It had both a table for eating and stools at the counter.

"The furniture is included, Tracy?" Caitlyn asked.

"Yes, it is. Part of the rental agreement and the purchase price." Tracy smiled.

Most of the downstairs was a great room, with a lovely open area connecting the living room, which had a cathedral ceiling, and the kitchen—an area that seemed to encourage gatherings. A bathroom and laundry room branched off a hallway leading to the garage. The upper level had three bedrooms, with one bathroom off the master bedroom and one for the other two bedrooms. A small loft with a railing overlooked the living area.

The front of the house was almost entirely glass and overlooked the large deck.

Caitlyn turned to Tracy. "It's perfect. I'll take it."

"Wonderful. I brought a copy of the rental agreement so you can look it over." She fussed through her briefcase, pulling out a stack of papers.

"No, you said the house was for sale, didn't you?"

"Yes, but it's going for almost a million dollars. It has a sizeable lawn in back in addition to the one in the front, since this is one of the larger lots on the lake."

"Well, could you please find out the exact amount so I could put an offer in? I'd like to buy it."

Tracy and Ryan both gave her stunned looks, but she continued. "I don't think I'll find anything that suits me better than this. I don't want a house that needs lots of updating. This is perfect."

Tracy smiled. "All right, then. Let's decide what you want to offer, and I'll check with the local banks to see who will offer you the best rate for the mortgage. Then we'll get the paperwork started. Where do you work?"

"Oh, I don't have a job yet, but I'm a nurse, so I'm sure I'll be able to find something. I've heard there are openings at the hospital."

Ryan asked, "Are you sure you don't want to think this through for a few days? You could get in touch with my aunt. She's in Human Resources at the hospital. My dad would be happy to look over the property for you to see if it needs anything."

"No, I don't need to wait. This has public sewer and water, doesn't it?"

"Yes," Tracy answered. "You're very close to town and there's a huge Cutler's supermarket nearby. But if you don't have a job yet, you'll have to wait to make the application. You'll likely have to make a large down payment if you're a nurse."

Tracy and Ryan both stared at her, waiting for her response.

"Whatever you think will snag the property for me. I don't want to pay asking price if I can get it for less, but I don't want to lose it to another buyer either. And I won't need a mortgage. I'll be paying cash."

CHAPTER SIX

Ryan grabbed a cup of coffee before he sat down at his desk. He loved his job. His family had tried to talk him into taking some time off after his injury, but he'd refused. He needed a reason to get up every day. Summerville PD had accepted him with his injury, though he knew that other departments would have rejected him. He suspected his status as an army vet, along with the fact that he'd grown up in Summerhill, had helped him get the job, but it was an instance of favoritism he was okay with accepting. Summerville PD only employed fifteen officers, and he got along with most of them. It was also mostly fun to work with his brother.

As if picking up on his thoughts, Jake sauntered by. "Paperwork, brother?"

"Yeah." He sipped his coffee and turned on the computer.

"I'm hitting my cruiser unless you need help."

"No. I'm fine.

Jake smirked. "C'mon, what are you working on?"

"Cait asked me to see if I can find out anything about her aunt in Buffalo."

"Sounds like personal business to me."

"She asked me at dinner before you all interfered. We weren't involved at the time. She was asking for help from a police officer." He typed on his keyboard, ignoring his brother.

"Did she find a place to rent?"

"No."

"Well, I know a realtor who could help her. I know Tracy showed you around, but she doesn't always have the best rentals. She focuses more on sales."

"Cait is putting in an offer on a house—gray with white shutters on West Lake Road."

"She's buying? How does she expect to get a mortgage without a job? Or is she moving here?"

"Yes and yes."

"What the hell? Answer me, fool. Stop talking in riddles."

Ryan shoved away from his keyboard. "Yes, she's buying the house. She's paying cash, so she doesn't need a mortgage, and yes, she's moving here."

"No shit. She's loaded? Hell, I knew I should have gotten there first."

Ryan smirked back at his brother, but then rolled his chair back up to his computer. "Go check on Summerhill. I'll let you know if I need any help. It's Monday morning. Sarge said I could work on this until noon since there isn't much going on around here in the winter. Have fun."

Jake left and muttered all the way down the hallway to the exit. "He always comes first. Born first, finds the girls first. What the hell?"

Ryan laughed at his brother's ribbing and focused on his computer search.

Though he'd pretended it was no big deal to torture Jake, he couldn't have been more shocked when Cait offered cash for the house. After Cait had made her arrangements with Tracy, he had brought her to the inn to meet his father. The house would be inspected, but his dad had volunteered to take a look at it with Cait and give her his own impressions of any work that needed to be done. He trusted his dad to be more thorough than an outsider hired by the homeowners. They were probably at the place even now.

After their trip to the inn, Ryan had taken her out to lunch at the Bistro at the end of the lake. There she'd explained...slightly. The only thing he had learned was that she had inherited quite a bit of money, which certainly put a different spin on her marriage. Perhaps Bruce Dalton was a jerk who had married her for her money. She was still quite secretive about her husband.

But he couldn't blame her, since he had secrets of his own. He just wasn't ready to discuss what had happened to him in the war yet. He had the type of wound that could end a relationship. He knew, because it had already happened to him twice. The girl he'd been dating before his accident had dumped him two weeks after he returned home. One other girl he had started dating had run for the hills as soon as she found out. That's why he wasn't about to tell Caitlyn until he had no choice. Even his dad had advised him to hold off. It wasn't something that would be easy for a woman to handle. She needed to have a little commitment to him first.

Later that morning, Jake returned to the office.

"Need my help out there?" Ryan smirked without taking his eyes off his computer screen.

"Hell, yeah, dangerous day out there in January in Summerhill." His brother tended to be a bit sarcastic, a quality Ryan had always appreciated about him. "Dead. The snowstorms are the only excitement."

"We don't need another storm."

"No. What did you find out? Anything?"

"As a matter of fact, I did. Cait's aunt was killed in a motor vehicle accident back in December. Bad weather, nothing suspicious. But Cait's husband? Now there's a character."

"She's married?" Jake was as surprised as Ryan had been.

"Yeah, married for two years, getting divorced, though she didn't say why." Ryan didn't know why he had opted to check out Bruce Dalton, but he had. He thought it was pretty unusual when a marriage ended that quickly. His curiosity won out, and he was glad he had searched.

"Why did you call him a character?" Jake asked, his arms folded across his chest.

"Quite a gambler, apparently. Owes some money around Philly and online."

"Really. Maybe you better keep a closer eye on your woman."

"She's not my woman."

"Good. What's her number? I'll see if she's busy tonight. A hot woman with money. My dream girl." Jake leaned against an empty desk.

"Like hell. And you can wipe that shit-eating grin off your face." Ryan kept his eyes on his computer, not wanting to give

Jake the satisfaction of thinking he riled him.

"I thought so. Hey, I hope it goes well for you. She seems like a nice girl."

Ryan lifted his eyes to stare at his brother, and the look in Jake's eyes made him realize this was a rare instance of him being serious. "Thanks. We'll see how it goes. She's meeting the realtor there today and bringing her stuff with her. She's going to pay rent until the deal closes."

"Where did her money come from? Husband or family? No, let me guess. Her family, which is why she was married to an asshole who was trying to gamble her money away."

"Something like that. Her father was killed in Iraq, but his family owned a big steel company a while ago in Buffalo."

"This could be interesting. Did her aunt have a lot of money? Was she sister to Caitlyn's father? Any reason to question her death?"

"I'm not sure whether she had any money, but her accident seems to be normal enough. But I left my name with Buffalo PD and informed them Cait was her next of kin. If anything out of the ordinary shows up, they'll call. They said they'd keep me informed. Though I think Buffalo PD must have screwed up somewhere. How could they not have notified her aunt's next of kin? Things aren't adding up."

Jake shook his head, "Too bad. I can get really mad at my family sometimes, but at least we have one. No other relatives?"

"Not based on what she's told me." Ryan leaned back in his chair and crossed his arms in thought. "Did you check out the driver of the car that took off from the scene of Cait's accident?"

"Yeah, it was a rental car."

"Did you follow up to see who the driver was?"

"Nah, I figured he was long gone. Sarge said to let it go. Given how bad the storm was that night, he said he's not going to charge anyone. Even the jerk that ran from the scene." He walked into the other room to grab a can of soda. When he returned, he asked, "Why? What are you thinking?"

"You know I don't believe in coincidences."

"Yeah."

"Storm or not, don't you think it's a little strange that a wealthy heiress like Caitlyn was in a car accident three months after her one surviving relative was killed in an MVA?"

"Shit." Jake sat down at his desk. "I'll see what I can find out about the guy who was driving the rental."

"Thanks." Ryan got up and headed out the door. "Let me know what you find."

"You stopping at the inn tonight?"

"No."

"Why not? Caitlyn?"

"No, going to Erin's." The door slammed behind him.

Caitlyn followed Ryan's father into the main entrance of the Summerville Memorial Hospital. After examining the house by the lake, which he'd given his stamp of approval, he'd suggested bringing her here to meet with his sister, Ellen, who was now the Nurse Recruiter after working at the hospital for several years. An old feeling of comfort and safety crept over her as she walked through the door. Though she had no financial need to work, she loved being a nurse. All hospitals smelled the same, though some were cleaner than others. The entrance to the small two-hundred-bed hospital was inviting, low voices chatting at the information desk. Mr. Ramsay returned with a name tag for her and slapped his own on his jacket.

"Well, you've got yourself a lovely house, Caitlyn. Hopefully, we can find you a job in Summerhill to your liking."

"Thanks so much for helping me with the cottage, Mr. Ramsay."

"No problem. The house is sound with lots of land for a cottage on a lake. The plumbing has been updated along with the electrical system. I think you've chosen well. It has a lot of character, too. Are you ready to meet my sister?"

Caitlyn nodded. "A little nervous, but ready."

"I'm sure you'll do fine. The hospital is always looking for good nurses like you. I'll show you to Ellen's office."

He led the way down the hall, talking about the hospital the whole way, his pride in the place obvious.

"I hope you like it here. I know you're moving here from a much bigger city, so if this hospital is too small for you, we aren't far from Rochester, especially with the expressway and the thruway. But I prefer smaller hospitals. Mallory loves her job here. They're very good to her."

"They treated me well on my visit." Caitlyn smiled at Ryan's dad. She could see where Ryan got his good looks. His dad was handsome, very tall, and broad shouldered, though his hair was much darker than his son's with shocks of gray peppered through it.

"I feel terrible that you arrived in Summerhill in such an awful way, but you sure did find one of the nicest houses on the lake. It isn't one of the larger places, but the rooms are all decently sized. If you have family that likes to visit…oh, sorry. I think Ryan mentioned you don't have any family nearby. Forgive me, I'm just an old man who likes to run his mouth. Anyway, I'd be glad to see you find a place here at the hospital. I'm on the Board of Directors, so I have a special interest in Memorial."

"What drew you to that position, Mr. Ramsay?"

"Ryan, call me Ryan. But that's probably confusing for you. What do you call my son?"

"Ryan."

"Okay, then Mr. Ramsay is fine. I used to be an anesthesiologist up until a few years ago. I retired from practicing, but I still teach occasionally at the University of Rochester, and I like to keep my hands in the medical world." He held the elevator door open for her as they headed for the bottom floor.

"My apologies." She couldn't help but blush. "I should be addressing you as Dr. Ramsay."

"Mr. Ramsay is fine, since you aren't my patient."

Caitlyn didn't know many doctors who would have answered her that way, so she decided to change her form of address, whether he'd requested it or not. It was a matter of respect, which he deserved all the more because he was humble. "Did you practice here?" Caitlyn asked as he pushed the button for the basement.

"For many years. I was part of a corporation of physicians,

so I also worked at Rochester General Hospital and occasionally at the University of Rochester's Medical Center, though we called it Strong Memorial Hospital. This place is SMH too, so it gets confusing sometimes. I love working with students at the U. of R. med school.

"But now my new family keeps me plenty busy, especially since it's so large. Lorraine and I have been blessed in many ways. I enjoy all the Grant and Ramsay kids. They're each special in their own way." He gave her a serious look. "Though Ryan is my first and will always be special. Don't tell anyone I said that." Dr. Ramsay smiled.

They headed down the hallway and he stopped in front of an office door. "Here we are." He stood back as he pushed the door open and gestured for her to enter the room.

"Ellen, I have a new nurse for you." After the introductions, Caitlyn sat and Ellen ushered her brother to the door. He turned around before he left. "Caitlyn, lovely seeing you this morning. I have other places to go, but please stop at our house any time."

A short time later, Caitlyn followed Ellen Ramsay into the Emergency Room. After spending an hour discussing the hospital, the various units, and where Caitlyn would fit best, Ellen had offered to take her on a small tour of the facility. The last unit was the emergency room, where Caitlyn was most interested in working.

Summerville Memorial Hospital was much smaller than the hospital she'd worked at in Philadelphia, but it reminded her of a small facility she'd loved working in during one of her clinical rotations at Niagara University, where she had received her Bachelor of Science Degree in Nursing. Ellen introduced her to the charge nurse, Mary Decamp, and to the Nurse Manager, Susan White. After the tour, she was interviewed by Susan White and one of the floor nurses.

When she was satisfied with Caitlyn's answers, Susan said, "Well, if you're interested and we confirm your license and experience, we would be pleased to welcome you as a member of our staff. When can you start?"

Caitlyn smiled. She might have ended up in Summerhill by some fluke of fate, but everything was falling into place.

After Ryan pulled into Erin's apartment complex, he stayed in his parked car for a moment before summoning the will to go inside. Visiting was hard, though he came every few weeks.

Erin was his best friend's widow.

Chad Armstrong had been Ryan's best friend all through high school. They had enlisted together at the age of twenty, along with Jake, who had just turned nineteen. The three of them had pledged to come home together.

Unusual though it was, they had been stationed together in Baghdad. But they hadn't come home together like they'd planned. Ryan had come home first, disgraced. Jake had stayed on another year and come home as a hero.

But Chad? Chad never made it back. Well, in a way, he had, but it was in a body bag. Chad was dead. He could no longer breathe or laugh or kiss his wife. He would never see his son, never spend a fun-filled day with his family or his friends.

As Ryan climbed the stairs to her door and rang the doorbell, his stomach clenched again. When he had first returned from the service, he had visited Erin often, believing that he was obligated to take care of her. After all, Chad had been his best friend and had died in his arms. It was only right that he take care of Erin and their son, especially since Chad had said something to that effect before he had died.

But Ryan and Erin just didn't mesh together. He had asked her about dating, but she had turned him down. However, he couldn't just walk away, so he came back to visit at least once a month. They were both comfortable about it now, and their son had accepted him.

Erin answered. "Hi, Ryan. Come on in." Her long brown hair sat piled on top of her head, and her brown eyes warmed to his smile.

Ryan stepped over a couple of toys, then leaned over to kiss her cheek. "Hey, Erin. Everything okay? How's Sammy?"

A young boy came charging out of his room and ran into his arms. "Uncle Ryan!" A grin danced across his face. "I got the highest score on that new game you brought me. Come on, let me show you." Sammy grabbed both of Ryan's hands and tugged him toward the living room.

Ryan gave Erin a sheepish grin. "Sorry, I guess I'm wanted."

She waved her hand at him and returned the smile. "Go ahead, Ryan. He's just excited to see you."

Ryan followed him over to their big-screen television and grabbed a controller. "Fine. Show me how to play so I can kick your butt."

CHAPTER SEVEN

Three days later, Ryan had to admit he couldn't get his mind off of Caitlyn. He wondered how the day had gone with his dad. He pulled his phone out as soon as he arrived back at his apartment after work, searching for Cait's number.

Ryan: *Everything go ok?*

A minute later, she answered.

Cait: *Yes. Your dad is so sweet and your aunt is nice.*

Ryan: *New job?*

Cait: *Yes, emergency.*

Ryan: *Mallory will be happy to hear that.*

Cait: *I'm excited. Want to stop and see my new furniture?*

Ryan thought for a minute, then typed in: *Now?*

Cait: *Sure, come on over.*

Ryan smiled and backed his car out. *Gladly.* He had to admit he was very happy to spend time with Cait. He couldn't get his mind off the woman.

Caitlyn stood in the middle of her great room, looking around at the new furniture she had ordered and the new carpet. Everything was settling into place. She sighed and walked over to the sliding glass doors in front of the house, doing what she loved to do several times a day—stare out at the lake. She was glad Ryan had contacted her and was on his way over.

Nothing was more peaceful to her than the calm waters of a lake. Though she'd been to the ocean and loved the beach, there was something about this lake that spoke to her more than any other place. She couldn't wait to swim in the water once it was warm enough. Of course, she'd have to go out in the early morning, before the boats were out in the water. In the winter, it was quiet, but a part of her would welcome the sound of motorboats and jet skis, the laughter of families on the water.

She walked into the laundry room just off the bathroom and finished folding her clothes. Her first day of work was coming up, which both excited and scared her. Helping people was her passion, and she especially liked working in the emergency room, where she could help calm and reassure frightened people. She liked to help where help was needed most. Of course, there was a dark side to the work—many people died in the ER. But the good outweighed the bad.

Ellen had said she could wait to report to work until a week from Monday, but she hadn't pulled a full shift for a while, so she'd volunteered to come in on Friday to shadow her preceptor and gain some familiarity with the department. Orientation started on Monday, and it was the general hospital orientation, so she wouldn't get back to her department until Wednesday or Thursday.

The doorbell rang, and it was Ryan. She wiped her hands on her jeans just to make sure her palms weren't sweating.

She opened the door and smiled. "Hi, Ryan. Come on in."

Ryan stamped his feet and took off his coat. Glancing around the great room, he said, "Wow, Cait. This place looks great. You have an eye for decorating."

"You think so?" She crossed her arms as his gaze moved around her room.

"Yeah, nice job."

"You want a beer?"

"Sure."

Cait got one for him, and when she returned to the room he was standing in front of the sliding glass doors, staring out over the lake with a look of awe. It moved her to see that the lake affected him just as it did her. She handed him the beer and he opened it, taking a couple of swigs before he walked over to the coffee table and set it down.

"I was going to turn basketball on. Any special game you're interested in?" She grabbed the remote to turn on the television, noticing that her hand shook a little around it.

His voice turned husky. "Yeah, there *is* something I'm

interested in."

The way he said it puzzled her, so she set the remote down and stared at him. His gaze caught hers and he reached for her hand, pulling her toward him. "You. I'm interested in you."

His lips descended onto hers and he gave her a ravenous kiss, grasping her head in his hands, running his fingers through her hair as he ravaged her lips. Their tongues twined until they were both panting. When he ended the kiss, he said, "Sorry, but that's all I could think of doing when I saw you."

Cait was stunned, unable to speak. Forcing a quick recovery, she said, "Me, too." She settled onto the couch with a flop, unable to look away from Ryan.

"Would you like to turn on a game?" he asked as he sat next to her. "There's a big one between Michigan and Michigan State today."

"No." She could tell from the way he devoured her with his gaze, floating from her lips to her breasts, that he understood her simple answer. The desire flooding through him was practically visible, like waves of heat off a blistering road. No one had ever looked at her like that before, like she was beautiful and sexy and hot, but that's exactly how she felt. Ryan wanted her. Bad. And she wanted him just as much.

His hand settled on her leg. If the house had caught on fire right that moment, Caitlyn would have melted into the floor. Her legs would not have held her up. The heat from his hand spread straight up her leg to her sex, and she squirmed. Needing no further invitation, Ryan grabbed her shoulders and pressed his mouth on hers with a deep groan. They fell back onto the couch together, his tongue stroking hers, causing her breath to hitch and her heart to pound, sending blood roaring through her veins in anticipation of his next touch. He cradled her jaw so tenderly she wanted to cry, and she wove her hands through his hair to bring him even closer. When he pulled back, she could only gasp for her next breath. He was about to say something when his phone went off.

"Fuck." He sat up and grabbed his phone from his pocket, checking to see who it was before he shoved it back inside. He ran his hand down his face before he turned to her and helped her sit up. "Sorry. It's work."

"No, it's okay," she mumbled.

He grabbed the beer, took a swig, and brought it over to the kitchen counter. "I probably better go." He leaned over and gave her a quick kiss, then disappeared before Caitlyn could say a word. She ran her tongue over her lips after he left, savoring the taste of peppermint.

She woke up bright and early on her first day of work. Though she arrived at the hospital a few minutes early, the charge nurse, Mary DeCamp, was already there, and she brought her back into her office.

"Here's your badge, though you aren't set up for the med system until you go through orientation, so you can't administer any meds today. You remember your HIPAA laws, right? I have to ask because you don't sign all that paperwork until orientation."

"Yes, I will be discreet, I promise. I just wanted to get a head's start, so I'll be ready to dig in right after orientation. Where can I put my coat?"

Mary took her in back and assigned her a locker in the break room. As she put her things away, the door opened and another nurse entered.

"Oh, perfect timing," Mary said. "Caitlyn, this is Mallory Ramsay. She'll be your preceptor for the next three weeks until you're on your own."

Caitlyn tried to contain her excitement, so she just smiled at Mallory and said, "Nice to see you again. I'm excited that we'll be working together."

"Wow," Mallory said, glancing from Mary to Caitlyn. "I heard you took the job, but I had no clue you'd be starting this soon!"

Mary looked from nurse to nurse, a puzzled expression on her face. "You two have met?"

Caitlyn said, "Yes. I was in the ER last week and Mallory talked me into coming to work here. That's why I still have a bit of a limp, though I have no problem getting around anymore."

"Oh. I didn't know. Nice job, Mallory." Mary patted her on the back. "Well, I'll leave you both to it. If you have any questions, just let me know."

Right after Mary left, an older nurse came in, grumbling to herself. She stopped in front of Caitlyn. "Who are you?"

"I'm Caitlyn McCabe, a new hire." She held her hand out to the woman, but her gesture was ignored. The woman pushed past her without another comment.

Mallory said, "Caitlyn, this is Lucille. She's been here for many, many years."

Caitlyn smiled, though she could already sense that the other woman wasn't the type to respond to good cheer. "Hi, Lucille. Nice to meet you."

Lucille grunted. "How long you been a nurse? You aren't a newbie, are you?"

Caitlyn glanced at Mallory, catching her eye roll. "No, I'm not."

Grunting in response, Lucille hung her coat up and turned to look at her, hands on her hips. "Good, because I don't want to have to pick up your slack." With that, she left the room.

"Just ignore her, Caitlyn," Mallory said in an undertone. "Every department has their bitch, and she's ours. She's been here forever, and all she does is complain. Makes you wonder why she stays. Be careful with her, though, she can be very sneaky."

They walked back onto the floor and Mallory gave her a quick tour of the med room, the supplies, and the kitchen, providing her with the codes to get into all the rooms. Then she took her into the nurse's station so they could sit and go over the computer system. "You'll have your own computer, but I'm guessing you can't do much today besides shadow me to get a feel for the place."

Mallory had four patients to start and the ER was consistently busy. Caitlyn was glad to get back into the familiar routine, and she enjoyed talking to the patients and listening to their stories.

Before Caitlyn knew it, it was already mid-afternoon. But while all the other nurses were busy, Lucille was sitting at the desk, reading the paper and checking her phone. She didn't seem to notice or care that the others were overwhelmed. At one point Caitlyn passed her and Lucille stopped her, holding out her hand to give her something.

On reflex, Caitlyn reached out to take it. "Here," Lucille said, "go give this to my patient in #10. Thanks." She dropped two Vicodin into her palm and turned around to her paper again.

"Sorry, but I can't. I'm not cleared to give meds yet."

Lucille glared at her. "Yeah. Who's gonna know? Just give them to him."

Caitlyn set the wrapped pills back in front of Lucille. "Sorry, but I'm not willing to risk it."

As Caitlyn walked away, she heard Lucille's groan. "So that's how it's going to be with you. Nice way to help a teammate. Thanks."

When Caitlyn caught up with Mallory and told her what had happened, Mallory sighed and shook her head. "Like I said, be very careful with her. As soon as you took those meds down the hallway, she would have reported you."

"You mean she was setting me up?" Caitlyn had worked with some difficult people over the years, but she couldn't believe anyone would do something so conniving.

"Don't deal with her at all unless you have no choice. She's very sneaky. And she loves to go after newbies."

Caitlyn glanced back at Lucille. The older woman looked up from her paper long enough to give her a sneaky grin.

The rest of the day proved very busy. It must have been a full moon because patient after patient walked in or was dropped off by ambulance, some with some unusual injuries. At one point, Caitlyn went from cubicle to cubicle to see if she could do anything for any of the patients because the physicians were so behind. It gave her something to do while Mallory doled out medications.

She ran to get some ice chips for one patient and she heard someone call out her name. She swung around to see who it was and had to repress a groan when she saw it was Lucille.

"I hope that isn't for my patient."

Caitlyn said, "I don't know. I just answered the call light, and the woman asked for some ice chips. I'm only trying to help."

"Well don't. Stay away from my patients."

"Lucille, I can't refuse a direct request for help. I think it will help lighten your load a little."

Lucille glared at her. "Don't worry about my load. I don't give this warning lightly, newbie. Stay away from my patients."

That cemented what she already knew—working with Lucille was going to be a challenge. Too bad nurses couldn't interview the rest of the floor before they accepted their position in a unit.

At the end of their shift, she and Mallory walked out to the parking lot together. Caitlyn was just about to get into her car when a police cruiser pulled up next to them and stopped. Her gut clenched. What had they done?

The window rolled down and Ryan smiled at them. "Ladies."

Caitlyn couldn't help but smile back. She had fond memories of last night.

"Cait," Ryan said. "I have some information for you, and I have an hour for dinner. Do you want to go to the diner with me?"

Caitlyn glanced at Mallory. "Um, sure. Right now?"

"Well, this is my break. Can I meet you there?"

Mallory gave her a push. "Go ahead. Good job today. I'll see you next week." She headed in the opposite direction.

"Okay. I'll meet you there in five minutes." Caitlyn waved and headed to her car, just noticing that her heartbeat sped up at the sight of Ryan Ramsay.

She hadn't realized it, but she'd missed him, and it had only been one day.

CHAPTER EIGHT

Ryan stood up as soon as he saw Cait walk through the door of the diner. Damn, but she even looked great in scrubs. As soon as she slid in the seat across from him, he said, "First day go okay?"

"Yeah, I wanted to get to know the hospital and the department a bit before orientation."

"How'd it go?"

"Actually, other than one thing, everything went very well. Your sister is my preceptor, and I know we'll get along great."

"And the one thing?"

"Oh, just a nurse I had a couple of run-ins with. Mallory says it's not uncommon for this particular woman."

"Mallory won't let anyone walk all over her. You shouldn't either." Ryan waved to a couple he recognized as they walked through the front door.

"I won't. I held my ground."

Ryan shook his head. "I'll never understand why some nurses are such bitches."

"It happens frequently. Now they call it bullying. I'm sure I'll hear all about it in orientation next week."

The waitress came over, and they both placed their orders.

As soon as she left, Cait said, "So...you said you have news?"

Ryan sat up straight in his seat. This wasn't going to be easy, but Cait had already known her aunt was dead, so that part wouldn't come as a surprise. He decided to plunge ahead. "I checked on your aunt in Buffalo. She died in a car accident last December. Black ice, nothing suspicious." Well, there was nothing suspicious on the report. He had his own thoughts, but he wasn't ready to share them with her yet. Of course, he had found out quite a bit about her husband, too, but since he'd done that research on his own volition, he didn't feel it was his place to tell her what he'd discovered. He reached for her hand and covered it with his. "I'm sorry, Cait."

"Oh, a car accident?" She was quiet for a moment, and Ryan could tell her mind was churning with a million questions.

Guessing what she would ask next, he said, "She died instantly, Cait."

Her gaze shot up and caught his for an instant, enough for him to see her pain. "Oh, well that's good, I guess. Thank you, Ryan, for letting me know."

"I left my name and number with the Buffalo PD in case any issues arise, and I gave them your name as the next of kin. The sergeant I spoke to didn't know anything about her or the accident. He didn't remember it, because he wasn't involved."

"Okay. Well..." She nodded her head, then reached up to swipe the tears gathering at her lashes. "Well, at least I know."

They ate in silence, and Ryan couldn't help but worry about her. "Do you want to catch a movie or something when I get off at ten?"

"No. Thank you, but I think I'd rather be alone tonight."

Silence descended again while they both picked at their food. He wanted to respect her need to be alone. He hoped her rejection wasn't directed at him, but just the situation and the timing.

"All right." Ryan said. "I'll accept that. You probably had a long, tiring day. But I won't take no for an answer to this next question. How about if I pick you up in the morning and bring you over to the famous Ramsay picnic at the inn on Saturday."

"The what?" she grinned.

"My dad and my stepmom have a picnic every Saturday, summer or winter, rain or shine. They claim it's the only way they can keep track of all of us. It's always potluck, but my stepmother is a great cook. Mallory will be there and most of my other siblings. Plus my dad has been asking how you're doing in the new house."

She nodded. "I would like that. Sure. What time?"

"Can I pick you up around eleven?"

"Sure. Eleven it is."

Ryan breathed a sigh of relief. He wasn't ready to let her go yet.

Caitlyn set her phone down and sat staring out of the window overlooking Orenda Lake. It was over. Finally, her marriage to Bruce Dalton was over. She had just finished a conversation with her lawyer, who had informed her that Bruce's lawyer had accepted the terms of the divorce. Bruce had actually signed the papers. Her lawyer was just waiting to get the papers before it was official.

She was single again.

Bruce hadn't argued the terms of the divorce either, which surprised her. Her lawyer had insisted on a prenuptial agreement, and Bruce had willingly signed it. But the prenup had specifically stated that if Bruce was ever caught cheating, he would receive no settlement or alimony payment—that he would only be entitled to half of what they'd both made while married.

Bruce hadn't made much. He had managed a cell phone retail store for half of their marriage, but then he had been fired. He had been job hunting ever since, but he hadn't found anything. Caitlyn suspected he hadn't been searching very hard. He had been quite content to stay at home, though he'd refused to do laundry or anything to help her out.

She had been quite naïve about their marriage. One day, Caitlyn had been sent home early from a twelve-hour shift because they were slow. When she pulled into the driveway at their house, she had wondered why her friend's car was there, but she'd walked into the house without giving it too much thought. There, in the living room, her best friend from the hospital was on her knees servicing her husband, who sat splayed on their couch. Caitlyn had frozen in the doorway, not knowing what to do or say. What was the proper response to such a sight?

At least her friend had appeared to experience a little guilt. She had jumped up, grabbed her bra and shirt (her pants were still on), thrown them on, and ran out the door with a trite,

"Sorry," on the way out.

Bruce hadn't moved. Instead, he'd actually said, "Oh my God, Caitlyn."

She'd stayed at a hotel that night and contacted her lawyer in the morning before leaving for Buffalo. She never wanted to see Bruce Dalton again.

Caitlyn had offered to give him the house for two reasons. The first was that she never wanted to go back to Philadelphia. The second was that she wanted no part of that house after what she'd witnessed there, after the unhappy life she'd shared there with her sleazeball ex. Since he was unemployed, and there was no mortgage, maybe it would help guarantee that he'd stay in Philadelphia—and far, far away from her. She'd decided to settle a sizeable sum on him to help him get back on his feet for the same reason.

The sound of the doorbell shook her out of her trance. Ryan had arrived. She smiled and warmth washed through her body, spreading to her fingers and toes.

She answered the door and moved aside so Ryan could come in. He kissed her cheek and moved in past her. "Are you ready?" A few more steps and he whistled. "Cait, how did I not notice the television the other night?" His gaze stopped on the new fifty-inch television. "Nice, Cait, very nice. Do you watch any sports?"

"Yes, I love football. My aunt made me a Bills fan. How about you?"

"We're all Bills fans here. Too bad they didn't make it to the Super Bowl."

"No, but they did have a much better year. My husband liked the Steelers. Now I guess I'll have to root against them." She clapped her hand over her mouth.

Ryan gave her a puzzled look.

She dropped her hand to her side. "I promised not to mention my husband again, though I will mention that he agreed to the terms of the divorce and has signed the papers. It's official. I'm single again once it goes through the court system."

He crossed the distance between them and cupped her cheeks. He kissed her, a light kiss at first, then he pulled back.

"Well then, Caitlyn McCabe, let's see if I can make you forget him."

She moaned and leaned into him. He kissed her deeply this time, parting her lips and caressing her tongue with his. Oh, how she loved the taste of this man. She crushed her body to his and her nipples reacted, even through the heavy sweater she had on.

When he ended the kiss, he ran his thumb across her plump bottom lip. "Is that better?"

She sighed. "Yes, much."

"Your scratches are healing, Cait, but you're beautiful even with the imperfections."

She blushed, but didn't move. The way Ryan looked at her, she felt beautiful.

"Here. I'll get your coat. When you go to a picnic where there are fourteen or more people present, you need to get there on time or risk missing the best food." He grabbed her coat from the chair and helped her on with it.

"Then I guess we better hurry, because I'm starved. I slept in late, so I haven't eaten yet." She picked up the flowers she had purchased for his stepmother and headed out the door.

As soon as they arrived, a bevy of people rushed outside to greet them. Ryan introduced her to all his siblings: Lauren, Jake, and Mallory, whom she had already met; a brother, Blake; two sisters, Madison and Paige; and his step-siblings Matthew, Chloe, and Daniel. Colton and Lucas were twins, and they were both in the military. "Even though Lauren and Madison are both attending college, they still find their way here for Saturday picnic."

As soon as he finished, Lauren said, "First test, now repeat all those names."

Caitlyn attempted, but she forgot a couple.

"You did really well, Caitlyn. I think you should keep her, Ryan," Chloe said with a mischievous grin.

Once they stepped inside, she greeted Dr. Ramsay, and he introduced his wife, Lorraine, a beautiful older woman who managed to look serene even in the midst of the comfortable chaos of the big house and bigger family. Lorraine thanked Caitlyn for the flowers and headed into the kitchen to find a vase. Caitlyn and Ryan followed her to help slice rolls for the meal—a family favorite, Beef on Kimmelwick sandwiches. Potato salad, baked beans, and fresh fruit were already arranged on the tables in great big bowls.

They sat at one of the smaller tables with Jake, Mallory, Paige, and Lauren. Caitlyn loved listening to the chatter of the huge clan, never having experienced such a thing before.

"How many in your family, Caitlyn?" Paige asked, the youngest of the group at seventeen.

"I'm alone."

"Oh, sorry." Paige gave her a sympathetic look. "What happened to your parents?"

"Paige!" the others all cried out.

Caitlyn reached for Ryan's hand and covered it with hers. "It's all right." She turned to Paige. "My mother died when I was eighteen. She was an alcoholic. She couldn't handle the loss of my father."

"Why? What happened to your father?"

"My father was killed by a bomb in Iraq when I was thirteen."

The entire room became silent, every member of the Grant-Ramsay family staring at Caitlyn in disbelief.

CHAPTER NINE

Caitlyn glanced around the room and said, "What's wrong?" Her fork froze in her hand.

Dr. Ramsay cleared his throat and said, "Caitlyn, would you mind repeating what you just said?"

Caitlyn set down her fork and said, "I was talking about my parents, Dr. Ramsay. My father died in an explosion in Iraq when I was thirteen. My mother couldn't handle it and started drinking too much. She died when I was eighteen."

"How awful," Lauren whispered.

Lorraine gave her a sympathetic look and said, "We're so sorry, dear. That must have been very difficult for you."

"Yes, but I moved in with my aunt when I turned sixteen, so I wasn't alone."

Mallory reached for her hand. "Still. We all know what it's like to lose one parent. You lost both. I'm so sorry for your loss."

Caitlyn blushed and stared into her lap. "Please. Go back to this wonderful meal. Everything is delicious, Lorraine."

Bits of chatter popped up at each table grouping. Once she was certain she was no longer the center of attention, Caitlyn glanced at Ryan, "Sorry. I didn't want to put a damper on the picnic."

"Don't be. I'm sorry for your loss." Ryan swore his heart had stopped beating when Caitlyn said her father was killed in an explosion in Iraq. How could that be? He didn't believe in coincidence. He shoveled food in his mouth, unable to take part in the conversations around him, unable to even look at Caitlyn as he tried to process what he'd just learned. Then he froze.

Suddenly, he was back there, hearing the sound of the bomb exploding, reaching for his friend and searching for his brother. Lights flashed in his peripheral vision, a boom went off next to his ear, and he saw Chad grab his chest before collapsing. Yelling alternated with the strange silence caused by his temporary deafness. Then his voice, Jake's voice, gunfire, Chad screaming, pain, more pain, more gunfire…He grappled to get out of their upturned vehicle, to save Chad. More gunfire. Chad's voice telling him something. *What was it? I can't hear you, Chad.* His hand gripped something—a gun? his fork?—and he couldn't let go.

"Ryan? Are you alright? Ryan?"

A sweet voice beckoned to him, cutting through all the chaos around him. Cait. He turned his head and saw her staring at him, her golden halo of curls making her look like an angel. Her hand reached under the table and grasped his hand in hers. "Ryan." He heard her voice as if he was on a different plateau, above her but next to her. Was that possible? He stared into her eyes, not daring to look away…if he did, he'd see bombs exploding all around them, he was certain of it. Feeling a sudden slice of fear in his chest, he grabbed her arm to pull her away from the bombs before one hit her. He couldn't let that happen to her, too.

"RYAN!" Mallory yelled at him.

Mallory brought him back. He stuttered and set his fork down, reaching down into his lap for his napkin. "What, Mallory? I'm fine."

For a stricken moment everyone was silent, but then his siblings started to chatter and play with their food again. He glanced over at his father and saw his dad's keen gaze on him, measuring him, always assessing as he had been trained to do. Caitlyn's hand was intertwined with his and gave his hand a squeeze.

"Mallory, what shifts are you working this week?" she asked.

Jake was still staring at him with alarm, as he always did at times like these, but Caitlyn did not seem frightened of or for him. She held his hand and smiled at him every once in a while, carrying on her conversation with Mallory as if nothing had happened.

She hadn't left. She hadn't run away, run from *him*, the way everyone else had.

He peered at the beautiful woman next to him. Every other time he had slipped into one of his PTSD episodes around a woman he was dating, she had excused herself, never to be seen again…at least by him. The first time had been two weeks after he was released from the hospital. His girlfriend of three years had stared at him as if he were a stranger—and a dangerous one at that—and fled his side in a hurry.

The other woman he had dated since the *incident* had only lasted a few weeks. Then he experienced an episode while they were eating in a restaurant. She had faked an emergency and insisted on leaving right away. He had never seen her again.

Which was why he didn't date. Well, at least one of the reasons why. He knew his problems were the kind women ran from.

But not Cait.

This only verified what he already knew: Caitlyn McCabe was different.

He peeked at her from the side again as she was talking to Paige. His aura—or whatever you wanted to call it—was descending upon him. It was hard to explain what it was to someone who'd never experienced one, but it most resembled a fog or a haze. He could barely speak when he was in his aura; sometimes it came upon him before a full-blown episode, sometimes a minute or so after it. He couldn't take in all his surroundings when he was in his aura. Right now, he saw his father, Jake, Mallory and Cait. Nothing else existed; no one else existed. Not even him.

When he was in his aura, he couldn't feel anything. It was a protective cocoon, keeping things he couldn't handle at bay for a time. But this one was different because he could feel one thing.

Cait's hand squeezing his.

When it came down to it, the incident itself had seemed so minor. Ryan's fork stopped midair and stayed there, his eyes fixed on some far-off sight.

As soon as that had happened, Dr. Ramsay said, "Caitlyn, you know Ryan was in the army, right?"

Caitlyn nodded and glanced back at Ryan, still not moving. After Mallory yelled his name three times, he finally responded, setting his fork on the table and grabbing his napkin.

Since she could tell he was embarrassed and uncomfortable, Caitlyn reached for him and held his hand in hers to help him through the episode, whatever it was. She rested one finger on his radial pulse and felt it speed up as all his muscles stiffened. She rubbed her thumb across the back of his hand, just wanting to let him know she was there. A few minutes later, his body changed again. His pulse slowed, his muscles relaxed, and he scanned the room again instead of staring at her.

And he was back.

Caitlyn wasn't sure what had caused the change in Ryan, but she could tell something was very badly wrong from the look in his eyes...and in the eyes of his family. They shared the same haunted expression—concern, worry, and so much love. They all watched him as they continued their conversations, but they tried to be subtle. The exception was Dr. Ramsay, who only took his gaze off his son to look at her, as if he wanted to see her reaction to Ryan.

Well, she wasn't leaving. Whatever he was suffering from didn't matter. It didn't change how she felt about him. She wanted to know more about Ryan Ramsay, and if he suffered from some type of post traumatic stress disorder, she didn't care. He was a kind, hard-working gentleman, and she wasn't ready to walk away from him because of issues with his past. Her father had been forced to deal with similar issues before his death.

No, she wasn't leaving yet, not until he asked her to leave. They finished their lunch and Caitlyn helped Lorraine in the kitchen. Ryan didn't move out of his chair, but she didn't expect he *could* yet. Had he experienced a seizure? No, it couldn't have been a seizure because Mallory had been able to pull him out of it. It had to be something else.

Dr. Ramsay stepped into the kitchen and said, "Caitlyn, would you mind helping me get something out of my car?"

"Sure, I'd be glad to help." He handed her coat to her and led her out the door, away from Ryan.

As soon as they stepped outside, Dr. Ramsay said, "Don't give up on him, please."

Caitlyn shook her head in confusion. "I'm sorry. What are you talking about?"

Ryan's father sighed and ran a hand through his hair, his gaze fixed on the ground. He finally looked up and met her eyes. "My son, Ryan. Please don't give up on him yet. He has his issues, but he's a good man."

"I'm not ready to give up on your son."

A look of relief passed over his face, but then left in a hurry. He kneaded his forehead, as if to stave off a headache, then said, "I don't know how much he has told you, but he fought in Iraq. He has post traumatic stress disorder. He's getting better, and the episodes are much less frequent now. I guess it's strange of me to say this, particularly since I'm a man of science, but I think you're special, Caitlyn, and I think you're here for a reason. Your father, when you talked about him, I think that sent Ryan into one of his episodes."

Caitlyn nodded, finally making some sense out of what had happened at lunch.

"Has he told you anything about that?" He moved his hands into his pockets.

"No."

"Then I won't say anymore. It's up to him, but please be patient with him. This...well it hasn't been easy for Ryan."

Caitlyn could see his eyes misting before he turned his gaze to look at the sky.

"Probably should head back inside. Could be snowing before long. I think we're supposed to have a storm tonight." He grabbed the door handle to hold it open for her.

She stopped and glanced at him, her head tipped. "Dr. Ramsay, did you need to get something from your car?"

He gave her a sheepish look. "No, I did what I needed to do. Thank you, Caitlyn."

When they stepped inside, Ryan was standing there waiting for them in the kitchen, though he had trouble meeting Cait's gaze. "Are you ready to go? I'll take you home."

She said her good-byes and thanked the Ramsays for the meal. As soon as they were away from prying ears, Caitlyn said, "Ryan, are you okay?"

"I'm fine. Why?" He wouldn't look at her, but he held her door open before he climbed into the driver's seat.

She waited until he closed his door. "Do you want to talk about anything?"

He shook his head and started the car.

His gaze caught hers and the gamut of emotions that crossed his face twisted her heart. "Ryan, please don't shut me out. I can't imagine what you went through in Iraq. I remember my father's stories about it."

He thought for a second before he said, "No. I'm not feeling well. I think I need to go home for a bit."

They rode in silence—if Ryan didn't want to talk about it, Caitlyn didn't know what to say to him. She thought about everything Ryan's father had told her, and wondered exactly what horrors Ryan had lived through. Her heart swelled for him.

When they were almost there, Ryan reached for her hand and held it on his lap. "I'm sure my father told you I served in Iraq."

"Yes, he did. He's very proud of you."

"I was in the army, so I have a lot of bad memories from combat. I'm sorry to have kept that from you. I try to ignore that part of my life." He kept his gaze glued to the road, but he squeezed her gloved hand.

"Ryan, don't apologize. But it may help you to talk about it. I'm a very good listener."

He shook his head and glanced at her for a moment, the pain in his eyes wrenching her very soul. "No. Someday maybe."

Caitlyn decided to let it go. Somehow she knew talking about his experience would be a major milestone for him. Her training told her it would help him to unburden himself. She had to get him to talk. "How long ago were you in?"

"A few years ago. I'd rather not talk about it, if you don't mind."

Ryan pulled into her driveway, walked her to the door and waited for her to unlock it, then gave her a quick kiss and left.

Caitlyn didn't know what to think. Getting Ryan Ramsay to open up was going to be a true challenge. Could she handle it?

CHAPTER TEN

Great, just fucking great. What better way to make a girl want you than to have a freaking PTSD episode in front of her and then go into an aura. Ryan slammed the door of his car and pulled out of her driveway, heading to his apartment.

Making matters worse, his dad had actually pulled her aside to talk to her. And what the hell had he said? Part of him wanted to go back to talk to him right now, but he was afraid of what he'd say. Maybe it would be better not to know. He loved his father, no matter what, and he knew his dad had his best interests at heart. Still, sometimes he needed to learn to *butt out.*

And he knew he shouldn't have rushed her out of there so quickly—it had been rude—but he couldn't stand the look in their eyes whenever he showed any signs of cracking—that poor-Ryan look he hated. The only one who never had that look was Jake, who had his own special look, though Ryan had yet to figure out what it meant. Jake, the brother he loved like no other, but hated at the same time... Okay, so hate wasn't quite the right word, but even though he knew he should, he couldn't get over the fact that his little brother had come home a hero, and he'd come home...this.

Shit, he was messed up. Just when he thought his life was taking a turn back toward normalcy, his past had reared its ugly head again. What the hell business did he have getting involved with Cait, anyway? He shouldn't inflict his problems on a woman, particularly not one as nice as she was.

He kept beating himself up over his every action—from the way he'd avoided talking to her in the car to the middle-school kiss he'd landed on her outside her house—as he pulled into his apartment driveway. Running his hands down his face in frustration, he gave himself a silent lecture: *Go inside, sit in front of the TV, try to find a basketball game to watch. This day was and is no different than any other. You did your family duty, now you'll go home and stare at sports. The memories will stay away.*

Stalking into his living room, he tossed his cell phone onto the coffee table and his coat over the back of a chair before plopping down on his couch and grabbing for the remote. He found a North Carolina basketball game and leaned back on his couch. His text signal went off. He had heard it in the car a couple of times, but he'd chosen to ignore it. Maybe it was Cait telling him to get lost. There were tons of messages, but none from her.

Mallory: *Are you okay?*

Ryan Sr.: *She's a nice girl, Three.*

Jake: *Can I come over?*

Mallory: *Ryan, don't do this. I know what you're doing. She's an RN. She can handle it. Don't push her away.*

Ryan laughed. Little too late for that advice, Mal. Maybe he should have checked his messages sooner after all.

He reached the most recent message, the one that had just been sent. It was another one from Mallory.

Mallory: *Ryan, talk to me.*

Of all his siblings, Mallory was the most faithful, never-give-up, always-be-there-for-you sister. He picked up the phone and punched the keys.

Ryan: *I'm fine.*

He sent it to all three.

Jake: *Can I come over? NC is on.*

Ryan: *No. I'm tired.*

The phone quieted, and he settled in to watch the game, though he didn't really take in what was going on.

He must have fallen asleep for a while, because the next thing he knew, there was a blue line across the bottom of his screen.

"Winter storm warning for all counties in central and western New York. A winter storm warning is in effect until 10 p.m. tonight. Snow, high winds, and squall conditions will approach our region between 7 and 8 p.m. coming from the west, possibly bringing blizzard conditions to our area. Stay tuned for more information."

The local TV station interrupted, repeating the storm warning and requesting that people stay off all major roadways. Storms were always dangerous, so they often needed to do overtime at the station to help out with any problems that arose. He called his supervisor. "I just saw the weather report. Do you need me to come in for overtime? I'm available to work tonight."

"Thanks, Ryan, but not yet. Haven't seen the storm yet. Charge your phone though, we may need you before the night is over. They're expecting high winds, and you know how easily this town loses power."

Ryan hung up and plugged his phone and his laptop into his charger. Then he settled back onto his couch, staring at the basketball game he wasn't watching. He should probably call Cait, make sure she was okay, but he'd only just left her. It was five o'clock, and the storm wouldn't roll in for a while. Maybe it would be best just to leave her alone for now. He closed his eyes, hoping he wouldn't see any bombs in his sleep.

The next time he opened his eyes, all he saw was pitch black. The TV was off, the wind was howling, and his phone was ringing. He brushed the sleep from his eyes and sat up, adjusting his eyes to the darkness. No power. He fumbled his way to the kitchen to unplug his phone.

He held it up to his ear. "Yeah?"

Jake was on the other end. "What the hell? Can't you answer a text?"

"I was sleeping."

"Oh, well, the storm is here. I got called in to work. You?"

"No. I may have but I missed it. You need me?"

He heard some talking in the background on the other line. A few moments later, his brother returned to the phone. "Sarge said not yet. May need you later, so get some rest. Do you have power?"

"No. Is the whole town out?"

"Power's out on the west side of the lake and half of

Summerhill."

"Shit."

"What's wrong?"

Ryan grabbed his jacket and his keys. "I'm going over to check on Cait."

Jake said, "Good idea, but text her first. She may need some candles. Call me if you need anything."

"Yep." Ryan hung up and texted Cait.

Ryan: *You okay?*

Cait: *Yes, but no power*

Ryan: *Got candles?*

Cait: *1*

Ryan: *I'll be right over.*

Cait: *No, Ryan, it's too dangerous. Stay put. I'll be fine.*

Ryan: *Be right there.*

He shoved his phone in his pocket, grabbed matches and a few candles, including the girly one in the candleholder Mallory had given him, and left.

Caitlyn stood in the kitchen in the darkness, staring out the back window that faced the driveway, waiting for Ryan to pull in. Dr. Ramsay had showed her how to unhook the garage door opener manually in case she ever lost power. Thank goodness, because she hadn't pulled her car into the garage until after she lost power. As soon as she saw Ryan's lights, she would go open the garage door so he could park in the other space.

One thing she had already learned about the Ramsay men was that though they were men's men, they knew how to take care of a woman. She'd known there would be no talking Ryan out of checking on her, so she'd just accepted it. He was a bit stubborn, but she had to admit she was relieved he was coming over. Her husband would have used the slippery roads as an excuse not to help her, but not Ryan. Somehow, she knew he would always go out of his way—even risk his own safety—to be there for her.

As soon as his headlights appeared in her driveway, she ran out and opened the garage door for him before running back near the door to stay warm. She was still in her sweatpants and sweatshirt, but at least she was warm.

Ryan climbed out of his car and said, "Are you crazy? I could have done that." But even in the dark she could see his eyes were sparkling, and she was happy she'd thought to do such a little thing for him to show some appreciation for all he'd done for her.

He closed the garage door behind him and followed her into her house, knocking the snow off his boots and taking them off at the door before hanging his jacket on the peg above them. Caitlyn leaned against her breakfast counter, her one candle arranged on the coffee table between her two couches.

Ryan walked over and stood in front of her, setting the candles he'd brought on the counter.

Caitlyn crossed her arms in front of her in an attempt to ward off the cold. Though she felt bad he'd gone out of his way to be here, the truth was, she hadn't been this happy to see anyone in a long, long time. Ryan's brown hair curled over the collar of his shirt, and she wanted so desperately to reach out and run her hands through it. The soft glow of the candle highlighted his strong jaw line, and the scruff of his beard. She ached to touch him, but she didn't know how he would receive it after the awkwardness of this afternoon. It was just too dark to see him.

She smiled instead. "Thanks for coming over." The only thing she could hear was the howl of the wind outside and his erratic breathing. With one look, the brilliant green of his eyes just distinguishable in the glow of the candle, he lit her insides to a hot, raging flame of need.

"I had to," he whispered.

She had no idea what he meant by that, but the heat of his body made her want to lean forward to absorb it. As he stood there, his gaze took a slow meandering journey down her body, pausing at her breasts long enough to cause her nipples to harden. She remembered she was braless when her erect buds brushed against the soft fabric of her sweatshirt. Thank goodness for the dark.

"I'm sorry, you had to what?" she asked, trying to keep her voice level.

"I had to come over."

The desire in his gaze made her want to shout for joy. *Bring it on, Ryan Ramsay*, was all she could think. The way he looked at her made her feel like one of the most beautiful women on the planet. Visions of a shirtless Ryan standing over her filled her mind. She opened her mouth to speak, but nothing came out. She'd never wanted someone this way before; she'd never allowed herself to…

He cupped her cheeks and kissed her, a deep, ravishing kiss that invaded every inch of her, assaulted every nerve ending in her body. Her body had turned from an icicle to a pit of fire as he ran his hands down her back and tugged her against the bulge in his jeans. He pulled back for just long enough to say, "I needed to kiss you the way you deserve to be kissed…I didn't do it right before." He devoured her lips again, teasing her with his tongue until she wanted to strip in front of him and melt to the floor in a puddle at his feet.

Caitlyn tugged at his shirt, pulling it out of his pants. She wanted to squeal in delight as her hands met rock hard abs and then skated over a sprinkling of coarse hairs in the middle of his chest. She rubbed his skin, teasing him all the way up until she found his nipples and raked her nails across the tender tips.

He pulled away from her, sucking on her bottom lip before he reached for her sweatshirt. His hand stiffened as he felt her nakedness, and he sighed in pleasure. "You shouldn't leave those beautiful breasts out for me to feel like that. Now I want to see them, to feel how beautiful they are."

Caitlyn ripped her sweatshirt off and threw it across the room. "Here. They're yours. Do what you want with them." Surprised at her own boldness, she rested her hands on her hips giving Ryan a full view of her breasts.

Ryan groaned and leaned down to take her nipple in his mouth while he cupped her other breast with his hand. Caitlyn cried out as he suckled her, knowing she was beyond the point of stopping now. It didn't matter. She wanted Ryan Ramsay. And she didn't want to wait.

"Do you want this as much as I do, Cait?" His hand brushed her cheek as he waited for her answer. Always the gentleman.

"Yes. I want you, Ryan." Her hands reached up and wove into his hair just before he dipped his head back down to lave her sensitive tips. Every caress and lick was enough to make her moan.

"Good—" he brought his gaze up to hers, "—because I want you really bad right now." He kissed her neck and made a trail of caresses down her shoulder. "You are so beautiful."

Caitlyn tugged on his shirt and between the two of them, they removed it along with her pants. The sight of his muscular chest, dusted with the perfect amount of dark hair, made her lick her lips. "Ryan, a condom. Do you have one?"

"Yeah." His voice, deep and husky, shot straight to her core. He pulled one from his pocket, and she took a moment to appreciate the sight of him. She'd never been with a man like him before...all brawn and muscle and physicality. She reached his hands where he held the condom and she said, "Let me."

"No, I've got it."

"The couch, Ryan, the couch."

While his hands reached down to drop his jeans and put on the condom, he stared at her, want and desire painted all over his face. "No, Cait, right here. Right now."

He put his shirt underneath her and laid her carefully back on the lower part of the counter, moving her to the edge. And then he grasped her hips and slid into her, right there, on the kitchen counter in her brand new house. Ryan Ramsay made her scream and beg for more, something she had never done before.

CHAPTER ELEVEN

"Oh my God, Ryan," Caitlyn whispered.

"Was it good for you?"

"Huh?" She stared at him, dazed.

"You came, didn't you?" He stared at her as he fumbled with his pants, then reached down to help her sit up.

"Yes. Do you really need to ask?"

He laughed. "No. I could feel you. That was amazing, Cait." He kissed her and then found her sweatshirt and pants on the floor. "Here, it's getting a little cold in here." He helped her slide it over her head. "C'mon, I'll warm you up on the couch." She walked over to the couch slowly, as if she was still dazed, and Ryan grinned. He was satisfied, *very* satisfied. It was the best sex he'd had in a long time, and in the dark and in that position, he was sure she had no idea. There would be no reason for her to suspect anything.

"Does the fireplace work?" He walked over and moved the grates, locating the poker at the side.

"Huh? Oh, yeah. It does, the inspector said it was in great shape, but I haven't bought any wood or anything."

"Didn't I see a cord of wood in the garage?"

"I have no idea." Her voice was dusky, and he grinned again. She'd clearly enjoyed herself as much as he had. He covered her with the throw on the back of the couch and said, "I'll go check. I'll be right back."

A few minutes later, he returned with his arms full of wood. He set some in the basket next to the fireplace and arranged the rest inside it.

"Oh, is that what that's for?" She huddled on the couch, the blanket tucked around her.

"How much more wood is out there?"

"Enough for a couple of days. We won't keep it raging, just big enough to keep the chill away at night. You should probably close the door to the laundry room and the bathroom so we can keep this room warm."

"How long is the storm supposed to last?"

"I don't know. The warning was until ten tonight, but who knows how long we might be without power." Ryan got the fire going, then got on the couch and wrapped his arms around Cait. "You okay?"

"Absolutely. I'm so glad you stopped over."

"Me, too."

"Ryan, I'm really sorry about today." Cait rested her head on his shoulder.

"Why? You didn't do anything wrong." Damn, but he wish he could just get rid of the PTSD. Why did it have to continue messing with him? No, Cait hadn't done anything wrong. She had done everything right simply because she hadn't run away. That meant more to him than anything else she could have done.

"I'm sorry talking about my father brought up bad memories...and I shouldn't have pushed you to talk before you were ready."

"No problem. I should be the one to apologize to you. I regretted the way I rushed you out of there, then brought you home and dropped you at the door like an idiot. But when I have my episodes, I never talk much afterwards. They're strange. What else did my father tell you?"

Caitlyn paused a moment before speaking. "He said you suffered from PTSD from your time in the army. He didn't tell me what happened. He loves you very much, you know." She had her hand on his arm, rubbing him gently, and he let the sensation sink in and soothe him. "The fire is starting to warm the house. Thanks for doing that. I appreciate all the things you do for me."

"You're welcome. I know my father loves me. He's just trying to help, but sometimes he goes overboard." He stopped and took a deep breath. This was as good a time as any. He wasn't going to tell her everything, but it wouldn't hurt to tell her something. "My leg was badly injured by a roadside bomb in Baghdad. That's why I limp."

"Oh, I'm sorry."

His phone went off with four text messages that arrived one after another. He got up and pulled it out of his jacket. Not his boss, fortunately. He had no desire to leave Cait yet.

Ryan Sr.: *Thunderstorm*

Mallory: *There's a thunderstorm coming. Odd for it to arrive in a snow storm, but apparently it's already hit south of Buffalo. Where are you? Want me to come over?*

Jake: *Thunder snow in Buffalo. Working till eight a.m., but Sarge doesn't need you. Maybe tomorrow early.*

Blake: *Thunder snow. Get off the road if you're driving.*

Cait looked at him with raised eyebrows. "What is it? Is everyone okay?"

"Yes, but there's a thunderstorm coming this way." He texted his response, letting his family know he was safe.

Ryan: *I'm at Cait's. No problem*

"In the snow? I've never seen one in the winter before." She scowled at him. "Are you sure?"

"Yeah, I've seen them before. They're not nice. Maybe I should go home."

"Why? I have to be honest. I'd like it if you stayed. No power, storming, howling wind, thunderstorm. Please stay?"

Ryan sighed, letting himself bask in the warmth of her words as he drew her close and tucked her head under his chin. "I don't know, Cait. Thunderstorms bother me."

"Really?" It suddenly dawned on her why. "Oh, the thunder sounds like an explosion. That makes sense. I'm sorry, but wouldn't it be better to have someone around you? I'll help you get through it."

Ryan thought about how she had been at the family inn. She had simply held his hand to show him her support, not staring at him, not embarrassing him. Maybe he could chance it. His sister was right—she was a nurse. Even though his episodes weren't really seizures, they did wreak havoc on his mind. And it wasn't like anything bad had ever happened; he had never hurt anyone—at least not yet. It was just like his worst memories exploded in his mind and incapacitated him.

"All right, I'll stay. But don't take anything I say or do personally. Promise?"

"I promise."

Ryan decided to ask her about her marriage. "Have you heard from your husband?"

"No. I probably won't since he signed the papers."

Ryan had a hard time believing that he wouldn't have tried to get more money from her. She must have been very generous. From what he'd found out about Bruce Dalton—particularly the man's gambling problem—he'd assumed the guy would try to get a ton of money from Caitlyn. "If he ever bothers you, will you promise to call me?"

"Yes, I will. But I don't think he'll contact me if he hasn't done it by now."

"Even if I'm working, I want you to call me. I don't like that fact that you're here alone in this house." He kissed her forehead.

"I'll be fine, Ryan. Thank you."

He decided to ask her the tough question. "Pretty unusual for a marriage to end so quickly. Do you mind if I ask what happened?"

"I guess we know each other well enough now." She smiled and raised her eyebrows. "I came home early from a twelve-hour shift one day, and I caught him cheating with my best friend. She was on her knees in front of him in my living room."

"Ouch. I'm sorry." Ryan winced, then rubbed her back.

"I'm not. On my drive up to New York, I thought a lot about our last year together. Our first year wasn't too bad, but the last year was terrible. He couldn't find a job, not that he seemed to care, and he wanted to travel to places that didn't interest me. He really changed. Or maybe it just took me too long to figure him out."

"Really? Where did he want to travel?"

"Las Vegas for one. I never wanted to go, but he liked to gamble, which was another source of argument for us."

A bright shard of lightning streaked across the sky, followed by a loud clap of thunder. Caitlyn stared at Ryan, as if anxious to see his reaction. "Are you alright?"

"Yes, but you don't have to keep asking me that. You'll know." He stood up. "Do you mind if I close the blinds? I'd like to block out the lightning as much as possible." He walked over to the windows and was starting to close the drapes when another bright streak zipped across the sky, the thunder seconds behind. Ryan's arms came up in reaction, protecting his face from something.

They had been driving down a road in Baghdad when the bomb exploded underneath their vehicle. He and Chad were the only ones inside; Jake was in the vehicle in front of him. The entire vehicle flipped on its side, tossing him and Chad around. The door was blown off the one side and fragments of hot, jagged metal blasted everywhere.

And oh, it had hurt so very bad.

He closed his eyes as another loud clap of thunder echoed over the lake, and just like that, he was right back in Iraq, back in that awful, awful moment following the explosion. The sound temporarily deafened him. He stared at his friend, who sat slumped in the seat next to him, unmoving. He hung onto a metal bar over his head, but he couldn't figure out why he had to hang on. He didn't even know which way was up. Another explosion went off in the distance, the light blinding him, causing him to put his hands up to cover his face.

He tried to reach Chad, but he couldn't. Blood covered Chad's chest and he could tell he was gasping for air. He stuck his head out of the vehicle and saw Jake crouched on the ground shooting…and a line of insurgents firing back. He and Chad were directly in the line of fire.

He started to move toward Chad, but he yelled out as pain shot up his leg. He grabbed it and looked down at the blood soaking his pants. The material had been shredded by shrapnel, shards of the truck embedded in his leg, parts of his bone visible.

It didn't matter, he had to get Chad out.

The next thing he remembered, he was on the ground hidden behind a copse of bushes, Chad was staring at him, trying to say something. All Ryan could make out was that his friend was asking him to take care of someone. A shard of pain ripped through his body, arching his back off the ground. His ears were deafened by someone's screams, and it took him a while to realize they were his own.

Bombs went off around his head, getting closer and closer, each one louder than the one before.

"*Ryan.*"

He turned to search for whoever had called out his name. It was a beautiful, soothing voice. Not his mother, she was gone.

"Ryan!" A hand grasped his wrist and another one wrapped around his waist. "Ryan, please come sit with me."

He glanced at her. Cait. Damn, she was beautiful. Cait, the one who didn't judge him, didn't pity him. He stared at her, taking in everything about her. She was such a good person, and he wanted to commit everything about her to memory. Her eyes, her pouty lips, the concern in her gaze. It wasn't pity, which he appreciated more than he could express.

"Ryan, I'm cold. Will you sit on the couch with me and hold me? I need your warmth."

"Sure, Cait," he said simply, so grateful she wasn't asking him to talk about it. He put his arm around her shoulder and led her over to the couch. They settled on the chaise end of the couch and he wrapped her in his embrace. He settled his head on her shoulder and closed his eyes for just a moment, just long enough to stop the bombs in his vision. Something told him that he could stay with this woman forever.

The next time he awoke, he heard only silence. He glanced around the room and listened. The thunderstorm had ended, and the wind had died down. His arms were still around Cait, but his grip was looser now. He picked up his head and found her staring at him.

 She smiled. "Better?"

"Yeah. Thanks, Cait." He breathed in her scent, letting it calm him. This episode hadn't been too bad. In fact, he thought it had definitely been shorter than the last one he'd suffered in a thunderstorm.

And she hadn't kicked him out or turned away from him. Nor was she sending him away now that he was awake. Instead she was looking at him with kindness and understanding in her eyes—that special look that made him feel like it was all actually going to be okay. He remembered making love to her, remembered how glorious they had been together.

"It's all right, Ryan. I don't mind. Just tell me what I can do to help."

He didn't say anything, just kissed her cheek and grabbed for her hand. He rested his head back on her shoulder and sighed. "Cait?"

"Yes?"

"The bomb destroyed my lower leg. I wear a prosthesis."

CHAPTER TWELVE

"I had guessed." Snuggled up against him while he slept, she had felt the hard material beneath his jeans, a harsh contrast to the soft skin of his right leg. She wanted to cry for him, but knew better than to do that. He would take it as a sign of pity...and there was nothing she pitied about this man.

"Do you want me to leave?" He wouldn't look at her.

She brushed her hand through his hair, then turned his head gently until their eyes met. "No, Ryan. I don't want you to leave. The fact that you wear a prosthesis doesn't change how I feel about you. I'm thankful you survived so I can have the pleasure of being held in your arms. But thank you for telling me. It helps me understand you a little better." She paused for a moment before continuing. "Who's Chad?"

He stared at her, a myriad of emotions crossing his face before he spoke. "Chad was my best friend. He died in the explosion."

His phone rang. He reached over to the table and answered it on speaker. "Ramsay."

"Ryan," his sarge barked into the phone. "I need you. How fast can you get here?"

"If I can get out of the garage, I'll be there in fifteen minutes."

"The garage? Where the hell are you, at your folks?"

Rather than answer the question, he said, "I'll let you know if there's a problem. See you in fifteen."

He set the phone back on the table and cupped Cait's face. He kissed her deeply, with more feeling than he ever had before. "I have to leave. Probably a mess out there." He sat up and ran a hand through his hair. "Promise me you won't go anywhere?"

"I promise. Believe me, I have no desire to drive in this weather, and I'm not done with orientation, so I doubt the hospital will call me. What time is it?"

"Good. It's a little after four." He squeezed her hand, then got up to retrieve his belongings. "You have food?"

"Yes, do you want an energy bar or something to take with you?"

"No. I have some in my car." He put on his coat. "I'll come back and shovel for you tomorrow."

"Ryan, that's not necessary. I can shovel…that is, if I have a shovel." She gave him a lopsided grin, but his offer filled her heart with warmth.

"I'll check on my way out. I think I saw one hanging on the garage wall. Nice that the previous residents left a few things for you. If not, I'll grab one on my way over here tomorrow."

She stood up and walked him to the door. "Please be careful out there."

He nodded. "And Cait?

"Yeah?"

"I can shovel, too." He kissed her cheek. "I'm not an invalid."

She smiled. "Don't I know it…I think you've already shown me that in more ways than one.

He laughed as he walked out the door.

Still grinning, Ryan opened the garage door and backed out, then got out to close it behind him after checking to see that she had a shovel. This was unusual for him. It was the first time he'd left a girl's house with a smile on his face since before the incident.

The roads were a mess, but traveling was easier once he got on the main road, which had been plowed. Cars sat in the ditch on both sides of the road. People never knew enough to stay home in bad weather. He checked each one to make sure no one was inside before continuing on to the station.

His brother was emerging from the front door just as he walked up to it.

"Holy shit," Jake said, shaking his head.

"What?"

"You have a smile on your face, and it's early morning. What, you get laid last night?"

Ryan didn't answer him—he kept right on walking.

"No shit!" He slapped him on the shoulder. "Good for you."

"Shut the hell up, Jake."

His brother's laughter followed him as Ryan walked into the precinct building, and it was hard not to keep smiling.

The storm kept Ryan and his partner busy; they cruised around town, making certain no drivers or passengers were in any of the stranded cars, forming a list of all the cars that needed towing. By the middle of the afternoon, Ryan finally had the opportunity to head home. He decided to go to Cait's first to make sure she could get out for work tomorrow. Her driveway was short, so he thought he could handle it himself.

He pulled in and noticed Cait shoveling up near the garage. Hell, she shouldn't be out in this cold shoveling. She stepped aside so he could pull in the garage, and as soon as his vehicle was in park, he hopped out of his car.

"Cait, I'll do that." He headed straight for her and grabbed the shovel out of her hands.

"I can, too." She settled her hands on her hips and glared at him.

"Well, you did a nice job starting, but you should let me finish." He had to admit, Cait looked damn cute in her sweats and ski jacket. Her nose was pink, which made him grin.

"What?" She gave him a suspicious look.

He grinned. "I can tell you've been out here a while. Your nose is pink."

She scowled and tried to hide her nose with her gloves. "Well, this is heavy snow."

She let her hands fall to her sides. "Ryan, you look tired. Have you been working since four this morning?"

"Yeah, a couple of the guys live way out and couldn't get in. I stayed a few extra hours."

He shoveled the packed snow as he talked. It had taken him some practice to learn to balance with his prosthesis, but he managed pretty well now.

"Would you like some coffee or cocoa when you're done?"

He stopped and rested his hands on the shovel. "Sure, cocoa sounds good if you have it. I don't want any caffeine. I'm going to head straight home to sleep." He didn't want her getting any ideas of a repeat of last night, not in the daylight. Though she knew the truth, he wasn't ready for her to *see* everything yet.

Cait went inside and he kept going. He'd made his way to the end when his foot slid on ice and he fell face first in the snow. One thing he'd learned about his prosthesis was that once he started to fall, there was no stopping it.

Cait rushed to his side as he started to get himself back up. "Here, let me help." Her hands grabbed under his arms and she tried to lift him.

"Cait," he yelled. "I can do it myself."

Cait's hands dropped away and she stood back. "Sorry, I was just trying to help."

"I know, and I appreciate it, but I need to learn how to do everything myself." He pushed himself upright and finished shoveling, then walked back into the garage. Cait followed him without a word, and he felt a pang of guilt. He shouldn't have yelled at her, but it was important to him to be able to do everything the same way he'd done it before his injury.

Her smile was gone, but as polite as ever, she said, "Thanks for shoveling. Why don't you come in for your cocoa?"

Since he had asked for it, he couldn't very well decline, so he followed her inside. Rather than sit at the kitchen table, he stood just inside the door and removed his gloves. She handed him the mug in silence.

"Sorry, Cait. I shouldn't have yelled. I'm still adjusting to my injury, I guess."

"How long have you had the prosthesis?"

"A couple of years."

Silence again. It stretched on for a few uncomfortable moments before she spoke up again.

"Don't you think it would help if you talked about that day? Talking about incidents is the only thing that helps you get past them."

"I know. I talk to my counselor."

"Oh. Well, I'm glad you see one."

"It was a condition of my employment in the PD, but I like going to her, so I continued. Now I go whenever I feel the need."

She nodded. "Still, maybe it would help our relationship if you talked about it with me. I might understand better."

He handed the cup back to her and put his gloves back on. "Thanks for the cocoa. I'm tired, so I'm going to go home to bed." He thought about exactly what he wanted to say. "I don't want to talk to you about it." He turned to leave, but before he stepped out, he said, "You can't fix me, Cait."

On Wednesday morning, Cait strode into the emergency room at seven a.m., happy to finally be on her unit and done with the hospital orientation. She would still be paired with Mallory for three weeks, which would be fun and helpful, and she was anxious to return to patient care. She left her jacket, purse, and lunch in her locker, then headed to the nurse's station to find her new friend.

"Pull up a chair," Mallory said. "Not much happening right now. You know how the morning lull is. But it gives us an hour or so to go over all our paperwork and make sure everything is ready for the patients."

A couple of hours later, Mallory had finished with all her busy work, but things were still quiet. Sheri and Linda both had patients, so she and Mallory were up for the next admission. Caitlyn knew what emergency rooms were like. One moment no one was there; the next, it was overflowing. She had learned to enjoy the quiet moments. They were a chance for the nurses to chat and spend quality time together.

"So," Mallory said, "you lost both your parents at an awfully young age. That must have been really difficult. It was terrible for us to lose our mother, but thank goodness we still have my dad. I couldn't imagine what it would be like if they were both gone."

Caitlyn sighed. "Yeah, it was hard, especially because I was an only child. When my dad died, my mother was a wreck. Before long she started drinking and our roles reversed. I used to get her into her nightgown every night, then put her to bed. I cooked dinner usually. But I didn't do a very good job."

"But you were thirteen when your dad passed! I couldn't imagine having to take care of my mother at such a young age. It's not surprising that you weren't a stellar cook at that age."

"No, I mean I didn't do such a great job taking care of her. She had developed problems with her pancreas, then she caught a super infection that killed her. She had given up a long time ago. I think it really hurt her when I left."

"Why did you leave?"

"One day when I was fifteen, Aunt Margie came over to see us. She lived on the other side of town. She flipped when she saw the way we were living. My mother was in bed, but she'd vomited on herself and could barely converse. My aunt helped me clean her up and insisted I move in with her. She said no child should have to do that. She arranged for a home care agency to take care of my mother. So the following school year, I moved in with my aunt. Every time I visited my mom after that, she seemed weaker and weaker."

"You shouldn't feel responsible."

"I know. It was her choice. I tried to convince her to quit, but she couldn't. Drinking was an addiction for her. I know in her heart she wanted to stop."

"Is that why you became a nurse?"

Caitlyn crossed her arms and stared off into space. "In a way. This is going to sound strange, but I might as well tell you... I had to bring my mother to the emergency room a few times. I learned to relax whenever I stepped into the ER because I knew the nurses and doctors would take care of her for me. My greatest fear was that she'd die alone at home. The sounds and smells of the ER actually became a comfort to me. I think that's why I became an ER nurse."

The monitor barked nearby, and Mallory leaned over to answer. Caitlyn listened to the ambulance driver. "MVA, one patient with a possible leg fracture, stable vitals, ETA five minutes."

"Finally," Mallory quirked a smile at her. "I mean, I feel bad for the patient, but we'll have something to do."

As soon as they stood up, the automatic doors opened and

Ryan Ramsay came striding into the ER. Caitlyn froze behind the counter. She could feel the heat pool in her core just from staring at him. Sex the other night had been fantastic, but she hadn't heard from him since. And something about the look on his face when he left the other afternoon, not to mention his parting words, had told her she needed to wait for him to come to her.

The look on his face wasn't promising.

CHAPTER THIRTEEN

"Morning, Ryan."

He nodded, "Cait. I just thought I would stop in to let you both know there's an MVA with multiple injuries. Two ambulances on their way. Things will get busy soon."

"Thanks, Ry, but usually you text, not call, and we just got the message from one ambulance driver. What's up?" Mallory had a grim expression. She clearly sensed something was up, just like Caitlyn did.

"If you don't mind, may I talk to Cait for a few minutes? This won't take long, she'll be free before the ambulance arrives."

Mallory scowled and said, "Sure."

A strange, dark certainty clung to Caitlyn as she led the way into the break room, Ryan right behind her. Wrong, this was all wrong. As soon as they stepped inside, she turned to face him, her arms crossed in front of her. She knew what was coming; she could read it in his eyes. "What is it?"

Ryan cleared his throat. "Listen, the other night was wonderful, but I don't think this is working for me. I didn't want to lead you on, so I thought I would be up front. You might not believe this right now, but I have a lot of respect for you."

Caitlyn nodded. *So you screw me, then leave me.* Somehow she hadn't expected it from Ryan, which made it hurt all the more. He had made her *trust* him. She decided not to let him off so easily. "You have a lot of respect for me, so you're breaking up with me right after we had sex? There wasn't much there to begin with maybe, but after the other night, I expected there might be something. Didn't realize it was so bad for you."

"What? Cait, no. I meant what I said. The other night was amazing, but…"

"But what?" She wrapped her arms tighter in front of her body and fought to hold back the tears. How could she have been this wrong about his feelings for her?

"Look, I'm just not ready for a commitment yet. It's not a good time. You don't understand…"

"I never asked you for a commitment, Ryan, but it's fine. *I'm* fine." She waved her hand toward the door. "Go. Just go."

He stared at her for a moment, but he avoided her eyes. "I'm sorry." Just as he turned to leave, Mallory opened the door. "C'mon, Caitlyn. We've got plenty of folks waiting for us now." She scowled at her brother, then turned around and left without sparing a word for him.

A few hours later, after the chaos had finally calmed, Caitlyn and Mallory had the chance to grab lunch in the break room.

Once they'd settled around a table with their food, Mallory said, "What'd my brother want? He didn't break up with you, did he?"

"Well, truthfully, there wasn't much to break up. We had only gone out a couple of times."

"He brought you to the family picnic. That's dating to me. Ryan never brings a woman to meet the family."

"Well, it doesn't matter. You won't be seeing me at the inn again."

Mallory's head jerked up and she stared at her. "What the hell. That man is a fool if he can't tell when he has it good."

Caitlyn didn't say another word. She wasn't going to share any of her feelings with Mallory. It wasn't like she could tell his sister about what had happened the other night…or about how crushed she felt.

The afternoon grew wild and Caitlyn ran the ER like a woman possessed. One nurse had called in sick, so they were short, and she tried to pick up the entire load herself.

At the end of the shift, Mallory said, "You're running around her like a mad woman. Are you like this all the time?"

"What do you mean?" Caitlyn was in no mood to hear criticism from anyone. She had run herself ragged, sure, but it was the only way she'd been able to keep herself from crying. Everything had been so beautiful a couple of nights ago, and now...

"You've been helping everyone's patients, including ours. It's a good thing Lucille isn't here. She'd be in your face because you are everywhere."

"Sorry, Mallory. I was just trying to help."

"Well, you did a great job, but don't burn yourself out. We need you around here."

And just like that, it felt like all of the emotion of the day finally caught up to her. She'd always pushed herself hard when she was upset, as if doing so would prove to everyone around her that she was worthy of their attention and love and respect. Well, it had never worked with her mother. She had just kept drinking and punishing herself no matter what Caitlyn did. There was no point in driving herself crazy over Ryan Ramsay or trying to win his favor. She would only suffer disappointment again, just like she had with her mother.

Perhaps Ryan had done her a favor.

Ryan turned his car off after he pulled into the family inn. He hadn't wanted to go to the picnic, but he knew he'd have to face everyone eventually. He had felt like shit all week after talking to Cait in the ER, but there'd been no choice.

There were two big problems with Cait. One was she wanted to fix him and he couldn't tolerate that. Yes, he still had issues. He had been in Iraq, for God's sake. Who wouldn't have issues after having his leg blown off by a bomb *and* watching his best friend die? He saw a therapist for that reason. It wasn't something he wanted from his girlfriend. He knew he would have issues the rest of his life, but he couldn't spend his time with someone who was desperate to solve his problems for him.

The second problem had to do with intimacy. He had gotten lucky that night. It had been fast and furious and fabulous, but it had also taken place in the dark. He couldn't take the risk of her seeing him. There was no way he could tolerate the disgust he'd no doubt see in her eyes. It disgusted him to look at himself, so there was no way someone as beautiful and perfect as her could feel different.

He wasn't happy with what he'd done, but he had his reasons…and his family was just going to have to accept that. He walked into the back room, and dead silence greeted him.

Lorraine finally yelled out, "Hello, hero."

Ryan grunted a response, then followed her into the kitchen as he usually did. His youngest stepsister, Paige, almost walked into him because she was busy texting.

"Oh, sorry. Hi Ryan! I missed you. Glad you're here. Where's Caitlyn?" She glanced over his shoulder as if he might have left her in the other room.

"Cait's not coming."

"Oh." She moved past him. "Later."

Ryan grabbed some platters of salad and rolls from the kitchen and carried them into the other room. He could smell the pulled pork in the crockpot that was already set out on the center table.

No one spoke until Jake finally said, "Where's Cait?"

"I don't know." No need to explain. They'd all get on his ass anyway.

His father said, "Did you invite her?"

He stopped fussing with the platters and looked up at his dad. "No, I didn't. We're done. It just didn't work out."

Later that afternoon, Ryan sat down in front of the TV to watch the basketball game. Blake sat down beside him. "I thought there was something great between you. I really liked her and I thought you did, too. What happened?"

Ryan swiveled to stare at his brother. "What difference does it make?"

"Did she break it off?"

Jake and his father sauntered over to join them, but they stood behind the couch rather than sitting down. Matthew and Daniel were on the other couch, but they knew enough to stay out.

"No, I did," Ryan answered.

Blake paused for a moment, absorbing the information. "Why?"

"Since when do I need my family's permission to break up with a girl," he snapped. "It just wasn't working. Enough said. Leave it."

Jake circled the couch and sat on the arm of a nearby chair. "Oh, good. 'Cause if you're sure you don't want her, I think I'll ask her out."

Ryan bellowed, "Like hell! Stay away from her, Jake."

"Why would you care if you've decided you're not interested? She's hot and rich and nice. Give me her number."

Ryan shot out of his chair and pulled Jake off the arm of the chair by the collar of his shirt. "Stay away from her, and don't you dare disrespect her either."

Jake stood up and got in his face. "What are you going to do about it? I'll ask her if I want."

"I know what you're doing, and it won't work."

"Yeah, and what am I doing?"

"Trying to piss me off."

"Is it working?" Jake laughed and stepped back. "You know you want her, so what's your problem? You don't think you can handle her?"

Ryan lunged for Jake and shoved him over the coffee table and to the floor. Jake jumped back up and swung his fist back, aimed at Ryan, but he froze in midair.

"Good, hit me, Jake. I've been waiting for this. Take me on."

Their dad came over, his eyes wide with alarm. "Boys, not in the house."

He shoved Jake again, but Jake held his ground, his fist still pulled back.

"C'mon, hit me. You know you want to. You've wanted to for a long time."

Jake got in his face. "Damn right I have. You've got it coming."

"Then hit me, Jake." He pushed at his chest again. "Go on, do it. Hit me!"

Jake backed away and dropped his fist. "No."

"Why not?" He shoved his brother again. He could feel his dad and his brothers around them, but in this moment there was only him and Jake.

"Because, Dad…"

"That's not why. You punched me plenty of times as a teenager. Stop lying."

"Yeah, it is why, we can't damage the house, and I don't want to upset anyone."

"No, you won't hit me because of what I am."

"What the hell are you talking about?"

"I'm a cripple, and you won't hit a cripple."

Jake stared at him. "I can't believe you just said that. You're an ass." He turned away and stalked over to the chair and sat. "Deal with it, Ryan."

"You need to deal with it. Treat me like you always did before. I'm sick of being treated like I'm gonna break. I'm your brother, the same brother you had before Iraq."

"Then start acting like him," Jake shouted. "My brother wouldn't have run from a girl."

Ryan grabbed his coat and left, slamming the door behind him.

Fuck, he hated to admit it, but his brother was right.

CHAPTER FOURTEEN

Caitlyn threw her suitcase into the back seat of her car. Now that she was in the ER, she was back to working three twelve-hour shifts a week. She had worked yesterday, Monday, and didn't have to return until Friday because she and Mallory would be working all weekend.

Though it had given her some closure to know how her aunt had died, she wanted to know more—whether there was more to the accident, what had happened with her aunt's remains, where her possessions had been sent—so she decided to head back to Buffalo on her own to talk to someone in the police department there. Ryan had told her they didn't know much, but surely they could at least send her in the right direction.

Though she could have asked Ryan to give her the name of the officer he'd spoken to in the Buffalo department, she couldn't stand the thought of talking with him. Fears and insecurities had flooded her since their break up, and she couldn't bury the concern that she'd driven him away by being bad in bed. Maybe that was why her husband had cheated on her, too? Thank goodness she had found a job to occupy her time, or the dark thoughts would push her over the edge. Her new life was in a tailspin and she didn't know how to stop it.

The weather was much warmer than it had been, so she didn't need to worry about running into another storm. She would stay for a few days, if need be, and settle any issues relating to her aunt's estate.

Several hours later, after expending much of her patience in the Buffalo Police Department, Caitlyn managed to find the name of the local lawyer, James Watkins, who was handling her aunt's estate. There were a few sentimental possessions Caitlyn would love to keep, if she could. One of her aunt's hobbies had been quilting, and it would feel wonderful to have a few of her aunt's colorful creations in her new home.

When she arrived in the lawyer's office, she introduced herself to the administrative assistant as the niece of Margie McCabe and explained she was visiting for a couple of days.

The assistant's eyes widened as she stared at Caitlyn, temporarily at a loss for words.

"Just a moment, please."

She disappeared from her desk and slipped through a door.

Caitlyn sat down in one of the chairs arranged around the waiting area, hoping the lawyer would understand her need to see him soon.

A few moments later, the door the assistant had disappeared into reopened, and she emerged with James Watkins himself. The lawyer introduced himself and immediately invited her back into his office.

"Hello, Caitlyn," he said once they had both taken a seat— him behind the desk, her in front of it. "It is lovely to meet you. You say you are the only surviving relative of Margie McCabe?"

"Yes."

"May I see some ID?"

Caitlyn handed him her driver's license and her New York nursing license. Since she had gone to school at Niagara University, she had taken the NCLEX exam in New York, then applied for her license in Pennsylvania. Fortunately, she had kept her NYS license active.

"Do you know Bruce Dalton?" he asked as he returned her documents to her.

"Yes, he is my husband. Well, my soon-to-be ex-husband. We are in the process of divorcing."

"Well, then I think I have the answer to my question. You see, Bruce Dalton showed up here in my office claiming you had been killed in a car accident just off the NYS Thruway. He declared himself heir to Aunt Margie's fortune."

Caitlyn scowled. "My ex-husband was here?" She tried to process everything the lawyer had said, but it was too much to process. "He tried to declare me *dead*? And he knew about my aunt's death?"

Mr. Watkins nodded. "I'm afraid so. He had the letter we mailed to you a couple of months ago."

"A letter? But I never saw any letter. And you say Bruce had it?" He'd kept the truth from her for that long? She'd thought him callous and cruel, neglectful, but never so conniving...

"Yes. I'm sorry. We assumed you had seen it."

"No. *I'm* sorry, Mr. Watkins. Apparently, my ex has been keeping many things from me."

She stared at the floor, then came back to something else he had just divulged. "Aunt Margie had a fortune? That's a surprise. She lives....er, *lived* quite simply. I stayed with her for two years when I was a teenager."

"Why, yes. I remember. You see, that's why Margie rewrote her will, making you her sole beneficiary."

"Oh, I had no idea. I don't want him to have my aunt's money—he doesn't deserve a penny of it—but that's not what's most important to me." She thought about what she really wanted. "I was wondering if you could tell me where her remains are...and...and her belongings? She crafted a couple of quilted throws that I would love to keep."

Mr. Watkins smiled. "Yes, I do know where her belongings are, and I am happy to give them to you. Mr. Dalton was not interested in any of her possessions, just her money. I can tell you are her niece. She described you perfectly. What college did you attend?"

"Niagara University. Why is that important?"

"Just putting together the pieces of the puzzle. Margie left a sizeable amount of money to the university for a nursing scholarship. An imposter wouldn't know why she did it. She was very proud of you."

Caitlyn swiped the tears out of her eyes. "I had no idea she was gone. Why wasn't I notified?"

"I actually sent you two letters. You never saw either one?"

"No, I never saw any letter."

"Well, your husband has one in his possession, so my guess is that he kept both of them from you. He was very frustrated when I didn't write him a check the instant he showed up here, but he didn't have a death certificate for you, and something struck me as suspicious. By the way, I hope this doesn't upset you, but your aunt specifically requested that Bruce Dalton not be given any of these funds. I will send verification of that to your lawyer. Besides, these things take much longer than most people think... He's still here in town, hoping to wear me down. Now I don't have to worry about that because you are here."

Caitlyn stared at him in disbelief. "Bruce is here? In Buffalo?"

"Yes, I saw him last week. He came in twice. Is he in some kind of financial trouble? Knowing your family, I didn't expect you'd be in desperate need of money."

"No, I'm not. But my lawyer froze our joint accounts after we separated. The prenuptial agreement he signed said he would get nothing if he were caught with another woman. And that's exactly what happened, so now I guess he's scrambling for money. But I'd heard that he was happy with the proposed settlement, that he'd already signed the divorce papers."

"Did he receive any funds or assets in the settlement?"

"Yes, the house and a sizable payment. He isn't working presently, so I wanted to leave him with enough money to support himself until he got back on his feet."

"He hasn't been working?" The lawyer asked, his hands folded in his lap.

"No, not for the past year." Caitlyn scratched her head. Somehow the situation sounded even worse when she said it out loud.

"Has he looked for a job?"

"No, not recently. He says there's nothing out there."

Mr. Watkins nodded, his lips set in a grim line. "You know where I'm going with this, don't you? As Margie's lawyer, I feel compelled to tell you this could be a dangerous situation for you. You have no other siblings, correct?"

She just shook her head, but his suggestion terrified her. Bruce had used her and played her for a fool, yes, but was he capable of doing her real harm? He had kept the letter about her aunt hidden from her for so long, though...and he'd tried to rob her aunt's estate out from under her.

She wanted to call Ryan. Damn him.

"Mrs. Dalton, I've given you a lot to process. I have your aunt's belongings in storage. Can we set up an appointment for tomorrow or the next day? I'll make sure your aunt's belongings are here and give you a copy of the will. I'd be happy to go over it with you, though it's pretty clear cut. Other than the nursing scholarship, the rest of her sizable estate goes to you. I hope you're planning to stay in town for a little while."

"Yes, but I have to return home on Thursday. I can arrange for another trip here, if necessary."

"Where are you living? Still in Philadelphia?"

"No, I'm living in Summerhill, my father's favorite vacation spot."

"Oh, wonderful. Living in New York State will help speed the process up. Does your ex-husband know where you are?"

"No, and please don't tell him."

Caitlyn made an appointment for the next day with the lawyer's assistant, then walked outside as if in a trance, still attempting to piece everything together.

The cold nip in the air encouraged her to get into the warmth of her car. As she opened her door to get in, she could swear she saw Bruce's car out of the corner of her eye, just leaving a parking spot across the street. Another question flashed through her mind, one that had been waiting there, lurking in the darkness, throughout her visit with the lawyer: How had he known about her accident in Summerhill?

CHAPTER FIFTEEN

Ryan and Jake sat in the station house at the end of their shift, both finishing up paperwork. A few other officers were joking around, which was common at the end of a shift. Jake's phone rang. The call came in through the station's private line, and he could see the captain on the phone in his office, so it had to be from him.

He couldn't hear the captain, but he listened to Jake's end.

"Yeah."

Silence.

"What? I can't do that." Jake glanced at Ryan, then turned his back to him.

Silence.

"Yeah. But you know…"

Silence.

"Yes, Sir." Jake got his pencil out and started writing, his back still to Ryan.

Silence.

More silence.

"What's the name again and what kind of car?"

Silence.

"What street in Buffalo?"

Damn it, if that had something to do with Cait, Jake had better let him in on it. Mallory had texted him to let him know Cait had gone to Buffalo to see what else she could learn about her aunt's death.

He pulled his phone out to reread their conversation for clues.

Mallory: *Caitlyn's gone to Buffalo.*

Ryan: *Why?*

Mallory: *To find out about her aunt.*

Ryan: *When'd she leave?*

Mallory: *I don't know. If you weren't such an asshole, you would know.*

Ryan: *Mal…*

Mallory: *I think early this morning.*

Ryan: *Why the hell didn't you tell me earlier?*

Mallory: *Cause you're a shithead.*

Ryan: *She could be in danger.*

Mallory: *Why? Her aunt died in an accident.*

Ryan: *Because her husband's scum.*

Mallory: *and…*

Ryan: *He could be in trouble, which would put her in trouble.*

Mallory: *Did you tell her?*

Ryan: *No*

Mallory: *Why not, stupid?*

Ryan: *Because*

Mallory: *Ryan?*

Ryan: *Because it wasn't my place*

Mallory: *SHE DESERVES TO KNOW, FOOL.*

Ryan: *Never mind. If you hear from her let me know.*

Mallory: *Fine. Why did you shit on her?*

Ryan: *I didn't*

Mallory: *Yes, you did. And at work besides. And at a new job.*

At that point, Ryan had ended the text conversation to take a call.

The truth was, he realized that what he'd done wasn't forgivable. He should never have talked to her about something like that at her job, but if he'd gone to her house to talk with her, he would have grabbed her in his arms and done the very opposite of break up with her. She was too much of a temptation. Closing his eyes, he could still hear those little moans she made right before she came. Damn, what he wouldn't give to hear those sweet sounds again.

Jake hung the phone up and scowled at him. Shit. Sweat broke out on his forehead. There better not be anything going on with Cait.

"What are you working on?" Ryan asked.

"Nothing." But he knew his brother well enough to recognize his expression for guilt. Jake avoided his gaze and looked down at his keyboard.

"If it's nothing, why do you look so guilty?"

"Do you mind? I have work to do." Jake gave him his back again.

Ryan stood up and peeked over his shoulder at his pad. "Caitlyn's in Buffalo, I heard you say Buffalo, so I know this is about her."

"I can't tell you anything," Jake snapped. "Now sit down and don't bother me."

Dead silence rang out as the other officers around them stared at the two Ramsays.

"Uh-oh. Another argument between the loving brothers," one of them said.

"You mean kissing cousins, don't you?" Everyone laughed but Ryan and Jake.

Ryan moved around Jake's desk so that he was facing him, and bent over to glare at his brother. "Jake, I want to know. Tell me."

"Then you shouldn't have broken up with her."

A bark echoed through the room. "Both Ramsays. In my office. Now."

Ryan turned to see the captain glaring at both of them. Shit. He stalked into the office and stood there with his hands in his pockets, Jake right behind him.

The captain closed the door behind them. "Sit down, both of you."

They both sat, tension filling the air in the small room.

"I've received a request from a citizen of this town, Caitlyn McCabe. She is concerned her life might be in danger, and she's asked for her Police Department's assistance. The only reason I assigned it to Jake is because I know a bit about your background with this particular person, Ryan, but if you'd like to be involved, I have no problem with that. Now, can I count on you two to take care of it? Or do I have to assign the case to someone else?"

Jake said, "I got no problem. Case accepted."

Ryan muttered, "Fine."

"I don't know what's going on between you two, but you need to keep your problems out of the office. Understood?"

"Understood." Jake said.

Ryan mumbled a meek, "Understood."

"Good, now get your asses to work and I don't want to see you in here again. Stop wasting my time."

Their peers all snickered as they left the office and made the walk of shame to their desks.

"Problem, officers?" The captain barked.

"No."

"Nope."

"Not with me."

"Good. Now does anybody work around here, or do you all just sit around and suck down coffee?"

The office quieted as the sound of clicking keyboards filled the room.

"Fill me in," Ryan said as he sat in his chair and turned to face Jake.

Jake sighed. "Apparently Cait called Dad."

"Dad?" Ryan barked.

Jake glared at him, then gave a pointed look to their captain's office.

Ryan forced himself to calm down. "Okay, so she called dad."

"Right, she called dad because she thinks her husband is up to something. He's in Buffalo and she thinks he's following her. Dad called the captain for her. She didn't want to call you."

"Anything else?" Damn, he was pissed she hadn't called him, but he forced himself to keep his focus on his brother.

"Just that she saw her aunt's lawyer. Apparently her husband had already stopped in to see the guy. He tried to declare her dead, saying she was killed in an accident on the NYS Thruway."

"How did he know about that? Shit." He ran a hand through his hair.

"What? What are you thinking?"

"How would her husband know she was in the accident? Unless…"

"Unless what?" Jake's brow furrowed as he waited for Ryan's answer.

"Did you ever get the name of the guy who was in the rental car that hit her from behind?"

"Oh, shit." Jake pushed his chair back and punched his keyboard again. He was quiet for a moment, then he said, "Yes, it's in the report with the license plate of the car." Jake's fingers stopped moving as he stared at the screen.

"What?"

"John Smith. And the kid who rented it to him forgot to copy his license."

"Fake name and he bought the kid off." *Shit*. Cait could be in real trouble.

CHAPTER SIXTEEN

Caitlyn woke up the next morning in her hotel room, chiding herself for her behavior the day before. She had chosen a nice chain hotel in Cheektowaga, not far from her lawyer's office, but she'd been too afraid to leave the room, opting instead to order room service. Even so, she'd kept imagining that Bruce would burst into the room.

Today she regretted her frantic call to Dr. Ramsay. The lawyer already had her new address and phone number, so after she picked up her aunt's things, she'd go home…well, maybe not tonight. Given what had happened on the last thruway trip she took in the dark, it would probably be better if she waited until morning to head home. But suppose Bruce was still here, and looking for money. Maybe she should head home today. She'd wait until she left the lawyer's office to make that decision.

After showering, drying her hair, and dressing, she headed down to the lobby for the continental breakfast provided by the hotel. Breakfast was served opposite the check-in desk. She greeted the staff and poured a cup of coffee, then sat down.

The front desk clerk ran over to her and said, "Ms. McCabe?"

"Yes?"

"Message for you." She handed Caitlyn a sealed card.

Caitlyn didn't recognize the handwriting, so she opened the card. Inside sat a sympathy card. She opened it and saw a printed line of writing under the card's message. *I know where you are.*

She dropped the card in front of her, then ran over to the

desk. "Who left that card?"

The clerk backed away from her. "It was a teenager. He left it last night. Said he had a message from someone. Is something wrong?"

Caitlyn forced herself to smile. "No, no problem. Thank you."

She gritted her teeth and walked back to her table, turning her back to the desk, not wanting to show the woman how upset she was. It had to be from Bruce. Maybe he was just trying to intimidate her, and she'd do best to ignore him. But she wasn't sure... Apparently, she didn't know her ex-husband at all.

After a hurried breakfast, she got into her car to head to the lawyer's office. When she was just two lights away, she glanced in her rearview mirror. Two cars behind her was a vehicle that looked like her ex-husband's car.

She was starting to freak out in earnest.

When she arrived at the lawyer's office, the assistant ushered her into a back room with a couple of tables and two large boxes, one on each table. "Please feel free to use this room. These are the two boxes of personal belongings from your aunt's house. Most of her things were sold in the estate, unfortunately, since we hadn't heard from you or any other relatives. These were things we didn't feel right about selling. If you have any questions, please come get me. Mr. Watkins will see you in a couple of hours."

The assistant closed the door behind her. Caitlyn took the top off the first box and stared inside.

On the top sat something that brought a smile to her face. Her aunt's daybook. She had written in it each day, making a record of her chores for the day, any reminders, and phone numbers. Caitlyn thumbed through it for a moment before setting it in the pile of things that she would take with her.

An hour and a half later, she had quite a stack to take with her. Some costume jewelry, a few various Christmas decorations, and some pictures. In the bottom of the last box sat three of the throws her aunt had made. The one on top was quilted in fall colors—greens, browns, reds, and yellows—her aunt's favorite season. She ran her hand across it lovingly, tears welling in her eyes. She set the throws in the keep pile and reached into the box for the last item. To her shock, it was a letter with her name on it.

She opened and started reading:

My dearest Caitlyn,

If you are reading this, things can't be good for me! Smile, sweetie. I want you to smile. I am with my beloved brother and my mother, so don't feel bad for me.

I wanted to take the time to tell you how very much I love you and how proud I am of you. Your mother went through a very difficult spell, and the brunt of her troubles fell on you. I'm sorry I didn't notice sooner how difficult things were for you.

But my good fortune was to spend two years with you. Believe me, your mother has already thanked me for taking care of you. You were the light of my days. Such a hard-working, dedicated young lady you were, both in high school and in college. And your compassionate nature has always inspired me.

Caitlyn stopped to pull a tissue from her purse and swipe at her eyes. Then she continued:

You will make such a wonderful nurse. I hope you will find someone very special to love, someone who loves and supports you the way you deserve. I don't believe Bruce Dalton is that man, but I think you will figure that out on your own. When you do, move on, keep smiling, and continue to work hard. Your knight is out there somewhere.

Your mom, dad, and I will try our best to watch over you.

Love,
Aunt Margie

She folded the letter and placed it in her purse. As soon as she was able to regain her composure, she found the assistant and told her she had finished with everything. Mr. Watkins walked into the room to check on her a few moments later.

"Did you find anything you'd like to keep?"

Caitlyn nodded and packed all the things she wanted back into one of the boxes.

"And you found the letter she left for you?"

"Yes, thank you." She wiped her eyes with the tissue.

He sat across the table from her. "You should know your aunt loved you very much, Caitlyn."

As soon as she settled down, he continued. "I don't think I need anything else from you at the moment. I will stay in touch once we close the estate. We may have to file a return and pay state taxes, so I can't release any funds to you yet, unless you are in dire need. Are you?"

She shook her head.

"Good. If anything changes, here's my card. Just let me know and I can release some of the money. Otherwise, you will hear from me within the year. Do you have any questions for me?"

"No, I don't think so. Thank you so much. I will treasure these things."

"You are most welcome, my dear." He led her to the front door. "Have a safe trip back."

As soon as Caitlyn shut herself into her car, she started to sob.

The afternoon after Caitlyn left for Buffalo, Jake and Ryan sat in the office together, reviewing everything they had discovered.

"Ryan, this doesn't look good for her. Aren't you worried?"

"Yeah, but I want to know as much as possible before I contact her. Her aunt's lawyer said she had an appointment with him today. He hasn't seen Bruce Dalton for a week. Hopefully, he left town as soon as Caitlyn showed up. He has to know he's not going to get anything now that she's seen her aunt's lawyer."

"He tried to declare her dead just to get her money, Ryan. And these gambling debts... the piece of shit owes more money than even I can believe. How do you gamble that much money away? Her lawyer in Pennsylvania has said that all their combined assets are frozen until he receives the papers."

"His lawyer said he signed, but the papers haven't been delivered yet, have they?" Ryan stared at this brother. The enormity of the situation stood before him like a dark pit he was about to fall into. "I have a very bad feeling about this. Do me a favor and text her."

"You should text her."

"No, I don't want her to think I'm interested in her again."

"Why not? You are." Jake crossed his arms as he stared at his brother.

Jake had a way of hitting the nail on the head. "I want it to be a police matter."

"Fine. What's her number?" Jake grabbed his phone and punched her number into his contacts.

Jake: *Cait, I'm checking into everything. You okay?*

A minute passed before she responded.

Cait: *Yes.*

Jake: *Where are you?*

Cait: *Still in Buffalo. Going to dinner and heading home tomorrow.*

Jake: *Let me know if you need anything. You know your ex-husband has been in Buffalo recently?*

Cait: *Yes.*

Jake: *Be careful.*

Cait: *I will. Thanks, Jake.*

"She's fine, Ryan. Coming home tomorrow."

Ryan let out the breath he had been holding.

His brother stared at him. "I saw that. Bullshit you don't want her."

CHAPTER SEVENTEEN

Caitlyn drove around Buffalo, mostly sticking to her aunt's old neighborhood. Memories flooded her mind, some of them good, some of them not so good. Life with her mother and father had been wonderful. Life with her mother had been hard. How she wished she could have changed that part of her life. Where would she be now if her father had lived?

Time flew by as she explored her childhood hometown. She checked her rearview mirror often, but didn't notice any cars that resembled Bruce's. Before she knew it, her afternoon had slipped away. She drove back to her hotel and chose a nice restaurant across the street for dinner. Her aunt's notebook was a comfort for her, so she spent her time perusing all the details in the book as she ate her meal. After she paid for her dinner and walked out of the restaurant, she looked around for Bruce before unlocking her car. She had parked on the side of the restaurant, but still in good light.

Chastising herself for acting like a child, she climbed into the driver's seat and tossed her purse on the passenger's seat. She froze in place as she registered something that shouldn't be there. A slip of paper sat on the seat. She picked it up and stared at the bold lettering:

I'M WATCHING YOU.

She looked in the backseat, but didn't see anything amiss. Then she locked the door and picked up her phone, dialing Jake's number.

He answered after two rings.

Caitlyn did her best to keep her voice free of hysteria, "Jake?"

"Caitlyn, you okay?"

"Yes, well, *no*. I don't know."

"Tell me what happened."

Caitlyn was so thankful for his strong, calm voice on the other end of the line. She would rather it be Ryan, but Jake was the one who'd contacted her and offered his help. He must be the one who'd been assigned to her case. "I just found a note in my car, and I don't know what to do."

"Read it to me."

"It says, 'I'm watching you.'"

"Was your car locked?"

"Yes, I always lock my car. Bruce is the only person who could have broken into it. I took both sets of keys when I left Philly, but maybe he had another set made."

"Where are you now?"

"In my car. I haven't gone anywhere." She could feel the panic flooding her veins. "I'm outside a restaurant. He did it while I was eating dinner."

"Do you see his car in the parking lot?"

Caitlyn glanced around. "No, he's not here. And another thing. It's the second time it happened. I got a note earlier today, too."

"What did it say?"

"It said, 'I know where you are.' But that note was given to the hotel clerk at the desk. This one was left in my car...my *locked* car. Jake, what do I do? I'm scared."

Caitlyn could hear Jake talking to someone. She thought she heard Ryan's voice, but she couldn't be sure.

Jake came back on the line. "Are you finished with the lawyer?"

"Yes, I have my aunt's things. I'm coming home tomorrow."

"Why don't you head home now? Do you have your things with you?"

"No, I have to go back to the hotel. I don't know if I want to drive at night. It's dark here already." Her hand trembled at the thought of driving home alone right now. The other car accident was too fresh on her mind.

"Caitlyn, I would recommend you leave now. Go back to

your hotel, pack your things, and head out. I'll contact the Buffalo PD. If anything else happens, let me know, but there are no storms forecasted and the roads are clear, so it would be better for you to leave tonight if at all possible. While it could be your ex-husband leaving you those messages, we really don't know. I think you're safer back in Summerhill."

"Maybe you're right. I'll go back and pack my things. Thanks, Jake."

"Call me if anything changes. Let me know what time you leave so we can watch for you."

Caitlyn hung up the phone, more frightened than she had ever been in her life.

Ryan jumped out of his chair. "Get your jacket."

Jake stared at his brother. They had stayed at the station late to work on Cait's case. "My jacket? For what?"

"You're driving me to Buffalo so I can drive Cait's car back here."

"Like hell. I'm not going anywhere. She's only an hour and a half away." Jake stared at Ryan as if he'd lost his mind.

He couldn't help it. This was Cait and losing her would end him. And if that wasn't a telling sign of how he really felt about her, he didn't know what was. He raked his hand through his hair and tried to calm down. Maybe Jake was right, and he was being a little overprotective. They were pretty sure they knew who the perp was, after all, which was usually half the battle. It had to be Dalton. If he ever got his hands on the guy, he would kick his ass, prosthesis or not.

Still, Dalton had tried to declare her dead, and he knew about and had potentially been involved in her accident… There was a distinct possibility that he would escalate and try to kill her, since he would then be the sole heir to her fortune. If he had truly signed the papers as his lawyer claimed, it wouldn't matter. But Ryan had his doubts. He had contacted the Philadelphia PD to see if Dalton was home, but they hadn't gotten back to him. Apparently, he wasn't high up on their priority list.

As long as she did as they asked, though, and came home immediately, everything should be fine. After all, Dalton could hardly try to run her off the road in these conditions without getting caught. Ryan glowered at his brother. "Fine, we'll go home, but keep your phone on you. If we don't hear from her soon, we're going to Buffalo."

She parked on the side of the hotel near the entrance closest to her room. The elevator was right inside the door. Checking the area before she unlocked her door, she made sure no one was around before she got out. She had almost made it to the hotel door when a cackling laugh interrupted her thoughts. Glancing around, she saw no one, which only made her more afraid. As she held her key card up to unlock the door, the same sound erupted again, so she tugged the door open and flew inside, slamming the door shut behind her.

Standing in the hallway, she gasped for breath. Her entire body was on alert. As a nurse, she knew all the signs of the 'fight or flight' reaction. Her pulse had sped up, she was sweating, and her respiratory rate had increased. *Calm. You need to calm yourself.* Taking two deep breaths, she headed to the lobby instead of going upstairs, hoping to find a few people around. She sighed as she rounded the corner and saw five people in the breakfast room, drinking coffee and munching on cookies.

Safety in numbers, right? She headed to the desk and asked the clerk if any messages had been left for her today. There were none. Breathing a sigh of relief, she decided to take a short break before tackling her room. Besides, she wasn't sure she could make it without some extra caffeine. She grabbed a cup of coffee, a cookie, and the paper, and sat down in the gathering room. But though she played with the edge of the paper and pretended to read, not one word of it registered in her brain. Instead she found herself surveying the other guests, watching for suspicious behavior. Her text notification went off and she jumped.

Her hands trembled as she pulled her phone out of her pocket, but she smiled when Ryan's name popped out at her. She knew she shouldn't find it comforting that he was still looking out for her, but a wave of relief washed over her. Ryan would fix this if anyone could.

Ryan: *Everything okay?*

Cait: *Yes.*

Ryan: *Have you left yet?*

Cait: *No. Having coffee, don't want to drive without the caffeine.*

Ryan: *Alone?*

Cait: *No, in the lobby with five others.*

Ryan: *Be careful.*

Cait: *Thanks for checking, Ry.*

Ryan: *Call if any problems.*

Cait: *Okay.*

She put her phone back in her pocket. It was a deflating feeling—like she was putting him away, too. There was no denying that she still had feelings for Ryan, though maybe his concern for her was a sign that he cared. Ryan still had issues he needed to work through, though, and he clearly wanted to do that alone.

A little later, she walked up to her room on the second floor. She stood outside the door and took a deep breath. *Don't be ridiculous, Cait. No one could get into your room.* She slid the card into the slot and opened her door, peeking around the corner. Nothing looked disturbed, so she stepped inside and glanced around, then locked the door behind her. She checked the bathroom, too, and breathed easier when everything was in her place.

Relax, Caitlyn. Everything will be fine.

She tried to reassure herself that the Ramsay brothers had just been checking up on her—the same way she would do with a patient who had a recurring symptom. They weren't worried she was in any serious danger.

She opened her suitcase to pack her things, and a piece of paper fluttered to the floor from inside. Cait's heart skipped a beat as she watched it land. The back was blank. Bending over, she gripped the paper in her hand and took a deep breath before she turned it over.

HI CAITLYN

A small scream escaped her lips as she dropped the paper back onto the floor. She had to get out of here. Now. She grabbed the few clothes she had hung up and stuffed them into her small suitcase, then retrieved the things she'd left in the bathroom. Scanning the room, she didn't see anything else of hers, so she zipped her suitcase shut. At the last minute, she scooped the note off the floor and shoved it into her pocket. Maybe the cops could tell something from the writing or fingerprint it—anything.

What had she done with the other two? She set her suitcase on the floor and rolled it to the door, stopping to think about the other two notes. One was in a wad on the floor of the car. What had she done with the one from this morning? *Oh, yeah, it's in my pocket.* She stashed the other note in the same pocket and crept back out the door, searching the hallway before stepping out. The lobby was deserted when she stopped at the desk to request a copy of her invoice and hurried to her car.

As soon as she got to her car, she checked the seats for any notes. When she didn't find any, she threw her suitcase in the trunk and climbed into the driver's seat. Closing the door, she locked it and picked up her phone, dialing a number she knew by heart. She was done with allowing him to intimidate her.

Her ex-husband answered. "Yeah?"

Caitlyn screamed into the phone. "Why are you doing this?"

Bruce shouted, "Whoa, what are you talking about?"

"The notes. You're trying to scare me. You tried to convince Aunt Margie's lawyer I'm dead, and now you're trying to get to me so what? You can declare me insane and get my money? What is your problem? Didn't I give you enough? You were the one fucking around with other women, so you clearly wanted out."

"Stop, Caitlyn. I haven't left you any notes. Yes, I tried to get your aunt's lawyer to give me some money, but it didn't work. Can't blame a guy for trying. God knows you have enough money on your own."

"I was more than generous with you. And why didn't you tell me Aunt Margie had died? You lying piece of shit."

"Isn't that obvious now? I wanted her money. Besides, you were being a bitch. I tried to talk you out of working. You have enough money to never work another day of your life. We could have traveled the world together like movie stars, but you wanted to stay in fucking Philadelphia so you could wipe people's asses. Well, that's not how I pictured our life. I figured you'd be satisfied once you got your license. But you chose to work full-time, which really ended up being what— fifty or sixty hours a week? That's not the lifestyle I wanted."

"You never said you didn't want me to work."

"Yes, I did. When I lost my job, I wanted you to quit, but you refused."

Caitlyn rubbed her hand across her forehead, remembering the argument they'd had a year ago. "So why bother me now? Leave me alone."

"I'm not bothering you. I'm in Philadelphia. What exactly are you accusing me of anyway?"

"I hate you." Caitlyn hung the phone up. Hell, if he was really in Philly, who was bothering her here? She had to admit, none of the notes looked like his handwriting.

Who the hell had it in for her?

CHAPTER EIGHTEEN

Caitlyn sat in the parking lot until she had her breathing under control. She checked her Bluetooth set up to make sure any calls that came in would stream through the mic in the car. Texting while driving was against the law in New York, and she wouldn't have tried anyway. Finally calm, she pulled out into the road. At the next stoplight, she called Ryan.

He answered on the first ring. "Cait?"

"Yeah, I'm just leaving Buffalo. I should be home soon."

"Any other problems?"

The word *yes!* practically screamed out of her, but she clamped down on it. She didn't want to tell him about the note and her conversation with Bruce until she could do so in person. Besides, if she told him now, he might tell her to stay put, and staying put was the last thing she wanted to do. She wanted to get home, to Summerhill, her new house, and her new job. "No. I'm sure everything will be fine."

"Call me if you need me."

"I will."

She would have loved for him to stay on the line with her, but she didn't feel she could ask that of him. The drive was fairly uneventful—she stopped at a toll booth, then again to get gas. There weren't many other cars on the road, thankfully. After passing the LeRoy exit, she sighed in relief. She was more than halfway there.

Her music was loud enough that she didn't hear the car behind her until it was almost right behind her. The bright lights got her attention first, almost blinding her in her rearview mirror. Her heart jumped into her throat and she turned off her music so she wouldn't have any distractions in the car. He gunned his engine and pulled up right behind her, nearly colliding with her before backing off. Fear crept into Caitlyn's belly and slid up her spine and into her neck, flushing across her face. There were no other cars on their side of the two-lane highway heading east. The car repeated the same gambit three times, then sped around her. It was a gray Chevrolet with tinted windows so she couldn't see inside.

She sighed in relief when the car finally pulled around her, hoping it was some young kid acting like an ass. He pulled back into her lane after passing her and slowed down. She was going the speed limit, sixty-five, and she had to slow down to keep from hitting him. What the hell was he doing? The needle dropped slowly to sixty, then fifty, then forty. Shit! She could get hit from behind if she was going forty on the highway, especially at this time of night. Afraid to pull around him, she stayed on the right. She was only going thirty-five miles an hour, but at least he couldn't hit her from behind.

Her heartbeat sped up in her chest. *Damn it. Stay calm, Caitlyn.* What to do, what to do. She could go around him, but then she'd be putting herself at his mercy. The needle dropped to thirty, then twenty-five. No way in hell was she stopping on the NYS Thruway, so she pulled into the left hand lane and sped up, going around him, whoever it was. She tried again to get a glimpse of the driver, but the windows were just too dark. At least the license plate was firmly implanted in her brain. As soon as this foolishness stopped, she would call Ryan and give him the number.

As soon as she pulled back into the right hand lane, he gunned his car and came so close, she screamed and revved forward. Another set of headlights approached in the left lane. *Thank God, thank God.* The car went around them, but she sped up to stay behind it. The car behind her immediately fell back, in fact, he fell back a good distance.

As soon as he fell back, she pushed the button in her car and called Ryan using the car's Bluetooth connection. He answered right away.

"Cait? What is it?"

"Someone is playing games with me," she blurted out. "He

followed me, then sped up until he almost collided with me. He did that a few times before pulling in front of me and dropping to thirty miles an hour. I tried to stay behind him, but I didn't want to stop completely."

"Cait, listen to me. Do not stop your car, and do not get out of your car for any reason. I'm calling the State Troopers. Did you see this guy's license plate?"

"Yes, I got it." She repeated the number to him. "Another car passed me, so I'm staying behind him."

"Where's the guy who's messing with you?"

"He fell back quite a distance, but I can still see his headlights."

"Do not engage him. Stay with the other car until the troopers come. Where are you?"

"I don't know the mile marker, but I just passed the LeRoy exit not too long ago. It's very isolated here. Ryan, help me, please."

"I'm on my way. I'm going to run the plates, but I'll be there as soon as I can." Ryan hung up.

Caitlyn relaxed her muscles, relieved by the thought she was no longer alone in this nightmare. She would do just as he asked. She didn't have much farther to go. After LeRoy came the Henrietta exit, then Victor, then the Finger Lakes exits.

The car in front of her turned off at the next exit. Shit, that wouldn't help. The other car had stayed back, but now he had no reason to keep away. As if her thoughts had summoned him, the headlights grew brighter in her rearview mirror.

And he was coming up on her fast. Closer and closer. Shit, he was going to hit her. She stepped on the gas and sped up as the car tailing her scooted right up to her bumper. The needle passed seventy, seventy-five, then eighty. The guy swung around her and flew past her.

She called Ryan again, her hand shaking. "He's back. The other car took an exit, and he came up on me again and almost hit me. Then he went around me. What do I do, Ryan?"

"Keep driving, don't stop for any reason. Go the speed limit, but keep driving. I looked up the plate, but the car is a rental, so that doesn't tell me anything right off. I'm on my way. Hang in there."

"Ryan, don't hang up. Please?"

"I'm here for you. What mile marker?"

"I can't see one."

"Where is he now?"

"He flew way ahead of me. I don't know what he's doing. Maybe he's leaving."

Caitlyn slowed her speed to sixty-five miles an hour, hoping Ryan would be there soon.

Oh my God. Noooo!

She stared straight ahead, hoping her eyes had deceived her. The bastard had turned his car around and was headed straight for her. There were no other cars on her side.

"Oh my God," she whispered.

"What is it?"

"Ryan, he turned around."

"Okay, so he's in the other lane. That gives you some time to get away. I should be directly behind him in no time at all."

"No, he's not."

"Not what?"

"He's not in the other lane."

"What?"

Caitlyn screamed. "He's coming right at me! Help me, Ryan."

"Cait, stay calm. Are there any other cars near you?"

She glanced in her rearview mirror. "No, it's just the two of us. And he's headed straight for me."

"The trooper should be behind you soon."

"Ryan, what do I do?" She had reached full-on panic mode. She couldn't help it. The car was headed straight for her and she had nowhere to go. Some spots by the side of the road were full of trees, others were bare, but she was going too fast to plan where she'd end up.

"Cait, try to stay calm. Pull off the road and let him go by."

"He's almost here. Headed straight for me. OH MY GOD!" Caitlyn slammed on her brakes and skidded sideways. The car flew past her, narrowly missing her, before turning around again.

Ryan yelled, "Cait! Are you alright?"

Caitlyn didn't answer—she was too busy looking over her

shoulder to see where the maniac was.

"Cait, answer me. Are you alright?" he shouted.

"Yes, he missed me, but he's coming back. *He's coming back*, Ryan!" Tears slid down her cheeks.

As the car came closer, she noticed police lights in the distance. "I think the Trooper's on his way, but this guy is closer. He's…" Her voice stopped dead.

"Cait?"

She screamed as the headlights loomed in her rearview mirror. "He's going to hit me from behind."

Just then, something caught her gaze out of the corner of her eye. The same young boy she had seen after her accident stood in the median staring at her, a large dog next to him.

His voice came to her. "Missy angel, do not worry. I will protect you. Trust Loki." Then he disappeared.

"Cait!" Ryan's voice rang in her ear.

"Ryan, help me!" The car came right for her, slowed down, as if still teasing, then sped right into her. She careened off the road, and the car bounced off the end of a guard rail before coming to a stop leaning to its side in the ditch. The airbag deployed, knocking her back. As soon as she moved it out of her way, she could hear Ryan yelling into her phone.

"Cait!"

She tried to regain her bearings, but confusion and terror clouded her mind. Another accident, she had just been in another accident.

"Cait, answer me!" Ryan was frantic.

"Ryan?" she whispered.

"Are you okay?"

"I think so."

"Where is he?" She could hear Ryan gather himself, his voice returning to calm, cool, and collected.

"I don't know, I can't see. I'm in a ditch. I think the trooper just pulled in behind me." She could see the red and blue lights flashing around her, a sight that sent comfort shooting through her. It could have been so much worse.

A knock on the window captured her attention. She rolled her window down. A tall black woman in the NYS Trooper uniform stood just outside. Caitlyn wanted to jump out and hug her.

"Miss, you all right? Hurt anywhere? Bleeding?"

"No, I think I'm fine, just shaken up."

"You Caitlyn McCabe?"

"Yes."

The trooper opened her door. "Why don't you come with me? My car is nice and warm. I'll write up your statement in there. Ryan Ramsay from Summerhill PD is on his way. I'll call a tow truck for your car."

Caitlyn picked up her purse and phone, then allowed the woman to usher her into her police vehicle. She sat in the back. As soon as the door closed, the tears started.

"Miss, I know this is hard, but can you tell me what happened?"

Caitlyn explained everything. She ended with, "I thought it was my ex-husband, Bruce Dalton, but now I'm not so sure."

"Ryan Ramsay was able to verify that your husband was in Philadelphia this evening. The car is a rental, but we're tracking down the driver."

"Then who could be doing this?" It was more of a sob than a question.

Another car pulled up behind them and Ryan got out. Her whole body responded to the sight of him. She closed her eyes and took a deep breath. He was here in his personal car, not the cruiser. But that didn't matter. What mattered was he came for her. Maybe he did care. When he opened her door, she jumped out and hurled herself into his arms, sobbing on his shoulder.

He wrapped his arms around her and held her tight. "I'll take you home, Cait. We'll figure this out tomorrow. Officer, do you need anything else?"

The trooper got out of her vehicle. "Just a phone number. I already took her statement and called for a tow truck. Does she have anything else she needs out of the car?"

Caitlyn was still clinging to him. When she finally let go, Ryan led her to his car, helped her into the front seat, then returned to get her things.

How could he leave her tonight? He had to stay with her, he just had to.

CHAPTER NINETEEN

Ryan pulled out from behind the trooper. The thruway was deserted, which was highly unusual. He passed her car on the side of the road, saw the tire tracks of her vehicle and the one that had hit her.

His hands gripped the steering wheel, his knuckles turning white as he thought of what he would do to the bastard if he ever got his hands on him. Turning to Cait, he grabbed her hand, just now noticing that tears still slid down her cheeks as she stared straight ahead, her breath hitching to keep from sobbing, he guessed. "Cait, you all right?"

She nodded and turned to look at him. "Thank you for coming," she said in a whisper.

Damn it, he could see the fear in her eyes. The fucker would pay for this. He rubbed his thumb across the back of her hand, hoping to calm her. Wanting nothing more than to pull over and hold her, though he knew it wasn't the right thing to do. They had ended their relationship at his insistence, so it wasn't fair for him to get her hopes up again, not when he wasn't more prepared to be vulnerable with her than he'd been last week. He'd just have to take her home, check her house to make sure no one was inside, then go home.

But no, there was no way he could leave her alone tonight, not when he'd spend the entire night wondering if the bastard was still after her. The problem was they had no idea who was harassing her. It wasn't her ex-husband, though he could have hired someone. There were no other obvious suspects, which was maddening.

They rode in silence. He was afraid if he said anything else she would fall apart in the car, and he didn't want that to happen. Not here, not now, but maybe when they got back to Summerhill.

When he finally reached the right exit, he put his turn signal on, paid their toll, and got off.

"Where are we going?" she whispered, her voice barely audible. She stared out the side window, refusing to look at him.

"I was taking you home."

"No, not tonight. Please?" She gave him a pleading look that wrenched his gut.

His cell phone went off while he waited at a red light.

Jake: *Where are you?*

Ryan: *Just getting into Summerhill.*

Jake: *She okay?*

Ryan: *Fine. Tomorrow*

"Okay. Talk to me, Cait. What do you want?" He moved through the light only to pull up on another red. After he pulled the car to a stop, he gazed at her, waiting for her to answer him or look at him, whichever she chose. "Cait?"

Finally, she swung her head around and reached into her pocket of her jeans. "I don't want to go home. He probably knows where I live. He'll follow me; I'll never be able to sleep."

"Your husband is in Philadelphia, so the driver was someone else. Did you get a look at him?"

"No. I tried, but the windows were too dark. I couldn't see anything inside.

"It could have just been some wacko out for fun. We'll have to do some follow-up tomorrow." He paused, catching a strange expression on her face. "What is it?"

"This." She pulled one piece of paper out of her pocket and tossed it on the console between them. Reaching back into her pocket, she pulled out two more. "And this." She threw the second one down. "And this. Who's doing this? I thought it was Bruce, but I talked to him on the phone, and you're right... I don't think it's him. Who would do this to me?"

The light changed and he made the decision to take her to his place. "I don't know."

"Ryan, he followed me to the hotel, he got in my car. The last message was left in my suitcase in my hotel room. How did he get in? Who would have let him in?" Her hands came up to both sides of her head, tugging on her hair. "Oh my God, what is happening to me? Oh my God, oh my God." She stared straight ahead.

Ryan pulled into the driveway of his apartment building. "You can stay with me tonight. Whoever it is probably doesn't know anything about me." He turned off his engine and reached for her hand. "Cait, I won't let anything happen to you. I promise."

Picking up the three messages, he took a second to compare them, a fury building inside of him. How easy it was to terrify someone. Three little slips of paper had caused so much fear and uncertainty for Cait. He got out of the car and walked over to her door, which he held open for her. Then he grabbed her suitcase, leaving the box in his car, and led the way into his apartment, the first floor of a two-story house. They entered the foyer, and he led her to the couch, which sat opposite the kitchen in the great room. His bedroom and bathroom were situated toward the back. As soon as she sat down, he said, "Stay here, I'll check and make sure no one has been here."

Tossing his keys on the counter, he searched the small apartment, leaving her suitcase in his bedroom before coming back out and taking off his jacket and helping her with hers.

He sat next to her and held his arms out to her. "Come here."

She fell into his arms and the next thing he knew, his lips found hers as she clung to him. He'd tried to stay away, but he couldn't fight the way he felt. Not with her here in his apartment, so sweet and scared and beautiful. Not when every inch of him was suffused with relief that she was okay. That she hadn't been seriously injured or killed. His arms traced the line of her back and moved across her shapely butt, pulling her tight to him. She sighed and leaned into him, wrapping her arms around his neck.

She tasted every bit as sweet as he remembered. Parting her lips for him, she met his passion stroke for stroke as he swirled his tongue with hers. That small moan of hers, the sound he thought about when he was trying to sleep at night, greeted his ears and went straight to his dick, making him hard instantly. Hell, it wasn't supposed to go down this way, but he just couldn't let her go.

She fell back onto the couch and tugged him on top of her. Pulling on his shirt, she ripped it off and tossed it aside.

"Cait, slow down, sweetie."

"No, I want you now. Please, Ryan." She rubbed her hand across his hard length through his jeans and he groaned. The next thing he knew her sweater flew into the middle of the room, followed quickly by her bra. He sighed, "Cait, you're so beautiful." He leaned down and caught her nipple in his mouth, tugging and suckling her until it reached a taut peak.

Her hands were everywhere, on his biceps, in his hair, scraping his nipples, pulling the zipper on his jeans. She slipped out of her pants, and he slid his hand down her belly until he found her core, rubbing her clit until she moaned, then sliding his finger into her crease to make sure she was ready for him.

"Ryan, get your pants off, now."

Shit, who was he to argue? He stood up and kicked off his shoes and pants.

And she was too fast for him. He still had on his boxers when she reached for him. So hot for her, he wasn't thinking right when she tugged his briefs down and grabbed his cock with one hand and cupped his testicles with the other.

And she froze.

Fuck! How could he have let this happen? He had vowed never to put himself in this position again. His erection shrank faster than if he'd been submerged in arctic water, and she stared up at him, her eyes wide.

He waited to see her look of disgust, her rejection, but it never happened. Instead, she said the most beautiful words he had ever heard.

"Ryan, I don't care if you only have one testicle. I want you now." She caressed his dick and made him hard again, then helped him adjust his prosthesis and settle on top of her.

And he made the sweetest love to her he had ever made to anyone.

Caitlyn strained to catch her breath. She struggled to find words to describe the experience they'd just shared: powerful, mind-blowing, and sweet all at once. Was that even possible? She smiled and curled up close to him, laying her hand on his chest so she could feel the pounding of his heart, thrilled by this evidence of his reaction to her.

Then her heart broke a little as she remembered the way he'd looked at her. The fear in his eyes. "That's why, isn't it?"

She heard him sigh, so he obviously knew what she meant. "Yes, a large part of it."

She leaned up on her elbow and gazed down at him. "Ryan, it doesn't bother me that you lost a testicle to an injury. Did you really think it would?"

"If you were anything like a couple of other women I've allowed near me since the explosion, then the answer is yes. My injuries disgusted them."

"It doesn't make you any less of a man."

"I know that, or at least I hope it doesn't. The doctors told me I only need one to father a child, and my remaining one is healthy."

"Well, it doesn't matter to me." She searched his gaze, wanting so much to convince him it didn't matter to her. As a nurse, she'd met plenty of people who had been disfigured by accidents, and their self-esteem was often totally destroyed by their injuries.

"Cait, I know you're a nurse, but even you have to admit it is gross. The bomb left terrible scar tissue. I don't like to look at it myself."

She grinned. "Well, if my intended use for it was to set it on the table as a decoration, then maybe it would bother me. But it isn't something that I intend to stare at. And it doesn't bother me to touch you. Far from it."

Ryan laughed. He gazed at her and played with the curls around her face. "You really are special, aren't you?"

"Besides, at least I know it wasn't my inadequacies in the bedroom that sent you away."

"How could you possibly think that? We're amazing together."

She shrugged her shoulders. "I didn't know what sent you away." She played with his hair, not wanting to catch his gaze. "What an awful experience for you. That had to be extremely painful." She settled her head back down on his chest.

"I blocked much of it out. I was obsessed with Chad. I poured all my energy into him, trying to move him, save him, do anything for him." He ran his hand down her arm, caressing her as he talked. "When I finally realized I had lost him, I started to register the pain…and the expression on Jake's face."

"What do you mean?"

"Until then, I hadn't realized my leg was almost destroyed. I knew I'd been hit there, but I couldn't feel it. When Jake finally got the chance to take a good look at me, he ran behind a tree to puke."

"He did?"

"Yeah, he thought I'd lost them both, because he kept saying something about my balls. It really freaked him out. I was too upset about Chad. The funny thing was that we had just been talking about bombs and IEDs, about where they were usually hidden. The next thing we knew the bomb went off and all hell broke loose."

She didn't say anything, just held his hand.

"I couldn't stand the possibility of you looking at me like that…with disgust. I had hardened myself to the fact that my sex life was going to be almost non-existent."

She pulled herself up and kissed him on the lips. "Not if I have anything to say about it. That was amazing."

He sat up and pulled her with him. "Yes, it was. I don't know about you, but I'm tired. He stood and tugged her behind him. "Into my big bed, woman."

CHAPTER TWENTY

Ryan made Caitlyn breakfast after he made love to her one more time. She was still reeling from the whole situation. In a matter of days, her entire life had been turned on its head again. First had come the emotional trauma of seeing all the reminders of her aunt's untimely death. Then she'd been harassed by a dangerous unknown assailant.

But now she had plenty of reason to smile, too. She and Ryan had spent a wonderful night together, and she felt they were well on their way to overcoming the damage he'd done to their relationship that day in the hospital. He had to be very embarrassed about his condition, and it wasn't surprising he'd tried to hide it from her.

She hoped he believed her when she said it didn't matter…because to her, it didn't.

After breakfast, Ryan drove her to the station.

"Cait, you are aware your ex-husband likes to gamble?" he asked in the car.

"Yes, I know he placed bets. He played Fantasy Football online and bet in small pools. I know he wanted to go to Vegas, but I don't think it amounted to that much money. Why?" She stared at Ryan, suddenly feeling uncertain. "Or is he in debt?"

"He is."

"How much?"

"Twenty thousand dollars."

She gasped. "Oh my God. Twenty thousand? He can't pay that back. He doesn't have that kind of money."

"No, I didn't think either one of you would have easy access to that kind of money."

They arrived at the station a few minutes later. Caitlyn was surprised to see Jake inside already working on her case.

Jake stood up when they entered, "Morning."

"Hi, Jake."

Ryan said, "Anything new?"

Jake shook his head and sat down again. "Another rental car, another fake name. We have no idea who was in the car. It wasn't returned to the rental agency, but left down the street. They can't even describe the guy other than dark-haired white male."

"You don't think my ex-husband is behind this, do you?" She glanced from Jake to Ryan.

Ryan shrugged his shoulders. "He's definitely a suspect."

"But you said he was home in Philadelphia."

"Right, but he could have hired someone."

"Hired someone for what?"

Ryan glanced at her, and something in his gaze told her... she gave him an incredulous look.

"No, you don't think...My own husband tried to have me killed?"

Now she was truly scared. Bruce Dalton always got what he wanted.

Mallory picked Caitlyn up on the way to work Friday for a twelve-hour shift. Time went very fast, partly because the bitchy nurse wasn't working, and Caitlyn felt more acclimated to the department. She was able to do the work she liked—start IVs, give out medication, and take care of the patients. Mallory just helped her out with things like finding supplies, and mastering their hospital support system: who to call in the lab, which doctors to contact, and so on.

When she got home, Ryan was waiting in her driveway in his cruiser. He greeted her with a kiss that made her want to swoon, and then he checked her house for any signs of an intruder.

He kissed her cheek when he was done. "Call me if anything happens. I'll be on shift until eight, but I'm happy to come over when I'm done if you're nervous about anything...or if you just don't want to be alone. Are you going to be okay?"

"Yeah. I have to get used to sleeping in my house again. I missed my lake view."

"You look exhausted, Cait."

"I'm tired. I took care of a lot of patients today. It's stressful until you get used to it."

"It's stressful then, too. I know. I've seen my sister looking the same way many times. You're working tomorrow?"

"Twelve hours tomorrow and Sunday."

He kissed her until she moaned and leaned into him. "Nope, I know that sound. I'm out of here now before it's too late."

She smiled and held the door for him. "Thanks, Ryan. You better go, I'd probably just fall asleep on you anyway."

She slept like a rock that night and woke up just in time for work. Unfortunately, Lucille was the first person she saw in the locker room. It was Saturday morning, so she decided to be cheerful to everyone, even the resident bitch. "Good morning, Lucille."

All she got back was a grunt and a slammed locker door.

Caitlyn dreaded spending the day with the woman, but at least she wasn't in it alone. A minute later, Mallory came into the room.

"Morning, Caitlyn," she said. "Ready for another long one? It's the weekend, and we're usually hectic on Saturdays. Get ready."

Mallory was right. After seeing four patients with abdominal pain, three with broken bones in various places, two with head injuries, two with heart attacks, one with a stroke, one who was injured in a car accident, and two who were drunks, they finally got the chance to grab something to eat. The day was more than half gone. Caitlyn was following Mallory into the break room when she heard her name. She turned to see Lucille beckoning her into the med room.

Caitlyn knew the hospital required two nurses' signatures for wasting narcotics and insulin, so she followed Lucille inside. It was a sad statement about medical personnel that too many before her had pocketed excess narcotics instead of throwing them into a waste receptacle as they should, thus requiring someone to witness their disposal.

"Hurry up. I need a signature. I just wasted two mg. of morphine." She held her sheet up for Caitlyn to sign.

Caitlyn gave her a puzzled look. "Where's the morphine?"

"I just threw it into the container. I thought you were right behind me. How is it my fault you were slow?" Lucille's narrowed gaze begged for Caitlyn to challenge her.

She wouldn't bite, but while she wasn't willing to argue, she refused to be intimidated by the brute. "Lucille, I'm supposed to see the morphine. I'll sign it this once, but next time I need to see it first."

"I was throwing it in the bin just as you walked through the door. Are you blind?"

"Here," Caitlyn said as she handed the paper to her. "You have your signature."

"I don't like your attitude." Lucille's cold voice followed her out the door.

She told Mallory what had happened, and all her friend did was whistle and say, "Be careful of her. It's like I told you, she'll try and set you up."

During lunch, Caitlyn told Mallory all about the last couple of days, and that she was seeing Ryan again. Mallory seemed pleased to hear her news. She hoped so.

After lunch, they returned to find a full waiting room. Mallory said, "You know, if we're ever going to get out of here, we'll need to take more patients. Do you mind taking three on your own?"

"No problem." Caitlyn took the next three patients and ran herself until she hit a lull. The waiting room finally emptied and two of her patients had gone off for testing, so she volunteered to help the other nurses on the unit. Mallory's patients were fine, and another nurse, Jane, didn't need anything. Lucille's patient walked out of her cubby at one point and asked for ice chips, so Caitlyn got them for her.

The next time Caitlyn walked into the med room, Lucille was directly behind her. "Didn't I tell you to stay away from my patients?" she snapped.

Caitlyn spun around. "I only got her ice chips. You were busy with a dressing change, so I thought I'd help out."

"Well, don't."

Caitlyn was incredulous. Really, over ice chips? "Don't what?"

"Give my patients anything. I train them to understand I'm not going to be around much. You ruin their expectations when you take care of their needs. Stay away. Take care of your own patients."

Caitlyn stared at her in disbelief as she stalked off. *Trained them?* It was hard to believe Lucille still had a job if that was her attitude.

As soon as Mallory pulled into her driveway, she noticed Ryan's cruiser sitting off to the side. Mallory just smiled and waved her off, not bothering to speak to her brother.

"Another night shift?" she asked as he opened her front door for her.

"Yeah, it doesn't happen that often, but one of the night cops is on vacation."

"Okay. No matter, another night. I'm so tired right now I wouldn't make good company anyway. Any news on my case?"

"No, sorry." He kissed her after he searched her house, and she leaned right into him at the door, sighing and resting her head on his shoulder.

He leaned in and whispered, "Cait, I think you are about to fall asleep standing up. I'm leaving before my ego gets damaged beyond repair."

She giggled and held the door for him. As soon as she closed it, he yelled through the door. "Don't forget to lock it."

"I won't, Ryan."

"Yes, you will. You're overtired. I'm not leaving until I hear you lock it."

She chuckled and turned the lock. "There, happy?"

"Yes, now don't unlock it for anyone."

"Don't worry. I'll be fast asleep in about five minutes."

The next day, Ryan strolled into the ER about an hour after Caitlyn arrived. They weren't busy yet, so he grabbed Cait's hand and tugged her back toward the break room. "Mallory, I need to speak to your charge," he called out over his shoulder before they moved into the break room.

There was no one else around, so Ryan grabbed her by the waist and positioned her up against a locker and kissed her with a hunger that shot straight to her core. She threaded her fingers into his hair and said, "I missed you."

"I know. It kills me to go home alone. I liked you in my bed. I'm finishing my shift, but I wanted to see you first." He continued to nuzzle her neck. "Call in sick."

She laughed. "Kind of hard to do when I'm already at work, Ryan Ramsay."

He kissed her again and his hands skimmed down her back until he found her butt and pulled her close enough to feel his erection.

Just then, the door flew open. Ryan released her and Caitlyn stood up, befuddled by the sudden change in circumstances.

"Nice, newbie. Thanks for making me uncomfortable in my own break room." Lucille glared at her, then turned around and left, doing her best to slam the door on her way out.

Caitlyn sputtered, wanting to respond to Lucille in some way, but Ryan pulled her close and whispered in her ear, "It isn't worth it. She's been here a long time and she's always been a miserable bitch. Let her go."

"I know. I've worked with other nurses like her."

"Forget her. When are you working again?"

"Tomorrow. Mallory asked if I could come in."

Ryan's eyebrows rose. "Four twelves in a row? Isn't that a little too much?"

"I know. It'll be rough, but she wanted to switch with someone so she could have next Friday off."

"Then it's the perfect time for me to head to Philadelphia. I'll head out tonight, after I sleep for a while and watch some football with my dad. I'll be wide awake since I've been on the night shift, and no one will be on the road."

"What?"

"I'm off tomorrow because I worked all weekend. I want to go to Philly to check out some things with the police department there. It doesn't take too long to get there. We need to find out who's bothering you, and I've reached a dead-end here. I've come up with nothing but your husband." He nuzzled her ear again.

"Ex-husband," she scowled.

"Why don't you give me the name of your lawyer and I'll stop and introduce myself. And as long as you're writing, add the names and addresses of your ex and the girl you caught him with the night you left him. I'd love to ask her a couple of questions."

She grabbed a piece of paper and wrote down the information. "My lawyer said he received the signed papers. Why would Bruce have signed them if he's out to get me?"

"I don't know. Maybe I'll have a better idea after my trip."

He kissed her on the lips, a sweet kiss that made her forget where she was. "Be careful, Ryan."

"I'll text you. Call Jake if anything happens." He turned and winked at her. "Now I'll go fall asleep and wake up all sweaty thinking of you."

CHAPTER TWENTY-ONE

Ryan headed south to Philadelphia later that evening. Somehow he had to find out who had frightened and threatened Cait. If he had to search through half of Philadelphia, he would. He would do anything for her, for this woman who had made him feel normal for one glorious night. Somehow, she had managed to make him forget about the explosion, Chad, the army, his leg, and his missing testicle. Of course, his memories had returned, but how wonderful it had been to live without them for a while. Yep, Caitlyn McCabe had done the impossible.

Not only had he forgotten everything, but he had no longer felt like a failure. Every single day since the bomb had sent Chad to his death, he had wallowed in self-pity for failing his friend. He told himself over and over again that he should have guessed a bomb was planted on the road, or at the very least, he should have made Chad slow down. Yeah, his therapist had talked to him about letting go of that feeling, but words hadn't helped much. His dad's advice didn't do much either. But Cait? Caitlyn made him feel as if he mattered again.

At about four a.m., he found a hotel on the outskirts of Philly and slept for a few hours. He knew he would get more information from the day shift officers, so he waited until after nine before heading out.

Ryan had driven his personal vehicle in order to be as unobtrusive as possible. He parked his car outside the central office of the Philadelphia Police Department and strode inside, hoping it would be a slow day so he could find the detective he had been dealing with, Bachorski. After waiting fifteen

ONE SUMMER HILL DAY

minutes, he was ushered into a back room to meet with Detective Bob Bachorski.

"Officer Ramsay, pleased to meet you." He offered his hand and Ryan shook it. "I'm afraid I don't have any information for you."

"Nothing on Bruce Dalton at all?"

"Nothing new. He's got an expensive gambling habit, but that's it. No run-ins with the law as far as I can tell."

Ryan thought for a minute, then passed him the paper he had gotten from Cait. "Is this the correct address for him?"

Bachorski glanced at the paper. "Yeah, that's him. And the girl listed on this sheet may have been with him before as you stated, but not lately."

Ryan nodded, then stood up. His prosthesis caught on the chair, but he righted himself before he fell.

"You did duty?" Bachorski asked.

"Yeah, Iraq, army."

"Afghanistan, army. Bomb catch you?"

"Yeah." He held his hand out. "Thanks for your help."

Bachorski shook his hand. "Sorry we couldn't do more for you. Just couldn't get my sarge to free us up. Heavy workload right now."

"Understood." He gave him his card. "If you hear anything, call me. I'll be in town until tomorrow."

Bachorski took the card. "Sure. Good luck."

About two hours later, Ryan sat parked in front of Cait's old house. He had just finished grabbing lunch after talking with her lawyer, who'd confirmed his possession of the signed divorce papers. According to the lawyer, he'd already made a partial payment to Dalton, whom he suspected was in sore need of money. Dalton had been at home at five p.m. yesterday, but there was a slim possibility he could have chased Caitlyn on the Thruway later that night. But how would he have known she was there without following her from the hotel? The timing was all wrong for that scenario.

Now he would meet this Dalton character face-to-face. He climbed out of his car and trudged up the sidewalk to the door. The house was nice and appeared to be relatively new, but the outside was a mess. He hadn't pulled into the driveway because it had snowed here and no one had bothered to shovel or plow. Dalton's car sat in the drive covered in snow, another reason to doubt he had gone to Buffalo. After he rang the bell, he glanced at the neighborhood. Money everywhere, and her husband was a gambling addict.

The door flew open to reveal a man a couple of inches shorter than his six foot two frame.

"Yeah?" Bruce Dalton was dressed in jeans and a sweatshirt. Though he had nowhere to be and no job to go to, he had an air of impatience.

"Bruce Dalton?"

"Yeah?"

"I'm Ryan Ramsay from the Summerhill Police Department. I wondered if I could talk with you about your wife, Caitlyn."

"Ex-wife."

"Ex-wife." Ryan glowered at him.

Dalton shifted his feet before he answered. "Fine, I'll answer a few questions, but that's it. I signed her fucking papers, so what else does she want?"

Ryan's eyebrows rose at the man's crass attitude, and it didn't elude his notice that he hadn't been asked inside. "Someone has threatened Caitlyn McCabe. Do you have any idea who would do such a thing? Does she have any enemies?"

"Well, it wasn't me. Like I told you on the phone, I was home when it happened. Sure, I tried to get her aunt's money, but the lawyer wouldn't budge, so I moved on. I just wanted more money."

"She didn't give you any in the settlement?"

"Yeah, but I need more and Caitlyn has more that she could ever spend. Would it hurt her to share her wealth a little?"

"I heard she gave you a very generous settlement, especially considering your prenup."

Dalton scowled. "How the hell do you know about my prenup?"

"I'm not sure I like your attitude. According to her lawyer, you were also aware of an accident she had in Summerhill during a snow storm. How did you find out about that?"

"Somebody from the hospital called me, asked if I was next

of kin. There was something in her purse. I wasn't up there. I just figured if they called me, she had to be pretty bad and I could beat her to Buffalo. " Bruce showed a touch of guilt, but not much. Ryan guessed he was finally figuring out that with his background, he would be suspect.

"Just the other day, someone tried to run her off the road on the NYS Thruway. Maybe you should take this a little more seriously." Ryan wasn't going to let up on him. He wanted to see how he reacted to pressure.

"What?" Dalton paled. "I would never do such a thing. We're better off apart than together, but she was my wife... I don't wish her dead. Who would try to kill her?"

Ryan noticed the color in his face changed. Maybe he was innocent. A gambler and a sleaze, yes. Murderer? Probably not. "That's what I'm trying to determine. What about the woman you were having an affair with?"

"Lynn? Hell no. She liked Caitlyn. She was always talking about her."

"Are you still seeing her?"

"No."

"Why not?"

"Because I caught her going through my things. And she was always asking me to buy her something. Watches, bracelets. She wanted my debit card. Shit, I don't need that. I got rid of her."

"Can you tell me where she's living now?"

"Over on Brown Street in a townhouse. Ummm...2301, I think."

"Are you seeing anyone now?"

"No, I'm single and I'm loving it. I never liked to be tied down before Caitlyn and I got together."

"You mean before you found out about Caitlyn's money."

"Yeah," he grinned. "That's right. It was about money, and I got plenty for the couple of years I spent with her. But I never tried to hurt her." The door slammed in his face.

Ryan smirked at the thought of that guy being a manwhore. He certainly didn't look the type. How the hell had Cait stayed with him for two years? He climbed into his car and headed for Brown Street.

Lynn Palermo answered the door right away. After he introduced himself, she invited him in and they sat at her dining table. The house was sparsely furnished but clean.

"Oh my gosh, is Caitlyn okay? I worry about her so much. I feel horrible about what I did, and it was so stupid. I don't even know why I was interested in him. He's a fool. I'm glad she divorced him." She gave him a wide-eyed look of innocence that could have snagged her an Oscar if her life had gone differently.

Ryan stifled his grin. He wanted to ask her if she had been worried about Caitlyn while she was screwing her husband, but he didn't. "She is fine for now. But someone is threatening her, actually tried to drive her car off the road. Do you have any idea of someone who might want to hurt her?"

She didn't have to feign her shock. "Threatening her? What happened? Is she back in Philly? I'd love to see her."

"No, she's not back in Philly. Now, about her enemies. Anyone you would suspect?"

Lynn thought for a moment, then shook her head. "Sorry, I can't think of anyone. Do you know where she is? I would really like to talk to her, to apologize, you know."

Ryan thought she appeared genuinely concerned, but he wasn't willing to give her any information about Caitlyn. "I believe she's still using the same phone, so you can text her if you'd like. I can't tell you whether or not she's interested in talking to you."

"Did she move out of Philadelphia for good? You said Summerhill Police? Where is that anyway?"

"Summerhill is in New York State, as it says on my jacket. I'll let Ms. McCabe update you on her status and where she's living. Her car accident was near Summerhill. That's why I'm investigating. Is there anything else you can tell me about Caitlyn? You worked with her, correct? Was there anyone at work she didn't get along with? Any patients who argued with her?"

Lynn scowled as she chewed on a nail. "No. Hmmm...let me think." A moment later, her face lit up. "Wait a minute. There was one guy...yeah. A transporter. He was always hitting on her, so she had to tell him she was married. William somebody."

"Can you be a little more specific? Take your time, maybe you'll remember his last name. Does he still work there?"

"I haven't seen him in a while. William…Jenkins. William Jenkins. That's his name."

Ryan sighed with relief. Finally, he had a lead.

Caitlyn trudged into work on Monday morning, regretting that she'd agreed to work four twelve-hour shifts in a row. The night before she had gone home at eight thirty and fallen into bed as soon as she changed out of her scrubs. She had passed out until her alarm went off, and then she'd groaned loud enough to wake the neighbors.

Hopefully, the emergency room would be quieter today. When she walked in, only three cubicles were full, which was a good sign She noticed Lucille was also there, but at this point, she knew better than to try and talk to her.

Mid morning, her nurse manager, Susan White, invited her into her office. It made her nervous to be called into a meeting, but she was new and it wasn't unusual for managers to check on new employees. She made sure Mallory was free to cover her patients for her, then followed Susan into her office.

"Please have a seat and close the door, Caitlyn." Susan smiled and sat down behind her desk. Caitlyn didn't like the feel of this. "So how is everything going?"

"I think it's going well. I was here all weekend with Mallory. I've been taking more patients, so I'll be prepared to go out on my own soon."

"Well, I was thinking of moving you to your own schedule starting next week, if you're comfortable with that."

Caitlyn thought for a minute and said, "I think I'll be fine. Would it be possible for my schedule to line up with Mallory's for the first week so I have someone to go to with questions?"

"Absolutely. I think that's a wonderful idea." Susan quieted and steepled her fingers in front of her face. "How are you getting along with the other nurses on the unit?"

"Oh, no problem. I like everyone. I don't think I've met all your nurses yet, but I've gotten along with everyone I've met." Caitlyn hoped her lie didn't show. Anyway, it was mostly true—she got along with everyone but Lucille. Still, she would never run to her boss and complain about another employee.

"Well, I'm glad you feel that way. I have received a complaint from one of your peers about your willingness to help. She said you didn't want to watch her waste her narcotic and almost refused to sign off on it when she did waste it in front of you."

Damn it, Mallory had been right. The bitch had set her up and thrown her under the bus. "I didn't see the nurse waste the medication, so I didn't want to sign. That is your policy, correct? In orientation, I was told we had to actually see the vial or pill when it's discarded."

"Of course, that's our policy. And I am sure none of my nurses would expect you to co-sign if you didn't see the medication."

"I apologize." The sweat pooled underneath her shirt. What the hell could she say? She was screwed one way or the other. Either she signed without seeing it, or she lied to the nurse about seeing the discard. Both went against protocol. *Just apologize and get out of here.* "Apparently, there was a misunderstanding. It won't happen again."

"Thank you. We all work very hard here and we have to function as a team. I need team players, not loners."

Susan White smiled and stood. "That's all. I just wondered if you were having any problems. Remember, if you do, please come to me as soon as possible."

Lucille was going to be nothing but trouble.

CHAPTER TWENTY-TWO

Monday was not her favorite day to work because there were so many people around. Lots of tests, surgeries, and doctors everywhere. Caitlyn tried to stay out of the way and just do her job. Avoiding Lucille was paramount, but in the middle of the afternoon, she had no choice but to interact with her.

A patient had requested IV Dilaudid, so Caitlyn had administered the prescribed dose, but since it wasn't the entire vial, she had to waste the remaining medication. Of course, the only person around to witness her waste was Lucille, who was standing next to her at the med cart. Against her better judgment, she approached the miserable woman.

"Lucille, I need to waste some Dilaudid." She held the vial up for Lucille to check. "Would you witness for me?"

"Sure, no problem, newbie." Lucille took the vial from her so she could read it. "Yup, Dilaudid. I'll sign for you."

Caitlyn tossed the vial into the sharps container, the required waste receptacle because the vial was glass. "Here, would you sign for me?" She held out the paper and pen.

Lucille placed her hand on her hip and said, "Oh, you know, I don't remember if that was Dilaudid or not. Would you show it to me again?"

Caitlyn froze, unable to speak. She had seen her look at the bottle. The woman had actually said it was Dilaudid out loud. Damn the witch. "I just threw it in the sharps container."

Lucille grinned. "Well, why don't you reach in there and see if you can get it back for me?"

"In the middle of all those needles? Very funny, Lucille. I

can't believe you said that. You know I can't reach in there to get anything out. That's impossible." Caitlyn couldn't believe what Lucille had just suggested. Of course, no one was around to overhear her, so she was free to do as she liked.

"Humph. I guess I can't sign if I didn't see what you wasted." Lucille smiled and spun on her heel and walked away.

Caitlyn was dumbfounded. She didn't know what to do. Without a witness's signature, she could lose her job, particularly after the other waste-related debacle, but there was no one else to ask. Mallory came out of a patient's cubicle, and Caitlyn waved her over.

"What's wrong?" Mallory asked.

"I showed Lucille my Dilaudid waste, but then she refused to sign, saying she couldn't remember what it was. She actually asked me to reach into the sharps container to pull it out."

"Oh my God. You didn't, did you?" Mallory gave her an incredulous stare.

"Of course not. But I have no one to sign my form, and it's gone."

"I'll sign it for you."

"No, Mallory. I wouldn't ask you to sign for something you didn't witness." Her recent conversation with her nurse manager echoed in her mind. Caitlyn closed out of the med page without the extra signature. "I guess you were right. I just had a hard time believing she could be so nasty."

"You need to report her to the nurse manager."

"If I report Lucille to the nurse manager, then I'm a troublemaker. You know Lucille will have a reason for everything she did. Plus, Susan already called me into her office because she had a complaint about me."

"What?" Mallory stared at her. "Why didn't you tell me?"

"Because I was embarrassed. Who gets pulled into their supervisor's office after working for two weeks?"

"It's Lucille. She has done it before and she's doing it again. I can't believe Sue White listens to her. She has to know what kind of person she is after all these years." Mallory paced back and forth in front of Caitlyn as she spoke.

"Mal, never mind. It's over and done with. I'll know better than to ask her again."

"Either way. I'm going to keep my eye on her."

Ryan pulled the hanger out of his closet, the shirt still on it. He held it up to inspect it. Good enough, he decided. There weren't too many wrinkles. He put the shirt on and thought about shaving, but changed his mind, deciding instead to leave his beard scruffy.

He was taking Erin and Sammy out for pizza. It didn't happen often, but he had promised Chad to take care of them. At first, he had considered marrying Erin, but they had quickly agreed that it wouldn't work for them. The least he could do was pay for dinner once in a while. Visiting them only reminded him of Chad, of how much he missed him, wished he had made it out of Iraq.

Now that he had met Cait, he knew more than ever that he had made the right decision not to date Erin. Someday, he would tell Cait about Erin, but not yet. He had to make sure she wouldn't feel threatened by their relationship. He and Erin were strictly friends. Truth be known, he was falling hard for Cait, and he didn't want to risk that relationship for anything.

He got out of the car, walked up to the door and rang the doorbell. Erin answered a minute later, Sammy right behind her.

"Uncle Ryan, I'm coming, too. Right?" Sammy peeked around his mother, a wide grin on his face.

Ryan had told Erin he wanted to take Sammy with them. "Of course, buddy."

"This was nice of you to do for us, Ryan. He loves you so." Erin gave him an appreciative glance before turning to Sammy, "Get your coat and come on."

"I know, Mom!" Sammy yelled as he charged back into the house for his jacket. "Where are we going?"

"Well, how about that place where we can get pizza and play games?" Ryan ruffled Sammy's hair when he came out the door, fumbling with the zipper on his jacket as he ran to the car.

"Yes! I love that place. I can't believe I get to stay out late. Thanks, Uncle Ryan."

Ryan opened the door for Erin, then climbed into the

driver's seat. "Is that alright with you, Erin?"

"Pizza is fine, Ryan."

Sammy chattered all the way to the restaurant, and every time he glanced at Erin, she appeared extremely uncomfortable. He had no idea what he had done, but hoped he would get the chance to ask her at dinner.

Once inside the restaurant, they settled and Ryan gave Sammy some money to go play some of the arcade games.

"Aren't you playing with me, Uncle Ryan?" Sammy's face was lit with excitement.

"No, maybe after dinner. Right now, I want to talk to your mom."

"Okay, call me when the pizza is here." Sammy flew off toward the game room.

"Ryan, you're so good with him. I wish..." Erin's eyes misted and she turned away, staring out the window of the restaurant.

Ryan thought he knew what she was going to say, so he finished it for her. "I know. I wish Chad was here with us."

Erin shook her head and reached into her purse for a tissue. "You don't understand."

"I know how much I miss him, Erin, so I can only imagine how much you and Sammy do."

Erin rested her elbow on the table and leaned her head into her hand. "Ryan, why are you doing this? You don't have to, you know."

"Doing what?"

"Taking care of us. That's what it seems like you're doing. There's no need. I can take care of Sammy and myself."

"Because I want to be here for you two. It's just not right that he was taken away from you so soon."

"I know, and you have been a wonderful friend, but I think we have adjusted. It's been a few years. You don't have to fuss over us." Erin peered at him before staring out the window again. "I do miss him, but I know Chad. He would want us to get on with our lives and not spend all our time mourning, especially Sammy. He would want Sammy to be happy."

"I know, but I am only doing what Chad wanted. It was his last wish."

"Tell me again what he said? Please? Tell me exactly what you heard." There was some glint in her eyes he had trouble understanding.

Ryan glanced across the room and saw Sammy laughing and cheering with a couple of other boys.

"When the bomb went off, the look on his face was terrible. He was in awful pain." The words came out without any conscious selection on his part. He peeked at Erin. "I'm sorry. I probably shouldn't be so graphic."

Erin reached for his hand and covered it with hers. "No, I want you to tell me exactly how it was. I can handle it."

"I don't want to go into all the details about getting Chad out of the way, but I finally got him hidden in some brush off the road. He tried to speak, but he had trouble catching his breath. He grabbed my hand and squeezed it and said the same thing three times. *Please.* That's the only word he could get out at first, but then he tugged on my arm and pulled me closer. He said, 'Promise me.' I told him I would promise him anything. My gut felt like someone had punched it while holding me down."

"Not your leg?"

"No, I didn't know about my leg injury yet. The doctor said I was in shock, and I'm sure Chad was, too. I don't think he felt all the pain of what had happened."

"I'm sorry, Ryan, you don't have to continue if you don't want to."

"No, I do. He whispered something else, but I couldn't understand him. Then I put my ear down to his mouth and he said it again. All I could make out was the last part, 'Take care of them.'"

He rubbed the rough beard on his chin, wanting to make everything go away. But he knew he couldn't. That day, that moment, would live with him forever. "He said to take care of you and Sammy."

"I know I've asked you this before, but did he say our names?" Tears slid down her cheeks and she swiped at them with the back of her hand.

He scowled for a moment, trying to remember, but he couldn't. "No, but he meant you and Sammy. I'm sure of it."

Erin nodded and fussed with her purse, pulled out her phone to check it, then placed it back inside. Her text alert went off, so she tugged it right back out. "Excuse me, I have to answer this."

Ryan waved his hand at her and stared into the game area where the kids were playing. He stood up, stuffed his hands in his pockets, and strolled over to watch Sammy play. When he got close, though, the lights and the bells set off a feeling inside him. Suddenly he was back there, right in the thick of it. He could hear another bomb explode not far from them, and he heard the men from his unit yelling and hollering, some shooting at nearby enemy forces.

Then time moved backward. He stood in the middle of the street, laughing at some stupid joke Jake had just told them. They were about to climb into their vehicles for their ill-fated mission, and he wanted to scream at himself to stop.

Ryan relived it all. Once again, he carried Chad across the road, away from the insurgents and the gunfire. Ryan knelt by his friend's side in the brush, yelling at him to get some response. Chaos reigned around them, but he couldn't take his gaze from Chad's. It was clear his friend didn't have much more life left in him.

He thought Chad had grabbed his hand and said, "Listen to me. Listen. I'm dying."

Ryan had ignored him. Why? He couldn't remember why he had turned away from his friend for a few moments, but he had. A feeling of remorse swept through him, of pity, just as he had felt at the time. What could have prompted such a feeling?

And then Chad's voice changed, insistent, frantic. Ryan had tried to understand his words, but it was impossible. He had rambled out almost a complete sentence before a few of his words finally registered: "Take care of them."

Sammy's voice pulled him from his memories. He shook his head and stared at the little boy in front of him.

"Uncle Ryan, are you okay?" Sammy tugged on his arm, one of the few things that could actually pull him out of an episode. Physically yanking on him.

"Yeah, I'm fine. Let's go eat." He headed back to the table with Sammy, and Erin was already sitting there and staring at him, a strange look on her face.

What the hell had he done during his episode?

Damn it, why couldn't he remember everything?

CHAPTER TWENTY-THREE

Caitlyn finished her hair and smiled. She was excited to be going out with Ryan tonight. She hadn't seen him since his return from Philly, so she was anxious to hear how the trip had gone. Most of Tuesday had been lost to sleep, and she'd spent a few hours cleaning her house today. Ryan had invited her to go to The Cobalt Brew House again, a favorite spot of the younger crowd. She liked the Brew House, but someday, she hoped to take a tour of the many wineries in the area, since wine was her drink of choice. Maybe she and Ryan could take a weekend trip together once things had settled down.

When she was ready, she stood in front of her sliding glass doors, smiling as she took in the beauty of Orenda Lake. The Finger Lakes was such a beautiful area and she had fallen in love with it. No snow was predicted for the week, so they had a brief reprieve from the frequent upstate snow.

As soon as she heard Ryan's car, she headed out the door. When he saw her, he got out of the car and wrapped her in a hug, proceeding to kiss her senseless.

"Maybe we should skip dinner and go right to my favorite part of the night." He raised his eyebrows and grinned.

Caitlyn grinned back. "Works for me, but then we'll have to get take-out because you know what a mess I'll be after we roll around in my bed."

He laughed and said, "No, let's go now. I'm starving. We have all night to play." He turned her back toward the car and guided her into her seat.

When they pulled into the parking lot, Caitlyn was surprised to see how many cars were already there. "Wow, this place is really busy."

"It's a popular place. They have great burgers and chicken wings. Mostly bar food, but it's *good* bar food." He took her hand as they walked through the entrance, which made Caitlyn smile.

Once they were settled at a pub table and had put their orders in, Caitlyn folded her hands on the table. "Okay, out with it. I want to know everything you found out in Philly."

Ryan nodded and said, "I'll tell you what I learned, but it wasn't what I had hoped for."

She'd pinned all her hopes on his visit, desperate to find out who was tormenting her. Granted, nothing had happened since she'd returned to town, but there had to be some clues.

"You have my undivided attention."

Ryan wrapped his hand around hers and rubbed his thumb across the back of it. "I met your ex-husband." He paused.

Caitlyn couldn't stand the suspense. "And?"

"I don't think he's guilty. Let me think for a minute about how to explain this..." He glanced at the crowd before turning back to her. "He's an asshole, but he's not the right type."

"The right type? What do you mean? What did you think of him?"

"Cait, don't take this the wrong way, but you asked me. He married you for your money." His thumb caressed her skin again. "I think he would have stayed with you if you'd ignored his infidelity. He's a man who's interested in nothing and no one but himself. He wanted you to fund his games and indiscretions."

Caitlyn put a hand over her face to hide her misting eyes.

"Cait, please don't cry. I can't stand it. My true opinion is you are better off without him. You deserve to be with someone better, someone who loves you for yourself."

"And Lynn? Is he still seeing Lynn?" She swiped at her eyes, but she didn't let go of Ryan's hand. This man was so solid he anchored her, somehow making her more grounded, too. She took in his chiseled jaw, his green eyes flecked with brown, his dark hair curling at his collar. He was a man she would always be able to trust and depend on. He was a very serious man, but he was thoughtful and warm.

"No, they both denied it, and I believe them. How long did you know Lynn? She was your best friend?"

"I had only been there a little over a year, and I didn't know too many people. I saw a lot of her because we worked together at the hospital.

"Speaking of the hospital, do you remember an aide by the name of William Jenkins?"

"No, why? Should I?" The name sounded vaguely familiar, but she couldn't place it.

"Lynn mentioned him. She said that she thought he had a thing for you. According to her, he used to hit on you. Do you remember anyone like that?"

Caitlyn thought for a moment, but she still didn't recall any William.

"She said he was a transporter, does that help?"

Her eyes widened. "Yes. Bill. He was a big guy, not too smart, and he did ask me out once. But he didn't seem to be upset when I told him I was married. He was a little creepy, but that was the end of it. In fact, I'm surprised Lynn knew anything about it."

"Have you heard from her since this happened? She mentioned that she wanted to apologize to you."

The waitress brought their sandwiches, and Caitlyn chewed on a few sweet potato fries before responding. "Actually, I got a text from her the other day. She wanted to meet with me so she could apologize, but I told her I didn't want to see her again." She stared at her plate. "She's not who I thought she was."

Ryan leaned over and kissed her cheek. "Then don't see her. Forget about Philadelphia. You have a new life here—a good one. I tried to locate this Bill, but I haven't been able to find him. Trust me, I'll follow up on it. At least we have something."

She nodded and took a bite of her burger.

"You haven't had any other threats?"

She shook her head. "Thank goodness."

They ate in silence for a few moments, but Caitlyn didn't really feel like eating her burger. The talk of Philadelphia had brought back so many bad memories. She picked at her fries and the small salad she had ordered. Her life had been so awful and filled with phony people. Why hadn't she realized that until now?

"Cait? Talk to me. What are you thinking?"

Tears gathered in her lashes as she gazed at Ryan. He reached for her hand again, but she pulled away. "I can't even remember why I married him." She sniffled and pulled a tissue from her purse.

"Does it matter?" Ryan whispered.

"It does to me. Why was I so naïve? I mean, I know why I went out with him...my mother's death hit me really hard, so when he invited me over to his apartment for dinner one night, I figured why not? And he started asking me over all the time. It made me feel like someone was finally offering me a place where I could *belong*."

"I don't understand, though. You still had your Aunt Margie, right?"

"Yes, but when I went to live with her, I never felt like it was the right place for me. I belonged at home with my mother and my father. When I lost my dad, I still felt like I belonged at home with my mom. I loved her so much, but I just couldn't care for her anymore. Still, I always thought the arrangement with my aunt would be temporary."

"You thought you would move back in with your mother someday."

"Yes. I always believed or hoped that she would get better. Even when I went to college, I thought she would be so proud of me that she would stop drinking. See? Foolish and naïve."

"You were young, babe."

"When she died, I felt so alone, like I had nowhere to go." Her voice was coming out as a whisper now, and she barely recognized the sound of it.

"But your aunt would have taken you back, wouldn't she have?"

"Yes. She never sent me away. My room was still there in her house, and she told me I was always welcome. But..."

"It didn't feel the same."

"No. Suddenly, I didn't belong anywhere. But then I met Bruce."

"When you were way too vulnerable."

She nodded. "Exactly. He convinced me we belonged together, and I believed him."

Ryan reached for her hand again. "You were young and hurting. Don't blame yourself."

"I know, but I wasn't stupid. Why didn't I notice how much money I gave him? Why didn't I question him more about the sums he took from our joint accounts?"

"Maybe you weren't ready to handle it then. But Cait, it's in your past now. I think you need to leave it there."

"Thank you, Ryan." She set her elbow on the table and rested her chin on her hand, gazing at the wonderful man next to her.

"For what?"

"For being here and for listening. For being you."

Ryan paid the check and they left the Brew House hand in hand. When they reached the car, he wrapped his arms around her and cupped her face in his hands. "I'm sorry I brought up bad memories."

"It's okay. I need to work through this."

He kissed her and she ran her hands through his hair. He tasted like beer and Ryan, a now-familiar taste that she somehow found more enticing every day. He angled his mouth over hers to deepen the kiss, sweeping his tongue into her mouth until she gasped, a little sound in the back of her throat that erupted from sheer desire.

He pulled back and said, "I think I need to take you home and tuck you in."

She giggled and rubbed his erection through his pants. "I think you'd better."

Once they arrived back at her house, they walked up the stairs hand in hand, Caitlyn behind Ryan. When he stepped inside her bedroom, he turned to her. In a small voice, he asked, "Do you mind if I remove my prosthesis?"

Cait ran her hand through his hair as she stepped close to him and whispered, "No. Why don't you show me what you need to in case you ever need help with it?"

"You're sure it won't bother you?" His gaze caught hers and his expression pierced her heart.

"I'm sure."

They sat on the side of the bed, and he did what he needed to do while she watched.

When he finished, she smiled at him and said, "Ryan, it doesn't matter to me."

He made sweet love to her twice before they fell asleep, arms and legs all tangled together.

In the middle of the night, Caitlyn awoke to a deep moan. She sat up and stared at Ryan, who was tossing and turning in bed. He swung his arm and nearly hit her with his fist, so she grabbed his arm.

"Ryan, Ryan, wake up. You're having a nightmare." It took a few minutes, but she finally managed to jar him awake.

He stared at her as if he didn't recognize her, then awareness kicked in. "Sorry," he gasped, trying to get his uneven breathing under control.

"Are you okay?"

He nodded, then put his prosthesis in place so he could pace the room. "Maybe I should go."

"No, you can't leave in the middle of the night. I'll worry about you. What were you dreaming about?"

"Nothing." He avoided her gaze.

"Nothing? You can't remember?"

"It doesn't matter."

"Does your therapist know about your nightmares?"

Ryan still paced the room like a caged animal, running his hand over his beard and through his hair. "Yes, yes. Many times. She knows everything."

"Are you sure? You shouldn't be having nightmares after all these years."

"How the hell would you know?" he said, glaring at her with eyes that flashed fire—so different from how he'd looked at her just a few hours before. "She says what I'm going through is normal. It's all because I keep trying to remember."

"Trying to remember what?"

"I'm sorry. I didn't mean to yell at you. It's just frustrating because I get so close, but..."

"Close to what?"

"Never mind. I'm sorry." He found his briefs and his pants and started to get dressed.

"Why are you leaving? Maybe you should talk about it. Talking helps, you know. Maybe we can figure this out together. You've helped me with my past. Give me the chance to do the same for you."

"You can't, Cait." He sat on the bed and put his shoes and socks on. "You can't, so forget it. I don't want to talk about it."

"It's not good to keep so much hurt buried inside."

"I don't. I talk to my therapist." He stood up and leaned over to kiss her. "Gotta go. See you later." With that, he pivoted and left the room.

Caitlyn hopped out of bed and followed him. She just couldn't let him leave like that. "Ryan. It isn't good to run from your issues. We need to talk about it."

When they reached the bottom of the stairs, he jerked around to stare at her. "Look, Cait, I know you have good intentions, but you can't fix me."

"Well, I could try to help you. I want to."

"No one can fix me." He reached for the doorknob and turned back to her. "I have been trying for years. It can't be done."

He slammed the door behind him. Caitlyn just stared at it, feeling numb. What was she getting herself into?

CHAPTER TWENTY-FOUR

The next night, Ryan headed over to his grandfather's. He couldn't stop thinking about the things he'd said to Cait the night before, and the heavy guilt had made for a terrible day at work. Somehow, he needed to stop his nightmares.

He and Jake had tried to find information about William Jenkins, but to no avail. The only thing they did discover was that William Jenkins fit the description of the man who took out the rental car in Buffalo, both times.

Every time Ryan got this frustrated, he needed to talk to his grandfather. For some reason, Ryan James Ramsay, Sr. could always help him reason through his troubles.

His grandparents lived in a small house just down the street from the family inn, but not on the lake. A little stream ran behind their house, and his grandfather had a deck built off the back so he could sit and listen to the sound of running water during the summer. Though they'd lived in a house on the lake for years, Gramps had tired of the sounds of the boats. Here he could listen to the sweet sounds of the birds that came to the many birdfeeders in his backyard.

Ryan pulled in and was surprised to see his father's car there. Oh, well, his grandfather would no doubt end up telling his father everything he said anyway. All of them were close. He sat in his car for a moment, organizing his thoughts, then sidled up the sidewalk and onto the porch to ring the bell.

His father answered the door. "Three. Come on in. I brought Gramps a bowl of chowder Lorraine made and he just finished eating."

Ryan stepped into the small living room and headed back to

the kitchen. His grandfather sat at the kitchen table, munching on a cookie his stepmother had no doubt sent with the soup.

"Three! How are you doing? It's about time you came by. Sit down, sit down."

Ryan shook his grandfather's hand. "Hi Gramps. How was the soup?" He pulled out a chair and took a seat at the same old-colonial, walnut-stained table he had sat at since he was a little kid. Gram had covered it with a plastic lace tablecloth after the years had faded the finish.

"Damn good. Lorraine is a helluva cook, but I think you know that." He chuckled as he ate the last bite of his cookie. "She takes good care of me when Gram is gone."

Ryan got up to grab a glass of water and returned to his chair. One, Two, and Three. That's what his grandmother had always called them. Her eyes always glittered with pride whenever she talked about her husband or any of her kids or grandkids. "When's Gram coming back from visiting her sister?"

"Oh, not for another few days. I'll have to eat more of Lorraine's good cooking." He laughed again, grabbing Ryan's hand on the table. "What's bothering you? I can see it in your face. Spill the beans, young man. How's that new blonde your dad told me about?"

Ryan glanced at his father leaning against the kitchen counter before he answered his grandfather. "She's good. Actually, that's what I came to talk to you about."

"Female advice? Well, you're asking the experts, isn't he, Two?" He laughed as he looked at Ryan's dad.

"This is serious, Gramps. I need to be sure I'm doing the right thing."

"Okay." He reached over with his arthritic hands and patted Ryan's arm. "I'm ready to listen whenever you're ready."

Ryan cleared his throat before he began. "Well, you know the situation with Chad and his wife, Erin."

"Oh, yes, yes. The young man you saved. He has a son, right?"

"Gramps, I didn't save him."

"Oh, right, right. Go on."

"When Chad died in my arms, he asked me to do something

for him. He asked me to take care of his wife and his son." He watched his grandfather to make sure he understood the importance of those words. His grandfather was quick, but sometimes he had trouble hearing. It seemed to register, so he continued, "Chad wanted me to take care of Erin and Sammy, so I originally thought the only way I can honor his request was to marry her. But you know Erin and I decided we weren't right for one another."

"What brought this up again? I thought it was settled in your mind that you wouldn't marry her." His father came over to the table and sat down.

"I've been seeing Cait, as you know."

"What's really going on?" his father whispered.

Ryan sighed and dropped his hands to the table. "I'm having more nightmares. I don't understand why, and all I can think of is because I'm seeing Cait."

His father and Gramps nodded in unison.

"I haven't told her anything about Chad and what he asked me to do. I have been afraid to tell her that I see Sammy and Erin every once in a while. I'm afraid she'll get angry, and I don't want to lose her. How do I tell her I'm seeing Erin?"

"You aren't really interested in Erin, but another woman will see it that way. You better tell her. Don't try to hide anything. Just be honest with the gel. Tell me more about her," Gramps said.

"Her name is Caitlyn, Caitlyn McCabe."

"Och, a fine Scottish lass, aye?" Gramps winked at him, a grin on his face. "You know how I feel about Scottish lassies."

His grandmother was Scottish, with red hair and a temper to go with it. "That's my issue, Gramps. And I need some advice. I think I'm in love with Caitlyn, but I'm having nightmares, and I'm wondering if it's because of Erin. I must be feeling guilty about not marrying Erin."

His father came over and grasped his shoulders from behind. "Three, I don't think you'll ever be able to resolve that issue until you recall Chad's exact words. Maybe you need to reconsider hypnosis."

"Dad, the thought of hypnosis makes me nauseous."

"I know. But I think it's time. Hasn't the issue haunted you for long enough?"

Gramps said, "Ryan James, you are a young man, and it saddens me to see what the war had done to you. The physical issues you can live with when you find the right lass, but the emotional scars you carry need to heal. Please do everything you can to fix them. It's time for you to live your life to the fullest, the way it was meant to be lived as a Ramsay. Do whatever it takes, and don't be afraid of life."

He nodded. Yep, he needed to tell Cait everything, and he needed hypnosis. It was time to settle things in his mind. "Thanks, Gramps." He got up and walked out the door with a heavy heart.

Ryan's father followed him out to his car. "Son, you and Caitlyn are a perfect match. She's a gift to you. Do what you need to in order to enjoy the gift you've been given."

He wanted nothing more than to do exactly what his father suggested. He was just afraid to find out exactly what Chad had said.

Caitlyn stood outside Ellen Ramsay's door in the basement of the hospital. She had decided to talk to someone who knew more about Ryan than she did. She wasn't sure if talking to Mallory would be appropriate or not, so she'd decided to visit his aunt while she was on her lunch break.

The door opened and Ellen welcomed her inside. "Caitlyn, how good to see you. Come on in. I love to chat with our nurses, especially our newest ones. How can I help you?"

Caitlyn sat down opposite Ellen and fidgeted for a moment, wanting to make sure she approached this delicate issue in the right way. "It's nice to see you, too. But I'm not here about a nursing issue, it's a personal matter, and I wondered if you would mind answering a question for me."

"Well, I'll try. What is it?"

"It's about your nephew, Ryan." She stared at her hands again before raising her gaze to meet Ellen's. "We've been dating, and I'm just wondering about his return home."

Ellen acted a bit surprised, but then returned quickly to her professional composure. "Okay, can you clarify a little more for me? How much do you know about Ryan's army experience?"

"I know about his injury and his prosthesis. I know about how Chad died in his arms. But I don't understand something and I don't want to dredge up a sore subject for him, so I thought it would be better to ask someone in his family."

"Go ahead, I'm listening."

"He has said some things that led me to believe he was not discharged honorably, yet I don't understand how that could be. Wouldn't the army reward someone who was wounded in action?"

"Oh, absolutely. And I don't feel that I am giving away any of Ryan's secrets away by telling you something that's a matter of public record. He received a Purple Heart for his duty and a Silver Star for what he did for Chad."

"Then why would Ryan think he isn't a hero? His stepmother called him a hero and he said he didn't like that label."

"Well, a little history. Ryan is the third Ryan James Ramsay, as you know."

"Yes, and he doesn't like to be called 'Three' either."

"No, he doesn't. Both his father and his grandfather each received a Medal of Honor for their bravery during wartime. Unfortunately, that put quite a bit of pressure on Ryan to do the same. I almost wish they didn't give him the family name because of the pressure it placed on him. Nevertheless, Ryan believes that since he couldn't save his friend, he failed in the military. It doesn't matter what anyone else tells him. I don't know what we can do to help him see otherwise. You know from your nursing experience that he needs to come to the right conclusion on his own, and I believe he will. He has all the support a returning soldier could."

Caitlyn reviewed Ellen's word in her mind, trying to make sense of the man she was falling in love with, but something else bothered her. "But didn't he receive a hero's welcome when he came home?"

"Oh, he most certainly did by Summerhill's standards. But Ryan was dealing with the loss of his leg and his best friend, and I don't think he could appreciate his homecoming when Chad didn't return with him."

Caitlyn smiled. "Thank you, Ellen. I appreciate your honesty."

"Well, as I said, I didn't tell you anything that isn't public knowledge, and I don't think I should tell you more than I have. But trust there are many people in Summerhill who love and support him. I hope you remain one of them." She stood and came around the desk, enveloping Caitlyn in her arms. "I hope I didn't say anything to scare you away, my dear. He needs someone like you in his life."

"No, you didn't."

"And how are things going in the emergency room for you? You have a good preceptor?"

"Oh, absolutely, Mallory is my preceptor and things are going well." Caitlyn couldn't look her in the eye as she told her little white lie. Everything was going well if you didn't count Lucille. One person was upsetting the entire applecart, and she couldn't decide what to do about it.

She would worry about Lucille tomorrow.

CHAPTER TWENTY-FIVE

Ryan sat in the diner waiting for Cait. He had asked her to meet him so he could discuss the case with her. Besides, he still felt bad about how abruptly he had left her the other night. She didn't understand how the nightmares affected him. He needed to apologize for his rudeness.

He had seen his therapist earlier that day, and they had talked extensively about Cait and Erin. His therapist had tried to talk him into hypnosis. She had agreed with his father that it might be the only way he could remember everything. His therapist believed that the memory was buried inside him for some reason, and he wouldn't stop having the nightmares until it surfaced. Much as he tried, only bits and pieces came back to him.

Somehow, he had hoped Gramps would come up with a different solution, but no matter how he tried, everything pointed to the same result—he needed to find out exactly what Chad had said. Hypnosis seemed to be the only surefire way to get answers to his question.

He ran his hand across his chin and glanced up in time to see Cait step inside. With just a glance, his dick took notice. She was gorgeous. He jumped up and made his way over to her so he could kiss her cheek.

First things first. As soon as they ordered, he started in on the case. "Cait, we believe William Jenkins was the one in Buffalo who followed you onto the thruway and forced you off the road. We're not certain, but he could have been the one that hit you from behind in Summerhill. He quit his job before your incident on the thruway, so it is possible he was in Buffalo.

Unfortunately, we don't have enough proof to arrest him.

"The new information we have is that he is presently in Florida and has been there for a few days. Why he's in Florida, we don't know. Hopefully, he has given up on you and plans to move south for good. If so, your worries are over."

"Do you think he did all that because I turned him down?"

"Who knows? He could have done it for a lot of reasons. Men get crazy over women, especially when they have little self-esteem. We're just hoping he has given up and is on to a new one in Florida." He reached for her hand on top of the table.

Caitlyn stared at their intertwined hands. "It all seems so unreal now, so distant, almost as if it never happened. I'm glad you were there to see my car, or I'd almost believe I had dreamed the entire episode."

"I know. Nothing else has happened, which is good, but it isn't helping us catch the perpetrator. Even though Jenkins is our primary suspect and he is out of town, if anything at all happens, please let me know. Don't wait until you see me. Text or call me right away."

They ate their dinner in silence. Finally Cait said, "Maybe you should try hypnosis, Ryan. That would help you remember what happened."

He kicked himself for not speaking up sooner. "I'm sorry about the other night. I shouldn't have run off the way I did. Maybe you're right. My dad thinks I should try hypnosis, too. I just feel like I didn't hear everything Chad said to me. There was more, I just don't recall what it was."

"Why not give it a try? It could help with your nightmares."

"Like I told you, that's completely normal for someone who's been through trauma. I'll make sure it doesn't happen again around you."

Cait peeked at him through her lashes. Damn it, he wasn't handling this right. Hell, he loved her, didn't he?

Dead silence hung between them. He suddenly couldn't finish his dinner, and he noticed she wasn't eating either.

"Aren't you hungry, Cait? You hardly ate anything. Sorry for my comment. I don't know what's wrong with me." Actually, that was a total lie, but he wasn't about to tell her that. The most logical next step was to explain about Erin, but he didn't think she was ready for that after the conversation they just shared. He had to get answers before he could give himself to her completely. There was no other way.

Cait played with her food, but refused to look him in the eye. "It was a long day, and I have to work tomorrow. I think I just need to go home to bed. I have to get through another day before I can sleep in."

He walked her out to her car and opened her door for her. "You all right going home alone, or would you like me to follow you and check out your house?"

"Don't bother. I'm fine. I just need sleep." She climbed into her car and drove off.

Great. Just great. He'd fucked things up again.

Caitlyn trudged into work the next morning, still trying to figure out what had gone wrong with Ryan at dinner. She made a mental note not to ever mention hypnosis to him again, though it bothered her he didn't know he needed help.

She could barely put one foot in front of the other as she sat through the report on her patients. Mallory had ended up working after all, and Lucille wasn't around yet, which was a relief. Still, she realized it wasn't a good sign that the quality of her days was based on the absence of a peer.

It wasn't particularly busy in the ER, just busy enough to keep her going. Slow days were torture when she was overtired, so she appreciated the steady pace. Around four o'clock, Susan White called her into her office. She only had two patients at the time, and the census was low. Susan instructed her to give Mallory a full report on her patients, then head to her office.

After she finished the report, Mallory said, "What's going on?"

"I don't know, but I don't have a good feeling about this. It's probably about the waste from the other day. Remember when I didn't get the required second signature?"

"You're just coming off orientation with me, so maybe she just wants to see how you're doing. Or maybe you forgot to give an antibiotic or something. Have you given all your meds on time?"

"As far as I can recall, I have. But maybe I missed something. She wouldn't fire me for that, would she?"

Mallory waved her hand. "Oh, no. I think you have at least three instances per year or something. I don't know for sure, but I've had two med errors over the years, and I'm still here. I'm sure it's because you're new."

Caitlyn wiped her sweaty palms on her scrub pants. She had never been fired before, let alone reprimanded. "Thanks, Mallory. I'll see you later."

"Let me know what happens."

Caitlyn nodded and walked down the hall, dreading this meeting. Hopefully, she wouldn't get fired for the incident over the narcotic waste. And if Susan asked her about it, should she squeal on Lucille?

She took a deep breath and knocked on the nurse manager's door.

"Come in, Caitlyn. Please close the door behind you."

Caitlyn closed the door and sat down. All it took to speed her pulse up was the tone of Susan's voice.

"I'm sorry to say that I've received a couple of other complaints about you, and I wanted to hear your side of it."

"Okay." Caitlyn couldn't think of another word to say to that.

"One of the complaints came from the chart review task force. They said you neglected to get a signature when you wasted Dilaudid the other day? Is that true?"

What the hell. She couldn't deny it. Of course, it was true. She thought carefully before she answered. "Yes, that's true. I was unable to find anyone to witness my waste at the time, so I felt I had no alternative." If she turned Lucille in, it would be her word against Lucille's, and Lucille had put in way more time here than she had. She might as well take the consequences. She had learned her lesson and would never ask Lucille again. Besides, she really didn't think she would get fired for one incident.

"I'm sorry to hear that. You know our policy for narcotics, and we cannot bend on that. I find it hard to believe there was no one available, but I'll take your word for it on this occasion.

Please see to it that it doesn't happen again." Susan's lips formed a grim line, showing no sign of a smile.

"Yes, ma'am. I'm sorry and I will make sure it doesn't happen again." Well, that wasn't so bad. That had to be the worst of it. What else had she done? Nothing she could recall.

Susan settled her hands on the desk in front of her. "On to the next issue. I have a complaint from one of your peers that you made her uncomfortable in your break room. She states that you were kissing a policeman during work hours and she was embarrassed by your behavior in front of her."

"What?" Fucking Lucille had thrown her under the bus again. She couldn't believe it.

"Did that happen? She claimed it was in the morning between eight and nine."

Caitlyn's hands clenched together in her lap. That bitch, that miserable bitch. "Yes, I did kiss Officer Ramsay in the break room when there was no one else in there. Lucille walked in on us and we stopped immediately. I don't know how that..."

Susan held her hand up. "You have told me enough. I don't think an employee break room is an appropriate place to be kissing anyone, and might I suggest that you could be compromising your care of your patients if your focus is on your boyfriend and not on them."

All of this over one kiss? She stared at her supervisor, speechless, trying to maintain her professional demeanor when she was feeling anything but.

"Caitlyn, I am sorry to have to do this, but I suggest that you search for another unit to work in. You already have three complaints in your file. One more incident and I would be forced to fire you. I don't think you want that on your work record, do you?"

Caitlyn stared at her "May I ask a question?" she finally managed to say.

"Certainly." Susan folded her hands on her desk and smiled.

"Were all the complaints made by the same person or different people?"

"I'm sorry, but I'm not at liberty to answer that question." She forced another phony smile.

"So you're taking the word of a miserable, unhappy

employee over mine?"

"Excuse me?" Her eyes widened in shock.

Caitlyn held up her hand. "Never mind. Please forget I said that."

"I'm going to send you home today, though we will pay you for a full day. Please use the next week to search for another position. After that time, I will no longer have any work for you here. I'll notify nursing administration, and nurse recruitment will be expecting you. Would you like to visit them tomorrow?"

"No, I would like a day to think about my choices. Let's make it next week, please. I'll be in on Tuesday."

"That will be fine."

Caitlyn was stunned. She put one foot in front of the other and walked into the break room to gather her things from her locker.

What the hell was she supposed to do now?

CHAPTER TWENTY-SIX

As soon as she got home, Caitlyn stripped out of her scrubs and stood in the shower, sobbing as she attempted to wash away all the atrocities of her day. She wanted to call Ryan, but their night had ended on a strange note, so she decided not to, choosing instead to sit at her table and stare out her window, transfixed by everything that had happened.

Staring at the lake, she meditated on her life and where it would go next. A knock sounded at her door and Mallory's voice rang out. "Caitlyn, are you alright?"

Caitlyn let Mallory into the house, then turned and walked back into the great room.

"What happened?" Mallory asked, following fast on her heels.

"I have to leave."

"What? You're kidding, right?"

"No, Lucille complained about me kissing Ryan in the break room. Lucille refusing to witness my waste was counted against me, too. That's three strikes."

"But they're all Lucille. Can't she see that? Did you tell her about what Lucille did with the Dilaudid?"

"No."

"Why the hell not? That woman is a menace. You have to defend yourself."

Caitlyn stared at Mallory, tears flowing down her cheeks. "Why bother? What chance do I have? Lucille has been there forever and I just started. Susan won't take my word over hers."

"Did she fire you?"

"No. She's giving me the opportunity to go to another unit, but now I don't know what to do."

Mallory walked over and pulled her into her arms. "Oh, Caitlyn. I'm so sorry. I've never trusted her, but I had no idea she would do this to you. What are you going to do?"

"I don't know. I have to think about it. Maybe I don't even belong in nursing." Caitlyn moved away and sat down on the couch, crossing her arms in front of her.

"Are you crazy? Of course you do. We need good nurses like you. You're kind, compassionate, responsible, intelligent, and wonderful with the patients. Lucille's the one who needs to go. Not you."

"And where is Lucille going to go? She has been there so long, she'd never make it anywhere else." Caitlyn mopped at her tears with a handful of tissues from the coffee table.

"No, you're probably right. I think she hates nursing, but she has nowhere else to go and it eats at her all day. That's why she's so miserable. But that's her problem."

Neither of them said anything.

"Cait, you aren't really thinking of leaving nursing are you? Why not try something completely different, like obstetrics or pediatrics? I've often thought about switching. I wish I had the nerve."

Caitlyn shook her head, her breath hitching. "You know, I wanted to be a nurse so I could help people like my mother. But she died, and now I can't help anyone else either. I feel like I should just give up."

Mallory sat down, hanging onto the edge of the table. "Your mother? What are you talking about?"

"My mother was an alcoholic. I told you that before."

"Yes. You had to take care of her?"

She nodded and stared out her window overlooking the lake. "She started to drink after my father died. I mean, she used to have a glass of wine or a beer once in awhile, but not like this. Over the next year, she drank more and more. Before I knew it, I would come home from school and find her passed out at the kitchen table."

"Oh, Caitlyn. I'm so sorry. How awful for you."

She turned and stared at Mallory. "But she was all I had left.

I loved her so much, and I tried so hard to fix her. I would bargain with her, beg her, promise to clean the house if she didn't drink, but it never worked. She just continued drinking and it got worse and worse.

"One day, when I was fifteen, I came home and she was lying in her own vomit. I could barely keep from puking myself, but I cleaned her up and got her into bed. Every night I would lie in bed and wonder if my mom would be alive when I woke up. I had nightmares about waking up and finding her dead."

"How awful. I can't imagine what that must have been like. And your poor mom to have lost her husband so young."

"One day, I bargained with God. I came home and I didn't think she was breathing so I called 911. While I waited for the ambulance, I promised God I would become a nurse if he would just bring my mom back to life. I didn't know it at the time, but she wasn't dead. They fixed her. I had to call an ambulance four more times later that year, and I always went with her.

"Eventually, I found the emergency room to be a source of comfort. I knew my mom was safe there, and the nurses were always so nice. They got to know me and let me sleep on a gurney when I brought my mom in. I slept so well because I knew I didn't have to worry about my mom when I was there."

"And so you became an emergency room nurse," Mallory whispered.

"Yep. My mom would always apologize to me the next day. I know she loved me, she just felt lost. So I vowed to help others. And I know she was proud of me. She always paid attention to my grades and bought me nice clothes. In fact, I think she watches over me. I can feel her sometimes, you know? You lost your mom. Have you ever felt that way?"

"Yeah, sometimes I do."

Caitlyn gathered her thoughts. She felt much better after talking to Mallory. Maybe tomorrow she'd be collected enough to tell Ryan about what had happened.

Mallory reached over and grasped Cait's hands in hers. "You know what I think? I think you should be in a different type of nursing. And I would love to help you figure out what that is. You're too good to throw your career away over this."

"Maybe you're right. I think I need to think about it for a couple of days. Then I'll go in and talk to the nurse recruiter, see what else they have available."

"There are lots of other kinds of nursing, Cait. You don't even have to work in a hospital. You could work in an office, an outpatient center, or even in rehab. We'll find something for you."

"As long as it isn't pediatrics. I don't think I'd do well with kids. I have no experience with them."

"I'm sure we can find something else." Mallory stood and leaned down to clasp his shoulder. "You're going to be okay? Is Ryan coming over or anything? Did you call him?"

"No. We had dinner last night, but it didn't go so well."

"I'm sorry. Ryan has his share of problems, too, but he is a good guy."

"I know. I'll be fine. I'm really tired right now, so I think I'll find a book and read in bed. I just bought a romance that's supposed to be good. I need to go live in another world for a couple of hours."

"Great idea." Mallory hugged her, then turned to leave. "Call or text me, anytime."

"Are you working tomorrow?"

"No, I'm off for two days, so I'll be around."

Caitlyn walked her to the door. "Thanks for stopping by, Mallory."

After Mallory left, she locked the door, climbed the stairs, and fell into bed. She was asleep in an instant, dreaming about a green-eyed policeman with brown hair and a scruffy beard.

Erin had called Ryan and asked if she could see him on Sunday afternoon. He had agreed. He paced in his front room while he waited for Erin, having no idea what she wanted. Cait, Cait was the woman he wanted, and the one he couldn't get out of his mind. He wanted to marry her and would propose immediately if he didn't have this entire other situation looming over him. Yes, she wanted to fix him, but didn't everyone in his life?

He jumped when the doorbell rang, and he was glad to see

Erin standing there when he opened his front door. "Hi, Erin. Come on in. I could have come to your house."

Erin stared at his feet. "I know, Ryan. But I need to talk to you, and I didn't want to do it in front of Sammy. So I came on my own. I hope that's okay." She lifted her gaze to meet his and smiled.

"Yeah," Ryan said, standing back. "Come in. Come in and sit down."

She sat down on the couch. "Do you want me to hang up your coat, Erin?"

"No, this won't take long."

Now he was really thrown off. What the hell was she going to say? Grabbing the chair opposite her, he sat down, trying to appear composed, when his stomach was in a knot. He wiped the sweat on his palms off on his pants and sat on the edge of the chair, resting his elbows on his knees. He hoped she wasn't about to tell him she had changed her mind about their dating. What the hell would he do then?

"Can I get you something to drink?" he asked.

"No, thank you." She took a deep breath. "I need to be completely honest with you, Ryan. I apologize that I haven't been before today, but Sammy adores you, which has made my decision difficult."

Ryan noticed the same signs of stress in Erin that he was experiencing. *Just get it out, Erin.*

She sighed before she continued. "I'm getting married next month."

Ryan was stunned. Hell, nothing could have shocked him more.

"What?"

"I know you feel some kind of responsibility toward us because you were so close with Chad, but things were not what you thought." She stared at her hands. Lifting her gaze to his, she said, "Sammy isn't Chad's son."

Shit, no, that *was* more shocking. He stared at her, not sure he'd heard her right.

"Please don't judge me. I couldn't bear it from you."

He could tell she was about to cry, her eyes misting as she spoke. She reached into her purse for a tissue.

"I missed Chad while he was away, and I was so lonely. I hated that he was in the army. I met this guy, and one thing led to another, and we fell in love."

Silence filled the room. What could he say?

"When Chad came home on leave, I told him about the pregnancy and said I wanted a divorce, but he wouldn't even talk about it. He just left without even speaking to me. I felt so guilty. But when he was deployed, I needed him and he wasn't here."

"Chad knew?"

She nodded. "John, my fiancé, told me to let him go. He thought Chad just needed some time to process what had happened." Erin wrung her hands in her lap. "The next thing you know, the army was at my door telling me of the accident and his death, and I fell apart. I was so afraid that I had something to do with his death, that he did something careless because he was upset..."

Ryan stood up. "No, there was no preventing his death."

"That's why I asked you about it again the other night. You know, I don't think he was asking you to take care of us, Ryan. I know you feel obligated to be there for Sammy and me, but you don't need to feel that way. He knew I was pregnant and that Sammy wasn't his. He knew I was in love with someone else, so he must have been trying to tell you something different. I just don't know what that was."

Silence descended again and all he could hear was the hitching of her breath. He thought about Chad and how devastated he must have been. Shit, he had been upset after leave, but Ryan had figured it was because he didn't want to leave a pregnant wife alone in the states while he was stationed in Iraq.

"When Chad died, I stopped seeing John because I couldn't handle the guilt. But we just recently got back together, and he proposed. I love John with all my heart, and it's time to make things right by him."

This changed everything.

Erin stood. "I guess that just about says it all." She stared at the wall. "Well, one more thing. John and I would appreciate it if you didn't come to see Sammy again. We're getting married and moving to Churchville on the other side of Rochester. John works there."

"Have you talked to Sammy about this?" He couldn't just walk out on the kid. Granted, he wasn't Chad's son, but he was still an important part of his life.

"Yes, that's why I waited until today. We're moving next week. I'm hoping to get everything sold and moved into a new house before the wedding. I gave birth to Sammy while I was married to Chad, so Chad's name is on his birth certificate, but John is his true father. He plans to adopt him, but our wish is to move away and raise him as our son, no questions asked. When he gets a little older, we'll explain everything to him, but John wants to start fresh. "

Ryan stood. Where did he go from here? He walked her out the front door and gave her a kiss and a hug. "Best of luck to you. Tell Sammy I'll miss him."

"I will. Thanks, Ryan, for everything." And just like that, Chad's wife walked out of his life.

He didn't have to feel guilty for not marrying Erin. For some reason, he wanted to jump for joy. But the thought of what his best friend had gone through stopped him.

So what had Chad been trying to tell him?

CHAPTER TWENTY-SEVEN

Caitlyn drove over to Ryan's house on Sunday afternoon. She just had to see him. Her life felt like it was falling apart and he was the only person she wanted to see. She hadn't even called before hopping into her car and driving over to Ryan's apartment. Just as she was about to get out of her parked car, she saw the door of his building open.

Out stepped a beautiful dark-haired woman. She turned and Ryan gave her a hug and a kiss. He spoke to her, but Caitlyn wasn't close enough to hear what he said. Her head had exploded...or at least it felt ready to explode.

She opened her car door and stood waiting for Ryan to recognize her. He didn't so much as glance her way until the mystery woman was in her car. When he finally noticed her, he smiled and said, "Cait? I didn't know you were coming over. What a nice surprise. Come on in."

Caitlyn glared at him. "You, too?" she said, in a whisper that grew to a shout. "You cheated on me? What am I, the biggest fool in the world?" She jumped back into her car and slammed the door, pulling away without waiting for a response.

She saw Ryan in her rearview mirror, chasing after the car and shouting, "No, Cait, it's not what you think."

Well, he had that part right, didn't he? He wasn't at all the man she had thought him to be. She had thought Ryan was her rock, someone she could depend on, someone who would always be there for her.

Tears flowed down her cheeks. Yep, he was there for her all right, he was there for her and any other women who needed him. How many people was he dating? Just the two of them, or were there more?

What was wrong with her? Why did men insist on cheating on her? Her vision blurred from all the tears. She swiped at them, only to have them quickly replaced by a new deluge. When she got home, she pulled into her garage and closed it. Once inside, she threw herself on the couch and sobbed, wrenching from her gut. How the hell had this happened? She'd lost her job and her boyfriend in just twenty-four hours.

Ryan stormed in behind her a few minutes later. "Cait, you have it all wrong. She's not who you think she is. Please listen to me."

"Who was that?" she wailed at him.

"You don't understand. That was Chad's wife, Erin. There's nothing between us."

"You haven't even mentioned her once. I don't understand why you wouldn't have said something if this thing between you was so innocent. When was the last time you saw her?"

She could see the panic set in Ryan's face. He was going to lie right to her face. He was going to lie and say they never spent time together.

"A couple of nights ago. We went out for pizza."

Well, he hadn't lied, but this woman was clearly a part of his life...and he hadn't said a word about her. Surely there was a reason for that. And experience had taught her what that reason likely was.

"Cait, I spend time with her and her son, Sammy. I promised Chad I would watch out for them...that's all there is to it. I...I don't know why I didn't mention her to you."

"And where was Sammy today? I didn't see any little boy with her."

"He wasn't there. She wanted to talk to me alone. She..."

"Have you been fucking her and me at the same time?" Rage raced uncontrollably through her body, driving her out of her seat.

"No. Cait, no. I would never do that. Erin has never been in my bed."

"I want to believe you, but I just can't. If that were the truth, you would have said something, Ryan. You would have *said* something." Her voice started to climb. She had learned what it meant when men didn't speak. When they made excuses to see other women. And the brunette—Erin—was beautiful, much prettier than Cait believed herself to be.

"Please, Cait, it's not like that. She and I are just friends."

"I will not be played the fool again," she said in a small, cold voice she barely recognized as her own. "Get out. I never want to see you again."

Ryan gaze caught hers. "I never meant it to be like this. You have to believe me."

"It's a little late for that. Just leave."

Ryan nodded and walked out the door.

As soon as he left, her entire world fell apart. She had no one, and no job. What the hell was she going to do now?

Ryan had managed to make it through the rest of the day, but not without feeling like a piece of shit. He couldn't believe how upset Cait had been and how she had twisted everything the wrong way. Yeah, he knew how it looked, and he knew that after what her husband had done to her, it was what he would have expected her to conclude. Erin had been walking out of his apartment after a kiss and a hug. He just wished Cait would have given him the chance to explain, but she clearly hadn't wanted to hear anything from him.

It would probably be best if he left her alone for a couple of days so she could calm down. Maybe after a few days he would try to talk to her again. He finally decided to head over to the inn to see if the family could help him out at all.

When they sat down for their meal, Mallory said, "Where's Caitlyn? Why didn't you bring her tonight? She really could use some friends right now. Jake said before he left that he thought you were going to see her today. How's she doing?"

"Cait won't be coming with me anymore." Ryan stared at his plate.

"What? Why not?"

"We're not seeing each other anymore." He played with the food on his plate, heaping on piles that he would never be able to eat.

Mallory stood up, her hands braced on the table. "What did

you do, Ryan Ramsay? Please tell me you didn't break up with her. Not now."

"No. Reality is she just broke up with me. I think her exact words were she never wanted to see me again." Ryan refused to look at anyone in the room, not wanting to see any derision.

"I can't believe that. She was in such a bad state after the situation with her job, I don't picture her breaking up with you unless she had a sound reason."

"What the hell are you talking about?" Ryan glared at Mallory. "What happened with her job?"

"Caitlyn was asked to find another position within the hospital last night. Lucille complained about her three times— one of which, I might add, was because of you—so our nurse manager told her to leave the department."

Ryan swallowed the huge lump in his throat. "How was I supposed to know that? And again, she broke up with me."

"What happened?" Mallory asked. "I'm calling Jake. He needs to be here to kick your ass for me."

"She saw Erin leaving my apartment and assumed we were seeing each other. You know that's not true, but she wouldn't listen and chose to believe the worst. Maybe after she calms down, she'll listen to me."

"Oh my God. She thinks you cheated on her like her husband, and within twenty-four hours of almost losing her job. Ryan. What have you done? I need to call her right now." She pushed away from the table and grabbed her phone out of her pocket.

Ryan said, "I had no idea, Mal. I'm sorry. She kicked me out of her house."

As she waited for Cait to answer, she said, "And how was she when you left?"

"Pretty upset." He glanced around the table, hoping someone would stand up for him, but they all stared at him with blank expressions.

Mal left the room to talk to Caitlyn. Ryan glanced at his father and the rest of his family. "I had no idea."

Lorraine spoke first. "Ryan, you told her Erin was just a friend, didn't you?"

"I did, Lorraine, but she wasn't ready to listen. So I left. If anyone has any suggestions on how to convince her there was nothing between Erin and me, I'm all ears."

"She probably just needs a little time, dear," Lorraine answered, loading his plate with more food.

Mallory strode back into the room, putting her phone back in her pocket. He didn't like the look on her face.

"Well? How is she?" Ryan was worried now. He knew how this looked to everyone and how the situation looked to Cait.

"I don't think she's doing very well, but it's hard to tell. I haven't known her that long, but she told me she doesn't want any company."

Their dad said, "Maybe you should go anyway, Mallory. With everything that has happened to the poor girl, I think she could use a friend right now. It wasn't that long ago that she left her husband and had to deal with someone stalking her."

"Dad, I know what you're saying, but I have to respect her privacy. She asked me not to come over. I'll go tomorrow. I promised to help her find another job."

Ryan stood up. "She shouldn't be alone. Somebody has to go over there. I didn't know about her job. And how did I have anything to do with that, anyway?"

Mallory's voice climbed as she spoke. "Because Lucille reported her for 'making out' with a cop in the break room. Unless you know of another cop she might have been kissing?"

"No." Ryan ran his hand through this hair. Oh, he had been a major fuck-up, for sure. Now what the hell should he do? "Mallory, you need to go over there. And who knows when the stalker could show up again."

"I thought her stalker was in Florida?" his father asked.

Ryan answered, "Well, he was there. We're not sure if he's staying, so she still needs to be on alert. She was getting a new security system installed. But again, everything about William was all conjecture. I'll go see her."

Mallory jumped in front of him. "Um, excuse me, but you lost the right to have any say about Caitlyn McCabe. She definitely does not wish to see you."

"I'm still the police officer handling her case."

Mallory got in his face and whispered. "I'll make sure Jake knows about everything, so I'll make sure he pulls you from it.

You need to stay the hell away from her."

Shit. He put his face in his hands. This wasn't how it was supposed to go.

CHAPTER TWENTY-EIGHT

Caitlyn had never been so down in her entire life, not after her father's death, her mother's death, or her divorce. She had no one, and she didn't know what to do. Mallory had been nice enough to offer to come over, but the last thing she needed right now was company.

She felt like a failure—she hadn't been able to save her mother or her aunt, and now Ryan had chosen another over her, just as her husband had done.. And the job she loved had slipped through her fingers.

Needing to be near the lake, she strolled out onto her deck, then down the steps to the part of the lawn nearest the water. All the while her mind was whirring with thought. The feelings inside her—the loneliness, hopelessness, and lack of control—were like a bottomless pit. It made her understand why people took their own lives. Not that she would ever consider suicide, but she could empathize with those that did.

This wasn't the first time she had felt destitute, she just needed to come up with a plan—something, anything to give her a reason to get up in the morning.

She thought about her nursing career. Maybe emergency nursing wasn't for her, she did often think of her mother when she was there. Perhaps she should consider ICU nursing or the PACU, where people came out after surgery. She wouldn't have to be so cheerful there, would she? The patients would be sleeping, and they'd probably never remember her. Eventually, she walked out to the end of her dock, arms crossed to warm herself...or was it to give herself courage?

As tears formed on her lashes, she stared at the icy glass

covering her beloved lake and wished it were summer. In summertime, she would have been able to dive and swim for long enough to forget her troubles, if only for a moment. But the healing powers of Orenda Lake were no good to her now, not in this cold season where the most you could hope for was the peacefulness of winter, or the sheer beauty of the sparkles on the crystalline surface of the water. She had believed she belonged at Summerhill, believed it down to her bones, but now that hope had been dashed for good.

Out of nowhere, a loud yelp sounded from under the dock, and a young lad slid across the ice on his bum, yelling as he struggled to slow his tumble across the freezing surface.

When he finally came to a stop, he scowled and placed his hands against the frosty plane. "Whoa, my laird. 'Twas a bit rough, was it not? Can you no' push so hard the next time?" He glanced up at Caitlyn and, scowling, said, "Your pardon, my lady." He brushed his hands off and lifted himself up, then strode directly toward her on the dock, slipping along the way but managing to keep himself upright.

What was this boy about? She'd seen him before. He looked vaguely familiar.

When he climbed up over the planks of the weather worn wood, he stopped in front of her and broke into a wide grin as his eyes met hers.

Caitlyn stared at the boy, dressed in baggy old pants, a small sword strung across his back, and a faded red tartan plaid wrapped around him. "I'm sorry, but who are you?" Totally perplexed, she had no idea where he had come from. Suddenly, she remembered. "No, wait. I know you. My accident, I saw you twice. With a big dog. Who are you?" Caitlyn's heart pounded in her chest as she remembered him clearly from the field in Summerhill and the median on the thruway.

"My name's Loki Grant and I'm your guarding angel." He straightened his plaid garment and rubbed his bum. "That ice is cold. Can we go inside? Do you no' have a hearth?"

Caitlyn hadn't budged, her gaze still locked on the urchin in front of her. "You mean my guardian angel?" She tried her best to stifle the small grin begging to break out across her face. He was a cheeky boy.

"I suppose so, but my sire said guarding, and I am a Grant warrior, so it must be guarding angel, not guardian. Guard because my sire is a warrior, and angel because my mama, Celestina, is missy angel." He patted his chest. "And I am a Grant warrior, too. My laird made me one." He chuckled and jumped up and down on the dock. "This does not move verra much, does it?"

"Your sire, your laird? Where exactly did you come from, Loki? How did you get under my dock? I didn't hear you walk across the grass or anything. Do you live down the lake?"

"Och, nay. I lived in Ayrshire when the Norse attacked us. 'Twas in the 1260s."

"1260s, huh?" Caitlyn rolled her eyes. This boy had a very active imagination.

"See, we each died when our time came, and now we live, well…we do not really live, but we are all together. We keep an eye on our family, on all the other Grants and Ramsays. That's our job. If one of our family needs us, we come to help. Sometimes we are old and sometimes young. I had to come to you as Lucky Loki. You'll see, missy angel. Can I find something to eat? Do you have a leg of mutton or boar stew or something? This trip made me verra hungry."

Caitlyn decided the least she could do was feed the boy. What did she have to lose? She had no husband, no boyfriend, no family, so she may as well make a new friend. She sighed and nodded, then beckoned for Loki to follow her up the slope to the stairs and her deck.

He ran ahead of her and peppered her with questions. "Is this your castle?" Then he glanced at it and scowled. "'Tis neither a castle nor a keep." His finger tapped his lip. "'Tis verra strange looking."

"No, this is my cottage on the lake."

"Cottage?" He grew wide-eyed. "This doesn't look like our cottages, or any huts I have ever seen. Or a tavern either. Look," he said as he bounced with glee. "I can hop up your steps on one foot. See?"

Caitlyn smiled. She might not know much about children, but this one was rather entertaining. She held the door open for him and he hopped up the last step and charged inside, coming to a halt in front of her fireplace. "Why, 'tis warm in here, and you don't have a fire in your hearth. How do you do that?"

"We heat our homes in the winter. Don't you?"

"Aye, with wood in our hearths. You must use magic." His brow furrowed as his gaze scanned her house. "Aye, 'tis different here, just as my sire told me it would be." His gaze flew back to hers. "Where are your kitchens? May I have something to eat?"

Caitlyn escorted him over to the fridge. She opened the door and searched inside for something to give the lad. "Hmmm...what could I give you? I wish I had some pizza."

"Some piece of what? Rabbit legs or a leg of mutton will do me."

She swung her gaze back at him. Rabbit legs? Where in hell had he come from? No one she knew ate rabbit. "How about a peanut butter sandwich? I have peanut butter and jelly."

"Aye, jelly! I like jelly. Strawberry?"

"Yes, strawberry." Caitlyn pulled out the bread, along with a knife and the peanut butter. The boy's hands rested on the edge of her counter as he watched her. "Who cuts your bread so nice and even? Ours never looks like that. And my mama makes strawberry jam, but where do you get the fancy label and the container? She just puts it in a bowl."

"I buy it at the store."

"What's a store?"

"A market?"

"Och, aye. We have a market. My sire buys ribbons for my mama there."

The glitter in the little imp's eyes was contagious. She desperately needed someone like him right now. Anything to take her mind off her present circumstances. She took one look at his dirty hands and said, "Why don't you wash your hands in the bathroom just down the hall?"

He peered at his palms. "They are not so dirty. And I don't need a bath, but can I use the garderobe?"

"The what?"

"The garderobe." He whispered, "I have to pish."

"Oh," she laughed and pointed down the hall.

He scurried down and headed into the door, but then stuck

his head back out at her. "Where are your torches? 'Tis dark in here. Uh, never mind, I'll leave the door open." He stepped inside and yelled to her. "Do not look, missy angel."

She grinned. Missy angel. That wasn't a term she'd heard before. She had been called an angel by a patient once, but never missy angel. The little Scottish lad was a puzzle, but a pleasant one at least. She would have to walk him home shortly. His mother had to be wondering where he was.

She hadn't heard anything from him in a while, so she stopped what she was doing to listen. All she heard was his laughter, which made her shake her head and laugh along with him. Apparently, he was entertaining himself with his stream of urine. Then she heard the shower turn on, followed by a screech. Oh, hell, what was he into now? Rushing toward the bathroom, she rounded the corner and froze once she turned the light on.

Loki stood in her bathtub, water raining down on him, his head tipped back in a screech. He continued to wail as she tore in and shut off the shower.

"Don't tell my laird. Please do no' tell him or he'll bring me back. I promised to be good. What is this? Why does water come out of your wall?"

Before she knew it, he was blubbering away, pointing to the drain and trying to wipe his face. She grabbed a towel and dried him while he continued to sob.

"My sire told me the garderobes were different and you had to wash your pish down with water. I hit the drain with most of my pish and I was just trying to wash it all down like he taught me. Please don't send me back yet. I have more to do. Please?"

"It's okay." She grabbed a dry towel and covered him. "Why don't you take those wet things off and I'll wrap you in a big towel. I can wash the clothes for you if you'd like."

As Caitlyn helped him remove his wet clothes and wrapped him in a towel, he pointed to the drain. "Is that not correct? Is that not where I was meant to go?"

Caitlyn hid her grin and shook her head, pulling the cover up on the toilet. She pointed to it and then flushed. "No, this is where you go."

He climbed out of the tub, the towel still wrapped around

him, and peered at the white contraption. "Oh, 'tis what my sire meant. My apologies. I did not see the hole there. I hope I did no' hurt anything."

"No, don't worry about it, Loki."

"Can I go in there the next time?" His eyes lit up and he grinned. "Will it splash out when I hit the water with my pish? In my castle, we just hit the stone wall inside the garderobe. I could always hit farther than Torrian."

"Of course you may use it, and no, it won't splash out. Who's Torrian?"

"Torrian's my cousin. I have lots of them. Lily and Torrian and Jake and Jamie and Gracie and Ashlyn and Bethia and Kyla, those are the older ones, but there are more bairns. I have a sister and brother, too."

"That's a big family you have. Come on. I'll finish your sandwich." She threw his clothes in the washer on her way. After settling him at the table, she placed his sandwich in front of him and a banana next to it.

"What's this yellow thing?" He picked it up and turned it over to look at it.

"A banana. You've never had one?"

He shook his head but bit into the peel and promptly scowled.

"No. Not like that." She reached over and peeled the banana for him. "Like this." She sat across from him at the table.

He took a bite, and his eyes widened. "This is good. Can I have it all? Or would you like some?" He held a piece out to her.

She shook her head. "No, you eat it." Unsure of what to make of her strange visitor, she reviewed everything that had happened since his arrival. Loki Grant, he had called himself. He chewed happily and stared out the window occasionally, humming as he ate and swinging his legs briskly under the table. He didn't know what a bathroom was or a shower or a banana or electricity or heat or...Was she dreaming?

Where had the lad come from and why was he here? At first she'd thought he was a neighborhood kid who'd come for some snacks. But now as she thought about the clothes she'd put into the wash for him, his comments about a garderobe and hearths and legs of mutton—it didn't make sense. All indications led her to believe he was not from this year or even this century. She chuckled. She had read too many time-travel books lately.

"Was it you I saw when I was in the accident, Loki?" Caitlyn was almost afraid to ask, but she had to know. Both instances had been fleeting images, but she was sure she had seen something both times.

"Aye, 'twas me. And Growley was with me. Do you no' remember? I told you I would take care of you. I just wanted to calm you."

"Growley? Why are you here, Loki Grant?"

CHAPTER TWENTY-NINE

The lad grew serious and stopped eating for a moment.

"I have two things to do. One is to deliver a message to you." He stood and walked over to stand in front of her, clasping his hands behind his back. "And I must do this proper or I will get in trouble." He waited to make sure he had her attention, then turned quite serious. "My laird sent me to tell you the souls need you."

"What?"

"My sire was afraid you might jump into the lake. Brodie said I have to convince you not to jump. You can't because the souls need you."

She stared at him, processing his words. Whatever task this lad had been given, he took it very seriously. "And how would you do that?"

"Were you going to jump?"

"No, the water would be too cold, and the ice is quite thick right now. Did you think I planned to take my own life?"

"You can no' jump. My laird said you have a lot of work to do on this plane. He was afraid. You have had too many troubles lately. It wasn't supposed to happen like this. You have to promise me before I can go back."

Caitlyn nodded, deciding to play along. Perhaps she was dreaming, and her little visitor was her subconscious way of helping her to deal with her troubles. Besides, what could it hurt to find out what work she had to do?

"And what work is it I have to do?" Her heart sped up at the thought. Right now, she had no idea what to do, so she'd be happy for any guidance, even if it came in the form of a dream.

"Pedi...ped..Pedia... Och, he made me say it many times and I still forgot." He scratched his head and stared at the floor. "Just a moment. Let me think of it."

"Pediatrics?"

"Aye, 'tis it. Pediatrics."

"Well, you must have remembered wrong, because I'm terrible with little ones."

"Nay, 'tis right. Working with bairns and weans. 'Tis your calling."

"My calling? And what is a bairn?"

"A bairn is a little one, a babe. Do you not know? This is the land of the Scots, is it not?"

Caitlyn stood abruptly from the table and walked over to stare out over her lake. Okay, this little guy was a bit too much. Pediatrics? The land of the Scots? She pinched herself, but nothing changed. The sharp burst of pain told her it wasn't a dream, at least not a traditional one.

She glanced at the innocent face of the lad in front of her, his jaw moving up and down as he chewed another bite of his sandwich.

After he swallowed, he tipped his head at her. "Do you not like me? I'm a wee one, and I like you."

Her face scrunched up at all the thoughts raging through her mind, all brought on by this strange boy she had never met before. Pediatrics? Could she do it? She did need a change. But such a large one?

"And the other thing, Loki? You said you had two things to do."

"You'll see. I cannot leave until he finds us. He's coming, don't worry."

"Who is coming?"

"Growley, my dog." Loki finished his sandwich and ran over to the couch. "I'm tired. I need a wee nap before I go back." He flounced on the couch, the towel still wrapped around him, and pulled the throw off the back of her couch. He smiled when he saw it. "Och, the Ramsay plaid. At least I am sure I made it to the right place."

"The what?"

"The Ramsay plaid. This plaid is the blue and greens of the

Ramsays. You are a Ramsay, are you not?"

"No, I'm not."

"You must be close to a Ramsay then. Or you'll marry one. Otherwise I would not be here. We only guard the Grants and the Ramsays." He cuddled onto the couch in his towel and covered himself with the plaid throw.

Caitlyn didn't approve of his last comment. Even if Ryan Ramsay came here on bended knee, she would never marry him. She didn't even want to see him again. The last thing she needed in her life was another man that would cheat on her. Thank goodness she had found out now.

Caitlyn headed down the hall and moved the boy's clothes into the dryer, then cleaned up the table, all the while unable to tear her thoughts from the suggestion she should become a pediatric nurse.

She turned on the television with the remote, but dialed down the sound. An ad for the Children's hospital near Rochester popped up. Dozens of small faces flashed across the screen: bald children, sleeping babies, teary-eyed families, and children with no energy left to fight. Tears threatened to spill down her cheeks, so she swiped at them.

At the end, a lone girl of about five sat up in her bed and said, "Please, come help me. You'll love working here."

Caitlyn shut the TV off and crept over to the couch, staring at the young boy asleep in a towel. The throw blanket had fallen off, so she picked it up off the floor and tucked it around Loki. He turned his head, smiled and fell back asleep. She found a spot to curl up at the end of the couch and cried herself to sleep, the vision of a child's haunted gaze foremost in her mind.

Ryan knocked on his grandfather's front door the next day.

"It's open."

Ryan walked in the front door and headed into the kitchen where his gramps spent most of his time. His father was already there, and he was leaning against the countertop with his arms crossed.

"Are you going to tell us what you discussed with Erin?" his dad asked. "I wanted to ask you last night, but not in front of

Mallory."

Gramps said, "Spill the beans, son. Are you feeling better about her or not?"

"She came to tell me she's marrying someone else, the father of her son."

Both men stared at him in shock, so he filled them in with the details.

Gramps said, "Better sit down, Three. I think you need it."

Ryan and his father both took a seat at the kitchen table.

Gramps said, "Holy crap."

His dad said, "Holy shit. Who knew?"

"Good," Gramps said. "Now tell me what happened with that Scottish girl. You know she's the one for you. Your dad told me you got in a little trouble with her, but buy her some flowers and she'll forgive you. She'll probably chew your ass a bit, but it'll be worth the effort." He chuckled. "Your grandmother sure chewed my ass a time or two."

"Did you deserve it?" Ryan's dad asked with a crooked smile.

Gramps grinned from ear to ear. "Aye, I did. Hellfire, she was a bonny lass when she was spitting fire. Go after that wee lassie and marry her, Ryan. I'd say it's your fate."

"I can't go just yet, Gramps."

"Why not?"

"Because I need to find out what Chad had been trying to tell me. I thought he wanted me to take care of his wife and baby, but that can't be it. He already knew Sammy wasn't his."

"So what's that have to do with marrying the lassie?"

"I have to settle this in my mind. I still have nightmares and I'm tired of it. I need to find out why."

His dad asked, "How are you going to do that? You've been trying to remember since you came back."

"I guess I'll go to my therapist and let her hypnotize me, see what comes out. I can't go back to Cait yet, it wouldn't be right. Not before I settle my demons."

"Well then, get yourself fixed, young man. You've got a life to live. I think Erin's message is for you to stop spending all your time on a memory. Time to live in the present."

Ryan just stared at his grandfather. Leave it to him to put

everything in such simple yet elegant terms.

Lynn Palermo paced in her tiny apartment. That foolish cop had disrupted her plans by arriving in Philadelphia just as she was preparing to head to Summerhill. It had taken her a while to figure things out, but she was happy with the adjustments she'd made.

She had planted the idea of William Jenkins as the stalker, and the cop seemed to have bought it. Maybe it wasn't the best plan, but it was the only one she'd been able to come up with on the spot.

Then she'd needed to send Will to Florida to throw the police off her tail. Hopefully, they would leave her alone now. And if she backed off—and had William do the same—the police would inevitably get lax. New problems would arise, better uses of their time.

And that's when she would go for the kill, so to say, when they least expected it. She had to admit she was pretty smart.

CHAPTER THIRTY

Caitlyn awoke to a loud barking and sat up on the couch, brushing the sleep from her eyes. The barking came from the outside, near the lake. Loki jerked up right after she did, then ran to the sliding glass doors facing the lake. The kid moved way too fast for her in the morning.

"Growley! There he is." He fumbled with the door and tried to open it, but he couldn't figure it out.

"Missy angel, we have to let him in. He's the other thing I have to do here." His eyes widened as he beckoned her to help him with the clasp on the unfamiliar door.

Caitlyn rushed over to the door, panicking at the thought of Loki letting any animal inside. "Wait, Loki. We can't just let a strange animal in the house." She glanced at him, secretly glad that he was still there. It made her hope she hadn't completely taken leave of her senses.

"But we have to. He's my dog and Torrian's, and he brought someone for you."

A huge deerhound had appeared outside the glass door, just like the one she had seen in the median. He stood there with his tongue hanging out and his tail wagging, waiting patiently. He seemed harmless enough, so she opened the door just a little. The enormous dog burst through the door and licked Loki's face until he fell on the floor giggling.

When the big dog finally settled, Loki hugged Growley before he stood and held his hand out to her. Then he looked down at himself in the towel and said, "Och, my clothes. I need my plaid and my sword."

Caitlyn traipsed down the hall with an awful thought in her

mind. When she returned with Loki's clothing, she asked, "Loki, does you being young mean you died young?"

"Nay," he shook his head while he wrapped his red tartan around himself. "I can be as old as I want when I come. Papa said everyone loved me when I was just a laddie, so he said I had the best chance to convince you to try children's nursing. I'm just a soul now. But here, I am cute. Do you no' think so?" He grinned at her while he dressed. When he finished, he turned to his big friend, "Show us, Growley."

Growley led them down the deck to a lump on the grass at the base of the steps. He nuzzled the brown lump and a small head lifted before falling back down. Growley trotted over to Caitlyn and nuzzled her hand.

She sighed, then crept over and sat on the steps, reaching for the animal. A thin dog with his ribs clearly protruding stared up at her with glassy eyes.

"Oh, Loki. What's wrong with him?"

"Her. Someone beat her and left her outside to die. Look at her bones, she hasn't eaten in a verra long time." Loki held his fist up to the heavens. "I'd like to find the surly pig-nut who did this." A moment later he hung his head. "Sorry, Da. I'll be nicer."

Caitlyn cradled the small dog on her lap and rubbed her head to calm her.

"She's still a pup, missy angel. She's only half a summer."

Caitlyn turned her head to Loki. "What? Half a summer?"

"She's not a full year yet. She's just a bairn." Loki stared up at the sky. "Aye, my laird. I'm coming." He turned to Caitlyn and said, "Bye, missy angel. I have to go back now. Thanks for the banana." He gave her a quick hug, then scampered off toward the beach. "Come on, Growley." The dog nuzzled Caitlyn's hand, then licked the pup before he lumbered off after Loki.

Caitlyn shouted, "Wait, Loki. I don't know what to do with her. Help me."

"Let me ask Aunt Brenna. She's a healer, you know." He halted and stared at the sky as if he were listening carefully to someone. After a few moments, he brought his gaze back to hers. "Aunt Brenna says to boil the chicken you just bought along with plain rice, just a wee bit, every two hours, until she gets stronger. She'll be fine."

Loki turned away and continued to run toward the lake with Growley.

"Wait, Loki. What's her name?"

Loki spun around to look at her, grinning. "Her name is Lucky. Do you know why?"

Caitlyn shook her head.

"Because that was my name, Lucky Loki, before I found my sire and my mama. And she has found a new mama just like I did." He whirled around again and yelled over his shoulder, "Bye, missy angel. My laird is hollering for me."

"But I don't know what to do with a dog." She tilted her head back and shouted to the sky as if someone in the heavens might be listening to her, as well.

"Aye, you do." Loki stopped and stared at the sky again. "Trust your heart. 'Tis what my mama says."

He ran toward the water and as soon as his feet hit the ice, he disappeared, taking the Scottish Deerhound with him.

Caitlyn was alone with a sick animal. What was she to do? She stared at the brown clump of fur in her lap and said, "Come, Lucky, I guess I need to get you where it's warm." She nestled the dog in her arm and carried her inside. She found an old blanket and placed it next to the couch, settling Lucky on top of it. "I'll go see if I can rustle up something for you to eat. Chicken and rice, hmmm."

The dog hardly moved when she walked over to her cupboards. She opened the fridge door, and there sat the chicken breasts she had just purchased. How had Loki known about that? Her brow furrowed, but then she decided the whole episode was much more than she could work through right now. She had something to do first.

As the food boiled on the stove, Caitlyn sat down next to the pup and petted her head. "You poor thing. How could anyone be so cruel to an animal?" She noticed Lucky winced when she petted one side of her, so that must have been where she was hit. One eye looked swollen as well. After she stroked the animal for a while, Lucky seemed to fall asleep, so she took her hand away and folded her hands in her lap, leaning over so she could look at the animal. A moment later, Lucky picked her head up and rested her chin on Caitlyn's foot, wiggling a little before finding just the right spot and closing her eyes again. "Awww. You are so sweet, Lucky."

Once the food was cooked, she waited for it to cool, then put it in a small bowl. Caitlyn worried the dog might vomit, so she picked Lucky up and settled onto the kitchen floor with the dog on her lap. She fed her with her fingers, offering her water intermittently. It took a while, but she ate almost a quarter of a cup. Lucky fell asleep, so Caitlyn moved her back to her blanket by the couch.

Lying down on the couch next to her new friend, she kept a hand on Lucky's back. The wee pup needed her, but maybe not as much as she needed the pup.

The next day, Caitlyn drove to the Children's Hospital in Rochester. Mallory had stopped over since she didn't have to work that day, and they had discussed the possibilities for her future. Her friend was a little surprised to hear she'd settled on pediatrics, but she offered her full support. Neither of them said a word about Ryan.

Mallory had instantly fallen in love with Lucky. Not willing to share the strange story of how she had come to find the pup, Caitlyn just said she'd found her in her front yard. Lucky was growing stronger every hour, and had actually gone to the bathroom outside. There hadn't been any accidents yet, but Caitlyn decided to play it safe and left her in a big box she had saved after moving. She put the dog's blanket in the box and a bowl of water and promised to be back before dinner time.

The drive was a little over thirty minutes, but it felt like an easy distance. There was a new Pediatric Hospital on the east side of Rochester, so she was excited about the prospect of working in a brand new facility.

After touring the different units, she decided to try the Pediatric Intensive Care Unit first. They had a good program for new nurses in the unit, and she liked the idea of working where she was needed most. Though she still struggled with the idea of changing her focus so completely—particularly since it was on the suggestion of a wee Scottish lad—

something felt right about it. When she thought about how dependent little Lucky was on her, she had a different feeling about it than she had in the past. Her brain couldn't believe she was thinking about doing this, but in her heart, she knew it was a good move.

Maybe her new life hadn't been destroyed as utterly as she'd believed it to be. She still had her beautiful house, new friends, and now there was the possibility of embarking on a new career. Yes, her relationship hadn't worked out, but maybe it was a good idea to date a few more men before choosing one for a serious relationship. She had never dated too much in Buffalo or at Niagara University.

Mallory had tried to talk her into returning to the local hospital, but Caitlyn wanted to get completely away from it. That ad she'd seen on TV after Loki had mentioned the idea of pediatric nursing to her had seemed like a sign.

She was offered a position, and would start the following week. There would be another round of orientation, but she would need it for pediatrics. Plus, any new facility took some adjusting, and she would take the time and not rush it.

On the way home, she stopped at a pet store and purchased a real bed for Lucky along with some dog food for pups with sensitive stomachs. After wandering down the different aisles, she found herself totally immersed in the dog toy section. She selected three toys she hoped would be appropriate for Lucky.

Her next step was a veterinarian in Summerhill. She wanted to make sure she was doing all she could for Lucky, so she made an appointment for the next day.

When she finally arrived home with all her purchases, she crept through the door quietly so as not to wake Lucky. Any nurse knew how important sleep was to someone who was healing from a sickness or injury. As soon as she closed the door, a pair of eyes popped out over the side of the box, and a thumping noise echoed through the house.

"Awww.... Are you happy to see me?" Caitlyn peered over the side of the box and saw Lucky's tail beating against the cardboard. She smiled and lifted the pup out, nuzzling her before she took her outside to see if she had to pee. As soon as Caitlyn set her down on the winter grass, Lucky squatted and did her business. Then she scampered over to a tree and sniffed it before returning to Caitlyn, her tail wagging. "You feel better, don't you?"

Caitlyn stared up at the moving clouds, wondering if Loki was watching her from up there. *Crazy*, she thought, shaking her head. She still hadn't been able to reason through everything. She scooped Lucky up and took her back inside to feed her again, then set out the dog's new bed and toys.

If not for Lucky, Caitlyn would have been able to convince herself that Loki and Growley had both come to her in a dream. But then she would have no answer for the puppy in front of her, who'd just picked up a stuffed squirrel in her mouth and shaken it from side to side, her tail wagging.

Where had the dog come from?

CHAPTER THIRTY-ONE

Toward the end of the week, Ryan sat in the waiting room in his therapist's office. His hands dripped sweat, so he wiped them on his pants with a scowl. What the hell, a little hypnosis shouldn't hurt him, no reason to stress over it.

But he *was* stressing. What if this actually worked? What the hell would he uncover about that day, the day Chad had died in his arms? He braced his elbow on his right knee, hoping to stop the incessant bouncing action. His leg finally stopped moving, so he leaned his face into his hands.

Part of it wasn't just nerves over his appointment. He missed Cait. No, that was wrong, he didn't just miss her, his heart ached for her. He stood up and paced. Shit, no, not his heart. He was a man, men's hearts didn't ache. It had to be his dick. That's it, his dick ached for her.

Well, he couldn't deny that, though he would never say it. Hellfire was the only word that came to mind. His grandfather was amazing sometimes. Hellfire, they had been great together in bed and out. He had glanced at a few other women since he'd split with Cait, but he had no desire for them. She was the only one he wanted—in his bed, in his arms, in his head. Cait was the only woman he wanted in his life. Period. He would marry her in a heartbeat.

But would she take him back? He doubted it. It had infuriated her to find out about Erin, which wasn't surprising after what her husband had put her through. He had hoped that after she had thought about it, she would have contacted him to discuss everything, but he hadn't heard from her. Maybe he never would.

The truth was, he had probably blown the only chance he had with the woman he loved. Yep, he could deny the whole heart aching bullshit, but he loved Cait. There was no doubt in his mind. If he wanted Cait, he would try talking to her again. He had to.

As Gramps had always told him, "You'll know, son, you'll just know." And he knew.

The door opened and his therapist came out to greet him.

"Are you ready, Ryan?"

He nodded and followed her into the other room.

It was time to fully face his past. Then, perhaps, he could start building toward the future.

Ryan and Chad were laughing about something another soldier had said the night before. His buddy was driving, and he saw a pothole in the road and tried to go around it. Ryan saw a dead animal carcass on the side of the road, directly in their path.

"Chad, no!" They had been trained to look out for animal carcasses, where the Iraqis often hid IEDs, or improvised explosive devices. They hid them in tin cans, dead animals, even in poles on the side of the road. Anything to take them by surprise. In fact, the pothole had probably been dug to try to get them to go around it in the direction of the bomb. Neither vehicle before them had gone around it, choosing to bounce into the hole instead.

"Chad, no! Turn the wheel back!"

Chad stepped on the gas.

A loud blast rent the air.

The next thing he knew, the memory sped forward, and he was trying to move Chad from the wreck, gunfire percussing all around them. Jake was covering them.

Ryan shook Chad until his friend stared at him. "I'm getting you out of here."

"Leave me. Get yourself out." Chad stared at his friend, an awful look in his eyes.

"No. I'm not leaving without you."

"There's gunfire. They'll come and kill you. I'm dying anyway. Leave me."

Ryan grabbed him by the collar. "Like hell you are. You are not going to fucking die on me. We're leaving. Together. You hear me?"

"Let me go, Ryan. I'm losing it, I can feel it...." His voice hitched and he fought to catch his breath.

Ryan climbed up to the opening of the wreck and tugged Chad next to him.

"Ry, you're bleeding. Let me go."

"I'm fine, I can't feel anything. You're coming with me." And he couldn't. Not anymore.

He would get Chad out of there, no matter what. He lifted his friend up over his left shoulder and pulled himself up with his right arm. He peered around him and saw Jake, still alive, flat on the ground and firing his weapon.

Jake yelled, "Stay there. I've got you covered." He fired again.

But Ryan wasn't staying. He saw what Jake couldn't see—a whole line of insurgents headed toward their vehicle. They wanted the bodies. He knew what they would do to them and he wouldn't risk it.

Ryan hauled his friend out of an opening in the wreckage and found a spot to leverage his right foot on the wheel, then jumped down and crouched, placing Chad behind him.

Jake took one look at him and said, "Holy shit, Ryan." He turned his head back and continued to fire at the insurgents coming toward them.

Ryan managed to get behind the vehicle, out of the range of gunfire, before he collapsed. He fell toward Chad, and Chad's eyes flew open again.

"Let me go. I'm dying. Save yourself."

"Like hell." Ryan searched the area for more cover and spotted a section of brush quite a ways behind them. It would be safer for Chad there.

Chad gave a weak push against Ryan's chest. "You don't understand. Erin..."

Ryan lifted Chad over his shoulder and hopped across the road into the brush well on the other side. He couldn't put all his weight on his left leg, but he didn't let it stop him. Gunfire continued to pop all around them, but he ignored it.

"I'll take care of Erin. If something happens and you don't make it, I promise." He fell on the ground and set Chad down, rolling toward him. He picked his head up. "I'll take care of your wife and son. But you're not dying on me or on them. Hear me?" Chad's eyes closed again. "Chad! Stay with me, damn it." He grabbed his shoulder and shook him.

Chad opened his eyes. "No, you don't have to."

"What the hell are you talking about? Of course, I will. I'll take care of them."

Ryan tipped his head to listen. The gunfire slowed. "We'll get you fixed."

"No, don't want to."

"What the hell is wrong with you? You have a brand new son at home."

He said something, but Ryan couldn't make out the words. Chad was losing strength, now gasping for each breath he took. He leaned his ear down and said, "Say it again. I can't hear you."

"Sammy's not mine. Erin wants divorce. Don't need to take care of them."

Ryan picked his head up and stared out over the fields, shocked by his friend's confession. Fuck. He stared into his friend's eyes and watched as the light drifted out of them. "Jeez, Chad." He picked his dying friend up and cradled his head, unable to look him in the eye. There might be pity there, and that was the last thing he wanted Chad to see in this moment.

He held his friend for what seemed like hours, but was probably only a matter of minutes. The next thing he remembered was Jake standing in front of him saying, "Jeez, Ryan. Your leg, your balls." And with that, Jake ran over to the bushes and heaved.

Ryan wasn't totally sure what his brother was talking about until he repositioned himself so he could see his leg.

There was little more than bone left on the inside of his left leg below his knee.

That was the last thing he remembered. The next time he reached consciousness, he was a below-the-knee amputee.

"Ryan, you can wake up now."

Ryan stared at his therapist, hardly able to believe the hypnosis had worked.

Everything, he remembered everything. The blast, the pain, the gunfire, Jake, his leg, and Chad.

Finally, after all this time, he could repeat everything Chad had said to him.

"Are you okay? Do you remember everything?"

"Yeah," he nodded.

She got up from her chair and brought him a glass of water. He took the cup and drank the whole thing down, as if he had just run a marathon.

"Does it change how you feel about the situation?"

He nodded, then stared out the window. He had been so wrong. Chad had known about his wife's infidelity all along, and in his last moments, he hadn't cared about dying. He had been ready for it. And the last thing Chad had said to him was, "Don't take care of them." Exactly the opposite of what he had remembered.

A huge weight had just been lifted off his shoulders.

Ryan finally felt free.

CHAPTER THIRTY-TWO

A few days later, Ryan was driving his cruiser at the busy area at the top of the lake. There was an ice cream shop, a couple of small restaurants, and a few touristy shops. The boardwalk and sidewalks ran through the entire area, all sitting at the top of the lake. The area had the most beautiful view. Not many were here in early April, but in a few months, this section of town would be the busiest, full of locals and tourists alike.

There were often concerts on the grass, the picnic tables situated under two separate pavilions were favorite places for barbeques or parties, and there was a small beach for the area's residents. In the summer, there were always kids out here running and playing.

"Dave, I have to check something out."

His partner just nodded.

There was a young woman up ahead walking a small dog, and he could swear it was Caitlyn. But when had she gotten a dog? He pulled the cruiser up next to her and parked and got out, saying to his partner, "I'll be right back."

"Cait?" She whirled around as he came up behind her.

"Oh, hi, Ryan,"

"When did you get a dog?"

"Not too long ago. This is Lucky."

Ryan bent down and petted Lucky on the head before he ruffled her brown fur. "Cute little thing. She looks like a chocolate lab. I didn't think you were the dog type."

"I didn't either, but it turns out I am. I just love her."

"Where did you get her?"

"Well, a little angel sent her my way, so I adopted her."

A little angel? What could she mean by that? No matter. He thought for a moment before he spoke. She looked radiant, and he couldn't help but feel a pang—apparently she didn't miss him the way he missed her. "Are you busy tomorrow? I wondered if I could stop over to catch up. See how you're doing." He plunged ahead. He had to get her back, somehow.

"Tomorrow? No, I'm working. I took a job at the new Pediatric Hospital in Rochester. How have you been?"

"Good." He nodded, lost in thought, tongue tied by the sight of her.

"How's Erin?" she asked with a smile on her face, but he could tell the expression was forced.

It was now or never, so he plunged ahead.

"Well, that's kind of what I wanted to talk to you about."

Damn it, the man looked so fucking hot in his uniform, she couldn't stand it. He wasn't wearing his jacket, so she could see every bulge and ridge of his muscles. She had to get the hell away from him or she would lose her dignity in a hurry. He had just asked her a question, hadn't he?

"I don't think that's a good idea." What the hell? He thought she wanted to hear about his new girlfriend? Men were such fools.

Ryan smiled, his hands in his pockets. "Another time? When are you off?"

He just wouldn't give up. Well, she wasn't going to allow him the opportunity to rip her heart in two again. Or maybe this time, he just wanted to tear it apart piece by little piece. "No, thanks, Ryan. Look, I've got to run. Nice to see you though."

She ran from him as fast as she could. Seeing Ryan James Ramsay III was just too painful. His scent had blown over to her on the wind, and it had made her think of waking up next to him in the morning. How comforting that had been. And behind the oh-so-familiar scent of Ryan had been the faint hint of peppermint. He was always sucking those peppermint candies when he worked.

How she wished he would suck on her again.

"Ooooh, shit. Stop thinking about him!"

Lucky stopped and peered over her shoulder at her. "I know, Lucky. I'm talking like a love sick fool." She walked with her head down all the way back to her cottage.

Two weeks later, Caitlyn stood outside Ellen Ramsay's door in the basement of Summerhill Memorial Hospital. Everything had gone well at the Pediatric Hospital, so she had decided to stay. She was still in orientation, which took her on and off the unit where she'd be working, but she had spent enough time there to know she would love pediatric nursing.

There was something about the innocence of the little ones when they were sick, and she saw so many different types of patients in the PICU: head injuries, motor vehicle accidents, infections, deformities, surgeries. The list went on and on.

The other day, she and her preceptor, a wonderful Haitian woman, had taken care of a one month old with a heart malformation, awaiting surgery. The only way she had found to calm the baby was to rub her head and sing to her, so Caitlyn had done just that. The baby's mother had come in while she was singing, and Caitlyn hadn't realized it until she heard the woman crying.

She had stopped instantly, embarrassed.

"No, please don't. You are so wonderful with her. You're like an angel sent from heaven."

And if that hadn't warmed her from head to toe. Somehow, after so many mistakes and false starts, she had found where she belonged, and she had Loki Grant to thank for it.

Mallory had tried to convince her to do the right thing for everyone else and report everything Lucille had done, but she hadn't possessed the self-confidence at the time. Now she did. Lucille was a menace to the ER patients and other employees.

Caitlyn had nothing to gain by reporting Lucille now that she was happily working at another facility. This would not be a showdown. She would tell Ellen exactly what had happened, and then would visit her nurse manager as soon as she finished here. After that, it was on them to decide what to do. But Lucille didn't deserve to get away with her behavior.

She stepped up to the door and knocked on it, entering as soon as she heard Ellen's voice.

After she had told Ellen everything, she picked up her purse and turned to leave.

"Caitlyn. Do you have a moment?"

"Sure." She sat back down in the chair, hoping to hell she wasn't going to have to listen to anything about Ryan and Erin.

"I'm so sorry things worked out the way they did between you and Ryan."

"Me, too. Ryan's a nice guy, just confused. Is he still seeing Erin?"

"Erin?" Ellen gave her a puzzled look.

"Erin, Chad's wife."

"Chad's wife? That's impossible. I know her family and she's getting married, but not to Ryan. I have never heard anything about Erin and Ryan. In fact, I'm sure she's marrying Sammy's father."

"Oh." Now it was Cait's turn to look puzzled. "I thought Chad was Sammy's father."

"No. It's a long story." She waved her hand. "Erin is moving to the other side of Rochester and getting married soon. They're very happy. The whole situation was so sad, so it's good for them to get this fresh start. I know Ryan tried to help Erin out with Sammy, but as far as I know, there was never a romantic relationship there."

Caitlyn stared at her hands. Was that what Ryan had meant when he'd said she didn't understand? She had to admit, she'd been so upset that she hadn't been able to listen to what Ryan had to say. The visual had been enough evidence for her. Well, even so. He couldn't be very interested or he would have found a way to tell her by now.

"I don't know exactly what happened between the two of you," Ellen said, "but he isn't very happy. I just wanted to tell you that. I think he misses you."

What could she say to that? "Oh, thank you," she managed to choke out. Then she gathered her things and left. It wasn't until she got into her car to leave that her heart started to sing just a bit. "Yes!"

Did she dare to hope?

She put her car into gear and headed back to her cottage. There was one more chore she needed to do first. All the money she had sitting in a bank somewhere was doing little good for anyone. After giving it a lot of thought, she had finally made up her mind on something she wanted to do for her new town.

She wanted to build a memorial and dedicate it to all the fallen veterans in the area. After searching the internet, she had located a design company she wished to hire for the task. They were presently working up several different designs to show her. She only needed one more piece to complete the puzzle—a place to put the memorial. Once she decided on that, she would bring her plan to the town council, and hopefully, be approved.

It had to be a very special place, because her father's name would go at the top. Chad would be memorialized, too.

Two days later, Mallory stopped by to see her.

As soon as Mallory came in, Lucky hopped up and down in excitement, but then she scampered back to hide behind Caitlyn.

"Oh, I just love your dog, Caitlyn. You make me want to get one. She's so cute. She looks like a chocolate lab. Is she?" Mallory bent down and called the pup, and Lucky crept over. As soon as Mallory raised a hand to pet her, Lucky cringed and ran back behind Caitlyn. "Oh no. Lucky, I would never hurt you."

Caitlyn sat on the couch and coaxed Lucky over next to her. Then she patted the seat next to her for Mallory to sit. "Sorry about that. You saw her when I first found her. She looked like she'd been beaten. I took her to the vet and he confirmed she had definitely been abused, but she's much better now."

Mallory picked up one of Lucky's toys and waited until the dog came over to her. Then she let the pup sniff her hand before she rubbed her behind one silky ear. Lucky's tail wagged. "You are lucky, Lucky. Caitlyn will take good care of you."

"She still runs and hides from most people, but she's coming out of her shell. How have you been, Mallory? I'm glad you stopped over."

"I'm fine. I just wanted to stop by and thank you for whatever you did to get Lucille ousted."

"Ousted? I wasn't trying to get her fired. I just wanted her to be more considerate of her peers."

"They didn't fire her; they moved her to an area where teamwork isn't required so much. She's down in medical records right now. I don't know for sure why she was moved, but I'm guessing it had something to do with you. Oh, and by the way, a physician who was nearby overheard her when she asked you to pull the Dilaudid out of the sharps container. He reported her, and it was mentioned in one of our meetings, so I think that forced the nurse manager to take action. Either way, if you had anything to do with it, thank you. And the floor's patients thank you."

She tried to stop herself from asking, but couldn't. "How's Ryan?"

Mallory let go of Lucky and stared at her friend. "I'm sorry it didn't work out between the two of you. Stupid, but my brother has a tough image to uphold. Both my dad and my granddad were army heroes, so he thinks he needs to walk in their footsteps. I think you were the best thing to ever happen to him, and so does he. I think he knows he made mistakes, but he doesn't know how to fix them. It's tearing him up inside, though he would never admit it."

"He could try talking to me." Caitlyn batted her eyelashes in an attempt to dry her misting eyes.

"I don't know everything that took place between the two of you, but Ryan doesn't have a lot of experience with women. He's hardly dated at all since coming home, and most of his experiences have been bad. Until you. But it's your business. I would only ask that if he reaches out to you, you'll give him the benefit of the doubt and listen."

"Of course, I will." She sighed and wrung her hands, inwardly cussing herself out.

Because Ryan had already reached out to her and she had shut him down.

CHAPTER THIRTY-THREE

Lynn Palermo stepped on the gas as the car crossed the border from Pennsylvania into New York State. "This time, we're going to finish this thing. We need that money. And we could have gotten it a while ago if your stupidity hadn't sent the police after us. Only because of your actions have we had to sit back and wait until the time was right."

"Yeah, well, I got a nice trip to the sunshine state. Worked fine for me."

"I had to send you away." Lynn glared at him from the side. "Never mind. Focus on today."

"We have everything we need. We should be able to get in and out of Summerhill in a couple of hours. You're sure you know where she lives?" her companion asked.

"I know everything about her. I've studied the maps of the town, so I know where all the banks are. We just have to convince her to give us the passwords. We have her credit card numbers and her social security number, so as soon as we get her ATM passwords, we're set. We'll hit as many as we can and withdraw as much as we can, then we'll drop her somewhere and leave."

"I'll take care of her when we find her. She'll scream the passwords to me. Let me handle it."

"Oh, yeah, right. Like you did in Buffalo or on the Thruway? You paid way too much money to secure the help to leave those notes. Then you were supposed to take care of everything on the thruway, but you let her get away."

"How the hell did I know the State Troopers would be after her?"

Lynn yelled at him. "They weren't after her. They were after you. You shouldn't have played around with her. You should have just stopped her and forced her to give you the information we need."

He grinned. "I was just having a little fun with her. I could almost see the tears in her eyes when I passed her."

"Fool. If you'd done it right, we wouldn't be in the fix we're in now. I didn't want you to hurt her. All I wanted was her passwords."

He glanced at his shaking hand, then put it under his other arm, trying to stop the tremor. "I know, I know."

"I'll handle her this time." Lynn stared at the road in front of her. Bruce had told her all about Caitlyn's money, and she deserved to have some of it after spending so many years working with bitchy nurses and doctors. Her time had come, unfortunately for Cait.

He pressed on his hand even harder. "You're going to have to handle her," he said through shaking lips. "I need a fix and it's getting bad. You should have shared the last one with me."

"Don't worry. We'll be in and out of Summerhill in no time. And I'll take care of getting what we need from Caitlyn Dalton."

"It's Caitlyn McCabe now."

Lynn took a long drag off her cigarette before she flicked it out the window. "Whatever. Won't matter soon."

Ryan walked into his grandfather's house. He needed a little encouragement to do what he planned to do today. Fresh from the shower, he had dressed carefully and shaved, putting on the cologne Caitlyn had told him she liked. He didn't know exactly what he was going to say, but he was going to apologize to Caitlyn and go from there. First he would explain everything about Erin and Chad, then he hoped she would accept his apology and let them start again.

He had to. He loved her. The more he was away from her, the more he missed her, the more he wanted her. But she had turned him down when she was out walking her dog, so he had to ask his gramps for a little advice.

"Ryan, my boy. Come on in."

He couldn't help but smile every time he saw his grandfather. "Hi, Gramps."

"Good to see you. Did you get back with that nice Scottish girl yet?" He pointed to the seat next to him at the table. "Sit down, sit down. What do you have there?" He grinned when he noticed the two containers in Ryan's hands.

"Oh, Lorraine sent some soup for you and some muffins."

"Well, store the soup in the fridge for later, but set those muffins right down in front of me. Have one yourself. What kind did she send me?"

"Blueberry."

"Blueberry? My favorite. She bakes a mean muffin, your stepmother does." He grabbed a napkin and set a muffin on top of it.

"They are good. I already had one, Gramps."

"Well, fine, fine. More for me." He chuckled, patting Ryan's arm. "Your father isn't coming?"

"Dad said he'd stop by later."

"What seems to be the trouble today?"

"No trouble, Gramps." He stared at his grandfather, suddenly registering how old Gramps was getting. What would he do when he passed away? He just loved talking to him. Yeah, sometimes he was a little goofy, but most of the time, he had so much wisdom to share. "I was just wondering…"

"Aye?" He bit into his muffin.

"I was wondering if you had any advice for me. I'm going over to Caitlyn's to apologize, and I want to make sure she doesn't slam the door in my face."

Gramps laughed and took another bite of his muffin, finishing his mouthful before he spoke. "That's an easy one."

"It is?"

"Aye, don't you know? Flowers or diamonds. And based on a policeman's budget, I would suggest flowers."

"Flowers? Really? That's it?"

"Hell, yeah. Women go crazy for flowers. Every time I got in hot water with your grandmother, I brought her a bouquet of flowers. She liked the really colorful ones."

"But aren't roses expensive?"

"Who said anything about roses? Other types of flowers

work just as well. Women don't care as long as they smell nice and are colorful. And don't get just one, get a whole bouquet. Stop in to see the florist on Main Street and tell 'em you want it for your girlfriend. Hell, Jerry does them all the time. Tell him I sent you, and he'll know exactly what you want. You think you're the only guy to ever get in hot water with his woman?"

"And they always work?"

"Well, not always. I recall one time your grandmother ripped them out of my hands and threw them at me." He laughed.

"Gram?"

"Yeah, I came home late one night smelling of perfume. She thought I had another woman. It took more than one bouquet that time. I had to go for diamonds."

"Gramps? You didn't cheat on Gram, did you?" Ryan couldn't keep the stunned look on his face. He just couldn't imagine it. He'd always thought their marriage the perfect union.

"Hell, no." Then he whispered. "But I did go to one of them strip clubs outside of Buffalo. Never went again. Hot-tempered woman made me pay dearly for that one."

So Ryan stopped at the florist on Main Street. He walked in and sighed with relief when he realized he was the only one in the shop.

"Hey, Three." Jerry said. "How are you? Haven't seen you in a while."

"Hi, Jerry. I need something for a special girl, so Gramps sent me to you. He said you'd know what I need." Shit, how embarrassing was this? Thank God no one else was around.

Jerry leaned toward him. "In trouble with the girlfriend, huh?" He winked at him. "Got just the thing for you. Coming right up."

Ryan paid for his flowers and carried them out to his car. Shit. He saw a cruiser coming toward him and damn if it didn't slow down.

Jake rolled his window down and yelled out, "Don't you look pretty carrying those flowers? Where's your nice dress?"

Ryan glared at his brother. "Fuck off, Jake." He climbed into his car, the echo of his brother's laughter following him.

Didn't matter. If it worked, it was worth it.

Caitlyn was huddling in the garage to get a bit of protection from the wind while Lucky searched for the right spot to do her business. A strange car pulled into her driveway and she peered through the front windshield to see who it was.

Lynn. *Shit*. She reached in her pocket to dial 911, but then remembered she had left her phone in on the counter.

"Lucky, come here." Lucky scampered over as soon as the car pulled in. Caitlyn ran through the side door and almost had it shut when a burly hand reached out and wrapped around the door, forcing it open.

"Caitlyn Dalton, how nice to see you," Lynn's voice dripped with sarcasm.

Caitlyn backed into her house, knocking over an end table as soon as she hit it. William advanced toward her, so she ran toward the glass door. He grabbed her and threw her down into the chair, then stood over her sneering.

"I got her, Lynn. She's all yours."

Caitlyn clung to Lucky, trying to protect her. "What do you want, Lynn?"

"Your money. Very simple. Hand over everything you have—your wallet, your passwords, everything."

"My wallet is right there on the counter, but I don't have much cash."

Lynn grabbed her purse and rummaged through it, taking what she wanted. "And your passwords?"

"Passwords for what?"

"For your checking accounts. Bruce said you had two different ones, and I want the cash from both. I'm going to the ATM from here."

Caitlyn made a quick decision to give her whatever she wanted. It was only money, and she didn't like the thug holding onto her shoulders. "Fine, here they are." She repeated the numbers and Lynn wrote them down.

"Good, now just to make sure you aren't lying about these numbers, you're coming with us. William, tie her up."

Caitlyn let Lucky go and stood up. "What? I'm not lying. You know me, Lynn. Leave me alone."

"No. Tie her up, William."

William grabbed her wrists and Caitlyn kicked him, catching him in both shins.

"Ow, you stupid bitch." He swung and punched her in the face hard enough that the chair she was in fell over to the side. Pain shot through Caitlyn's face as blood started to drip from her burst lip.

"William! Tie her up and don't knock her out. I need her."

"Well, she kicked me." He tied Caitlyn's hands together.

"Really, you baby? She kicked you? Let's go."

Lucky chased them all the way out the door, barking.

Ryan pulled into Caitlyn's driveway and noticed her garage door was up, her car still inside. That was odd. She usually kept it closed. Maybe she was having trouble with the opener. He knocked on her door, squeezing the flowers in his hands. Nothing.

He pressed the doorbell in case she was upstairs and hadn't heard his knock. Nothing. He pulled his phone out and texted her, but she didn't answer. All he heard was a low-pitched whining. A few minutes later he heard her puppy scratching at the door. Jeez, she probably wouldn't be happy to see her door all scratched up.

Then all the pieces fell together and he stopped to stare at her car. Where the hell was she anyway? She wasn't here, but her car was, so she couldn't be at work. He could hear her dog inside, so she definitely wasn't walking the dog. He dialed her number and he could swear he heard her phone ringing inside. Not at home, but she didn't have her phone? She always carried it with her in case she'd be needed at work. He tried the door and was surprised to find it wasn't locked. Something was definitely wrong—she never left her door unlocked.

He opened the door and the dog flew out past him, chasing around her entire yard, front and back, looking for Cait. Leaving the door open so the dog could return, he stepped into the hallway. What he saw sent a surge of sickness to his stomach. A chair and an end table were overturned—as if she had been running away from something or someone. He moved closer, and it was as if a fist hit him square in the gut.

There was dark fluid on the floor.

Blood. Shit. Her stalker was back.

Caitlyn squirmed on the floor in the back seat of the car, trying to loosen her bindings, but to no avail.

Bill Jenkins yelled at her. "Quit your wiggling, bitch. If we get pulled over, I'll shoot you before you have time to scream."

"Stop yelling at her," Lynn said. "Every time you turn around and look at the floor back there, you look suspicious."

"You need to get me my fix. I told you that."

"And I told you not yet. We have to hit as many ATMs as we can. They'll be on to us quick and we have to be on our way out of town way before they get on our tail. As soon as we have what we need, we'll stop in the city so we can get enough to hold us for a few days."

"And what are we going to do with her once you have the money?"

"Stop the car and leave her by the side of the road. We'll be long gone by the time they find her. We'll find some deserted back road."

Caitlyn tried her best to scream, but the sound was completely muffled by the duct tape over her mouth. She couldn't budge her hands either. Her head hurt from all the times Bill had slapped her, but at least Lynn hadn't let him punch her again.

Tears rolled down her cheeks. Her situation was hopeless. No one would miss her until she didn't show up at work tomorrow. *Loki, where are you?* She stared at the ceiling in the car. Many, many prayers to God had already been said, but hadn't Loki told her he was her guardian angel? No, guarding angel. That's right. If so, where the hell was he? Some guard she had. If he'd done his job, these fools would never have gotten into her house.

Loki, God, somebody help me!

CHAPTER THIRTY-FOUR

Ryan tossed the flowers on the counter next to her phone. The dog ran into the house and sat in front of him, barking, as if to signal something was wrong. "I know, girl, I know," he said. He took out his cell phone and called Jake and told him Caitlyn was missing, then climbed into the car and headed for the station. He was halfway there when the phone went off through the car's Bluetooth system.

"Yeah."

"Ryan, it's Jake. We just got a report of suspicious activity from Caitlyn's bank. Good thing you contacted them before. There have been three different hits at ATMs…each one for the max amount of cash."

"From where?"

"Right here in Summerhill."

"I'm on my way. They must have her with them."

"Sarge has called in five guys to stake-out the other banks. Hurry up."

Ryan flew down the road until he got to the precinct. He ran into the building and found his captain. "Anything? They have her. We have to find her."

"I know, Ryan. I have every available officer working on this case. Sarge is on top of everything. We already have officers at most of the banks. We'll get them."

The phone rang, and the dispatcher answered. "Where?" Silence while her pen flew. "How many?" Silence again. "Description?" Silence as she wrote.

Ryan glanced over her shoulder to look at her notes. "State Street bank. Just left. Black Ford Mustang, female, 30s, male...."

He tore out the front door, headed for his car.

"Ramsay!" his captain yelled.

Ryan turned around and his captain threw him a set of keys. He nodded, ran out, and climbed into the cruiser. As soon as he started the car, he called Jake and gave him the information. "What's your 1020?"

"We just passed the location. We saw a black mustang leaving the bank heading east."

Ryan heard the squeal of tires through the radio as Jake turned around and flipped on his siren.

"Unit 35 in pursuit, half a mile heading east on State Street."

Ryan called in. "Unit 40 in pursuit behind Unit 35." It didn't take him long to catch up with Jake. His siren was on and all traffic cleared for them both. Hell, she had to be all right. The thought of finding her dead made him want to vomit.

He'd held his best friend as he took his last breath. It just couldn't happen with the woman he loved. He couldn't handle it. Not Cait, not his Cait.

He floored it.

Cait's side was sore from banging against the hump on the floor. Lynn and Bill Jenkins had hit four ATMs so far and were planning on finding at least two more.

Lynn pulled out into the street. "Shit."

"What?" Bill said.

"Cops. Fuck. Hang on. I can get us clear of them. We're heading to the city now." Lynn stepped on the gas and Caitlyn was thrown around in the back seat. She heard sirens and Bill opened his window and started firing a gun.

"Bill, what the fuck? Stop."

He swung back inside and pointed the gun at Lynn. "No. I need my fucking fix. I'll kill anyone who gets in my way." He stuck his head back out the window and fired again.

Caitlyn panicked. She was going to die for sure. Her breathing sped up, and she tried to calm herself, but she just couldn't. Her eyes darted every which way and she tensed up, making the hits her body was taking even more painful. Tires squealing, gunfire, screaming, police sirens—all were doing a fine job at increasing her sense of panic.

Lynn kept screaming, "Fuck, fuck, fuck, this wasn't supposed to happen this way. You dumb ass, stop shooting."

Cait's vision dimmed, and a little voice whispered in her ear. "Don't worry, missy angel. Ryan's coming. Trust your guarding angel." Loki. Tears rolled down her face just at the sound of his voice. It was him. She was sure of it. Knowing how important it was not to go into fight or flight mode, she took a deep breath, followed by several more.

Bill pulled back inside the window and waved the gun at Lynn. "I hit one car already."

Ryan. No, please, not Ryan.

He stuck his head out again and fired two more shots. Lynn clipped something on the side of the street and swerved the car, braking to try to regain control. Bill pulled his head back in and said, "Don't you dare stop this car. Step on it."

Lynn said "No, we're done, stupid. Get rid of the gun. You can't shoot policemen, you idiot. You'll have every cop in fifty states after us. That was never part of the plan."

"Stop calling me names! Stupid? Idiot?" He turned on Lynn. "I'll show you idiot."

Caitlyn heard the gun go off and Lynn screamed—a piercing sound that faded into silence. With no one at the wheel, the car hit a guardrail first, then slid across the road and struck a pole.

Bill flew out the window on impact.

Ryan knew the fool was shooting, but that wasn't about to stop him. A bullet hit Jake's car once, and the vehicle careened to the side. Ryan flew past them as they struggled to right their car—both Jake and his partner seemed fine, he was relieved to see. Then he saw the perp stick his head back inside the car and discharge his weapon. A lump the size of a watermelon lodged in Ryan's throat. Not Cait, please not Cait.

The car careened out of control, which gave him hope he had shot the driver instead of Cait. A female is what dispatch had said. Had the guy gone crazy enough to shoot his own partner? The car seemed to move in slow motion as it hit the guardrail, then bounced off and spun to the opposite side of the street, hitting the telephone pole. As soon as the car connected with the pole, the shooter flew out of the car and hit the ground. Ryan stopped his car right in front of the guy, then opened his door and crouched behind it, gun in hand. "Police. Drop your weapon. Hands in the air!" Ryan yelled at the perp.

The perp rolled on his side, and Ryan couldn't tell whether he was still holding his weapon. He repeated himself. The guy stopped moving, but Ryan didn't think he was dead. All of a sudden, the man stood, his back to them.

Ryan yelled. "Drop your weapon. You're under arrest!" Still no weapon on the ground.

The fool swung around, his gun outstretched, and he fired.

But Ryan hit him first, right between the eyes. The guy crumpled to the ground and his gun fell away from him. Jake and Dave came up on either side of Ryan, then charged the perp when the gun fell away.

Ryan ran to the car and opened the door, praying he would find her. In the back seat, tied up, beat up, but the most beautiful sight he had ever seen, was Cait, tears rolling down her face.

"Cait, thank God." He climbed into the back seat and removed the duct tape from her face, then cradled her in his arms. "Are you okay?"

She nodded, and collapsed onto his shoulder sobbing. He picked her up and carried her out of the car, over to his. He sat in the back seat and held her on his lap. "I love you, Cait." He brushed the hair back from her face. "You scared the shit out of me. I'm never leaving you again."

She sobbed and sobbed, and in the middle of her hitching, she whispered, "I love you, too."

He smiled and cupped her face, kissing her. "Don't you ever scare me like that again." She shook her head, still hitching and sobbing. He untied the bindings on her hands and feet and she wrapped her arms around his neck, burying her face in his shoulder. And he just held her as she cried, wanting to never let her go.

More sirens echoed all around them. Jake stuck his head in the backseat. "She all right?"

"Yeah, beat up and bruised, but nothing serious."

"Cait, you need to see the EMT?"

She lifted her head long enough to shake it, then buried her face back in Ryan's shoulder.

"Come on, let's get you home."

CHAPTER THIRTY-FIVE

It was Memorial Day weekend in Summerhill, and it was one beautiful day.

The town had just finished the dedication of the new Summerhill Veteran's Memorial Wall on the hill at the top of Orenda Lake, dedicated to Ian McCabe, Caitlyn's dad, and Chad Armstrong, Ryan's best friend. The wall was shaped in a V, each side facing the water, and names were etched across its surface. Lights were arranged to illuminate the surface at night, so those names would never be in darkness.

The entire town had shown up for the dedication, and Ryan, Jake, and his dad and grandfather stood together in uniform during the dedication. Cait, Gram, and Lorraine stood proudly with them. The monument stood tall, and it was topped with the American flag and a flag for each branch of the service, just as he and Cait had requested. More and more names would be added to the wall—people's ancestors as well as their fathers and mothers, brothers and sisters, uncles and aunts, cousins, and friends.

As the crowd dispersed, Ryan James Ramsay, Jr., strode up to his son and clasped his shoulder. "Son, today is all about heroes. I want you to know you didn't have to save Caitlyn to be a hero to me."

Ryan jerked his head to stare at his father as he squeezed Cait's hand. The expression on his dad's face surprised him. Not sure what to say, studying his father, contemplating what had made him say such a thing.

"Any man who carries his dying comrade to safety through a barrage of gunfire and mortar rounds is a hero, Three. But I think you know that." He leaned over and kissed Caitlyn's cheek. "You make me proud to have you as a member of the Ramsay family, Caitlyn. The ceremony was lovely."

"Thanks, Dad," Ryan said. He had never heard those words from his father before, but he would never forget them. For some reason, he didn't mind his old nickname of Three today.

After they said their goodbyes to the others, Ryan grabbed Cait and they strolled down toward the water. They found a secluded spot and sat on a bench overlooking the crystal clear waters of Orenda Lake. He wrapped his arm around his wife. "Cold, Cait?" The crisp spring day was beautiful, with just a cool breeze blowing across the water.

She shook her head. "No, not with you next to me."

She smiled at him, a smile he would never tire of seeing. They had married just two weeks ago. Cait hadn't wanted another big wedding, and he had happily agreed with her. He wasn't the showy type of guy. With all his siblings, there would be plenty of big weddings in the Ramsay-Grant household.

His other reason to shy away from the large wedding had been fear of his spells, though he had kept this fear to himself. He still had occasional episodes of PTSD, but they were less frequent. Caitlyn was always there to help him through them.

"When you saw the crowd that showed up for this, Ryan, are you sorry we married so quickly? Did I deprive you of a big wedding in your hometown?" She rested her head on his shoulder, their hands intertwined.

"No. I loved our wedding. Just family. Quiet, not a big production. I'm not much into productions. I just hope you don't regret it."

"No. It was just the way I wanted it."

They both stared out at the lake in silence.

Finally he spoke, rubbing his thumb across the back of her hand. "Do you know how long I waited for you to come into my life, Caitlyn McCabe?"

She lifted her head from his shoulder to gaze into his eyes. "How long?"

"Forever. It's hard for me to explain it, and I've never been a man who's very good at expressing my feelings, but my soul felt like I waited for you forever. And when we stood up there at the dedication, all I could think about was how happy I am to call you my wife."

He thought for a moment before he continued, carefully choosing his words, feeling a need to share with her. He tucked a lock of her hair behind her ear.

"I've just felt so alone ever since the accident. I lost my purpose, my best friend, my leg... I don't know how a guy with eleven siblings could feel alone, but I did. And then one snowy day in Summerhill, there you were." He stared back over the water, noticing that she was swiping at the tears forming on her lashes.

"Oh, Ryan. You're going to make me cry. You know how much I love you."

"I'm glad we didn't wait to get married. I waited too damn long for you to come into my life as it was." He turned back to her and cupped her face in his hands. "I love you, Caitlyn Ramsay, and I know I will love you forever."

EPILOGUE

A month after their wedding, Ryan was playing tug of war with Lucky in front of the hearth, when Lucky stopped and ran over to pull the blue plaid blanket from its spot on the back of the couch. The puppy wrestled it and tugged it over to the door as if she were waiting for someone.

"Cait?" he called to her in the kitchen.

Cait washed her hands and dried them on the towel. She had just finished making a batch of chocolate chip cookies. "Yeah?"

He kept his eyes on Lucky as he got up off the floor and sat on the edge of the couch. "Why does she do that?"

"Do what?"

"Haven't you ever seen her grab the plaid blanket for no reason and bring it over to the sliding glass doors? Then she sits there and waits like she thinks someone is out there. Look, she just did it now."

Cait smiled as she watched Lucky. She knew what she believed, but she hadn't been able to tell Ryan about Loki yet. He would probably think she was out of her mind. She strolled over to the door and stood behind Lucky.

A few minutes later, Lucky's tail started to wag and she nudged the blue and green plaid throw.

"What do you think she's looking at?" Ryan asked with a furrowed brow.

Cait believed Loki was nearby, and somehow the dog could sense it. After all, Loki and Growley had saved the puppy from near death, so she didn't expect the lab would ever forget

Loki's scent or Growley's. Was it possible that the two came around once in a while just to check up on them?

Ryan walked over to the glass door. "There's no one out there."

Lucky raised her paw up to the door and looked at Ryan at the same time, crying to go out.

"Why don't we let her out and see," Cait said. She opened the door and Lucky flew down to the water's edge, barking twice before she sat down, her tail still wagging. Cait held her hand out to Ryan and said, "Are you open-minded, Ryan Ramsay?"

"What? Of course, I am."

"No, I mean really open minded." She leaned in and kissed him. "Do you believe in guardian angels? Because I think Lucky and I have one. And maybe he's yours, too."

He gave her a skeptical look. "What are you talking about?"

She led him down to the water's edge next to Lucky before answering. "I was never truthful about where Lucky came from," she said at last. "Do you remember the awful day I had after you and I broke up and I was told to change jobs at the hospital?"

"Yeah, I'm sorry you had to go through that." He tugged her in close and wrapped his arm around her so he could caress her bum.

"Well, I was a bit depressed and I came down to the dock. Come on, I'll show you." She grabbed his hand and led him out onto their dock. When they reached the end, she stopped and they gazed out over the sparkling waters of the Finger Lake. "I was standing right here when, out of nowhere, a young lad came out from under my dock and told me he was my guardian angel. And he brought Lucky to me."

Ryan looked at her, aghast. "Come on, Cait, You don't expect me to believe that, do you? A guardian angel? I mean, I'm not saying I don't believe in them, but I've never heard of one appearing in front of people before. That's a little far-fetched. I love you and all, but really? Don't you think it was a dream?"

Cait just smiled, grabbed his hand, and curled up against him. She laughed, and Lucky barked. As soon as she did, a huge splash landed right in front of them.

"What the hell?" Ryan's eyes were as big as saucers.

Cait grinned and bent over the water. "Hello, Loki."

Loki Grant stood up in the water, sputtering and brushing his wet hair out of his eyes. "My laird, must you push so hard? I think I could get here on my own." He stared up at the clouds in the sky.

Ryan looked at her in shock. "Where did he come from? I didn't even see him on the grass. Where does he live?"

She turned to him and shook her head. "Ryan, meet Loki Grant, my guardian angel. Or maybe *our* guardian angel."

Loki ran out of the water and said, "Missy angel, I told you I am a *guarding* angel, not guardian. Wasn't I guarding you when you were in the car with those bad people, the one who lied and said she was your friend?"

Ryan just stared at the imp. The information about Lynn being her former friend had never been released. "How does he know about that?"

"Thank you for that, by the way, Loki." Cait smiled at him, so happy to actually see him again, and moreover, for Ryan to meet him.

As soon as Loki got out of the water, Lucky ran over to him and licked everywhere she could, sending Loki into a fit of giggles. Then he stopped laughing and turned to Ryan, his hands clasped behind his back. Before he spoke, he tipped his head up to the sky and said. "Aye, I will, my laird. I promised." He leveled his gaze back at Ryan and said. "Hello, Master Ryan Ramsay. My name is Loki Grant and I am missy angel's guarding angel and yours, too."

Ryan just stared at him. Caitlyn moved toward the lad, tugging Ryan behind her.

Once they stepped off the dock, Loki ran over to them and said, "Missy angel, watch this." He waved at them. "Stand back, please. I don't want to get you wet from my big splash."

Caitlyn grinned and stood back, squeezing her husband's hand.

The boy scrambled down the dock and yelled, "Watch this!" With that, he hurled himself into the air off the end, landing with a huge splash. Lucky followed him to the end and barked at him. Loki's head popped out of the water and he yelled, "Come, Growley. 'Tis no' so cold." A Scottish Deerhound popped up next to him, swimming frantically to the water's edge before climbing out to shake the water off his fur.

"Holy shit." Ryan said. "Any more?"

Cait shook her head. "No, just Loki and Growley."

Lucky ran over to Growley and bounced in excitement around the big hound as he lumbered across the lawn. Growley nuzzled the smaller dog, then lay on the grass.

Loki climbed up the ladder and stared at them. "Master Ryan, missy angel, watch this one and tell me which one was bigger." He walked to the end of the dock, but then stopped. "Wait. I need to run, it'll be a bigger splash." He scooted back to the beginning of the dock and paused. "Are you watching, missy angel?" Then he launched himself down the dock and into the air, shouting, "Watch me!" as he hit the water. Lucky chased him again, her tail wagging in glee.

When he came up for air, his face had changed from joyful to serious. He whispered, "I know, Papa. I'm coming."

He trudged out of the water and shook himself off. "Missy angel, I can't stay long this time. I only came for two reasons. One is to meet Master Ryan and 'troduce myself." He stood directly in front of her and peered up at her, wide-eyed and grinning.

"And the other reason? Because I really don't need you this time," Caitlyn said. "But I'm glad you came to meet Ryan. Lucky told me you were coming."

"I know. I told her. And I know you missed me." His face lit up again at this last comment. He scampered up the lawn and toward the house.

"Loki, what's the other reason?" She followed him back toward the house, tugging a befuddled Ryan behind her.

Loki opened the door and ran into the house, then came out with a small container. When he ran past her, he stopped and ran back to hug her, Ryan, and Lucky. As soon as he was done, he took off running toward the water again.

"Loki? The reason?"

He giggled. "Chocolate chip cookies. You make the best ones, missy angel. We don't have any where I come from and I promised Lily and Torrian they could have a warm one." He yelled back over his shoulder. "They cannot get sick anymore where they are now. Come on, Growley."

As he continued toward the lake, he tipped his head to the heavens, "Coming, my laird." He peeked back at her, shouting as he pointed to the sky. "I think my laird wants one, too."

Loki and his lumbering friend ran toward the water. Before they jumped, Loki turned back to her. "Missy angel?"

"Yes, Loki?"

"This is where you belong." He and Growley jumped off the end of the dock and disappeared in midair.

Caitlyn swiped at her tears and said. "I know, Loki." She wrapped her arms around her husband and allowed herself to indulge in the peace and happiness of finally being home.

THE END

Dear Reader,

Thank you so much for reading my first contemporary novel from the Summerhill series. I know brothers aren't allowed to serve together in the army, but this is fiction, so please forgive me.

I grew up not far from the Finger Lakes and have always loved the area. I actually have been swimming in Conesus, Honeoye, Canandaigua, and Keuka Lake. Since I couldn't decide which one I like best, I decided to create my own Finger Lake.

Since many of the Finger Lakes have the names of Iroquois tribes, I searched for an appropriate name, and finally chose Orenda Lake, which means:

"extraordinary invisible power believed by the Iroquois Indians to pervade in varying degrees all animate and inanimate natural objects as a transmissible spiritual energy capable of being exerted according to the will of its possessor"

Citation: "Orenda." *Merriam-Webster.com.* Merriam-Webster, n.d. Web. 11 Jan. 2015. <http://www.merriam-webster.com/dictionary/orenda>.

I think of Orenda Lake as having transmissible spiritual energy for guardian angels. Did Caitlyn have the will to transmit her guardian angel?

So do you believe in guardian angels? I do, so I thought I would introduce them in my novels, and what better way to do that than using the characters in my Clan Grant Series? What if it were true? What if, when you die, your job becomes that of being a guardian angel for one of your descendants? I hope this leaves you thinking, as I always hope to do through my writing.

If you enjoyed Loki Grant, also known as Lucky Loki, his first appearance was in LOVE LETTERS FROM LARGS, and he has popped up in many other places as well. I love him and so do many readers. Each of my novels can stand alone, so you don't need to read the entire Highlander series if you wish to just read about Loki. I also promise no cliffhangers at the end of any of my novels!

I hope this was a good read for you, and if so, I have at least eleven more novels coming in the Summerhill series, because there are eleven more siblings in the Ramsay-Grant clan. You haven't become familiar with them all yet, but you will. Down the road, I also plan to tell Ryan and Lorraine's story, and maybe even Gramps's story someday. He's a character, isn't he? And wait until you meet Gram! For those of you who love my Highlander Clan Grant Series, don't worry, I'll keep writing them as long as you keep asking for them. For those of you who read both series, your challenge will be to match the souls of two characters. This one I made easy, as Caitlyn and Celestina have similar souls (and both are missy angels). I'll include clues in each novel to help you find the one soul match in each story. Soul mate and soul match are *not* the same thing.

Thanks so much for your continued support, and someday I hope to tell you that I am writing one of my Summerhill novels from the banks of a real Finger Lake.

Here are some ways you can let me know what you think of my novels or just to get in touch with me:

1. **Write a review on Amazon or Goodreads:** Please consider leaving a review. They can really help an author, particularly one who is self-published as I am. I don't have a marketing department or an advertising team backing me. Any reviews are appreciated, and yes, I do read them all. If you didn't like the novel, then please offer constructive criticism so I can improve. You do not need to use your real name for Amazon, Barnes and Noble, or Goodreads. These reviews are also helpful for other readers.
2. **Send me an email at keiramontclair@gmail.com.** I promise to respond!
3. **Go to my Facebook page and 'like' me:** You will get updates on any new novels, book signings, and giveaways. Here is the link: **https://www.facebook.com/KeiraMontclair**

4. **Visit my website: www.keiramontclair.com:** Another way to contact me is through my website. Don't forget to sign up for my **newsletter** while you're there.

5. **Stop by my Pinterest page: http://www.pinterest.com/KeiraMontclair/** You'll see how I envision Ryan and Caitlyn.

Next up – Book #6 in my Clan Grant Highlander Series featuring Micheil Ramsay and a Grant cousin. After that will be two Summerhill novels – Jake's story, then Mallory's.

Keep reading!

Keira Montclair

NOVELS BY KEIRA MONTCLAIR

Made in the USA
San Bernardino, CA
27 April 2015